I AM BLUE, *IN* PAIN, *AND* FRAGILE

ILLUSTRATION: Fusui

Seven Seas press and purchase enquiries can be sent to Marketing Manager Lianne Sentar at press@gomanga.com. Information regarding the distribution and purchase of digital editions is available from Digital Manager CK Russell at digital@gomanga.com.

Follow Seven Seas Entertainment online at sevenseasentertainment.com.

TRANSLATION: Diana Taylor
COVER DESIGN: H. Qi
INTERIOR LAYOUT & DESIGN: Clay Gardner
COPY EDITOR: Jade Gardner
PROOFREADER: Meg van Huygen
LIGHT NOVEL EDITOR: Mercedez Clewis
PREPRESS TECHNICIAN: Melanie Ujimori
PRINT MANAGER: Rhiannon Rasmussen-Silverstein
PRODUCTION MANAGER: Lissa Pattillo
EDITOR-IN-CHIEF: Julie Davis
ASSOCIATE PUBLISHER: Adam Arnold
PUBLISHER: Jason DeAngelis

ISBN: 978-1-63858-110-9
Printed in Canada
First Printing: March 2022
10 9 8 7 6 5 4 3 2 1

I AM BLUE, *IN* PAIN, *AND* FRAGILE

WRITTEN BY

Yoru Sumino

TRANSLATION BY

Diana Taylor

Seven Seas Entertainment

And so we grew up,
never leaving those years behind.

EVERY ACTION YOU TAKE has the chance of making someone else unhappy.

That was the philosophy by which I was raised for eighteen years of my life, up until I graduated high school. So as a freshman at university, I decided to make this the principle by which I lived my life. In other words, never would I carelessly approach others, nor would I ever speak up enough to voice an opinion which might contradict anyone else's. Thus, I believed, I would decrease the possibility that I might ever inconvenience anyone else, as well as the chance that anyone who was ever inconvenienced by me might wound me in return.

And so, when I first laid eyes upon Akiyoshi Hisano at my university, I thought very little of her. Here, I thought, was proof of how foolish, overconfident, and dull the people of this world could be.

It was the second Monday of my first freshman term. For the most part, I had finished selecting my courses, and starting this week, my studies would begin in earnest. On such a day as this, where I was possessed of such righteous motivation, I, who had yet to join any clubs or take part in any of the usual freshman activities, found myself sitting alone in the corner of a large lecture hall. All I hoped for was some measure of peace in my university life.

Third period was a general civics course of sorts, I believe. As I thumbed idly through my textbook, the lecturer finally took quietly to the lectern, a respectful hush falling over the room full of freshman. Of course, throughout the ninety minutes of undivided attention that such a lecture demanded, that dutiful focus began to wane. The hall was soon abuzz with chatter. Even the teacher, likely accustomed to this annual progression, paid this little mind, simply continuing the lesson.

I was no exception here as one of those people who could never even maintain my attention in my high school classes. Those ninety minutes of class felt like an eternity beneath the spring sunshine, a feeling that I wasn't sure I would be able to bear for the next four years.

The lesson quickly became tedious. From my seat at the edge of the room, I could see outside of the window. The laughter of out-of-class students and the chirping of the birds melted into the sunlight. It was just as my head began to droop and my chin was about to slide from my hands that I heard a voice come crashing through this beautiful, sunny day.

"Pardon me, can I ask a question?"

A loud, vivacious voice echoed across the quiet lecture hall. Everyone, startled into attention, began glancing around, looking for the source of the disturbance. I was similarly intrigued, but there was no need for me to look around myself. I had heard the voice straight from its source—a girl sitting one seat over, to my right. I furtively glanced over to see her right hand thrust straight up towards the ceiling, achingly self-assured.

I had not been paying attention to the lecture, so I thought that perhaps the teacher had opened the floor for questions. However, the aged lecturer merely met her piercing gaze with a dull stare, urging her to lower her hand with a, "Save your questions for the end." I kept watching the girl out of the corner of my eye; she eventually lowered her hand, but the sour expression she made must have been visible even from the teacher's podium. "All right, *now* is fine," the lecturer relented. She instantly perked up, her thanks echoing throughout the room.

As I think about it now, I'm sure that if she had presented some kind of jaw-dropping opinion that no ordinary student would ever have thought of and started a debate with the professor, I might have started to develop an actual interest in the creatures known as college students. I might have thought that there were some truly spectacular specimens out there in the world, and that would have been that.

However, that was not the case.

"I don't think that violence is necessary in this world."

Hearing this question, or rather, this expression of an opinion that had merely been disguised as a question, and an opinion that, quite frankly, belonged in an elementary school ethics lesson, I was filled with secondhand embarrassment.

I suppose she was something of an idealist. Not even attempting to hide his sneer, the lecturer replied, "I'm pretty sure we're all aware that a world like that would be ideal."

I know my ears were not just playing tricks when I heard the murmured, "Yeesh," "What the hell," and "Ouch"es from all around the room.

Having thoroughly embarrassed herself, the girl fell silent. The teacher then continued as though the girl did not even exist, as though he were simply ridiculing some formless, theoretical idiot somewhere out in the world.

When I looked back at her again, it was not because I was curious to see what sort of person would be so excited to voice their own opinion that they would bother interrupting a lecture. It was merely because I enjoyed seeing the looks of disappointment upon idiots' faces when their own foolish words were rebutted. Thus, while I would not call the look that I saw on her face when I glanced over disappointing, it was at least unexpected. She looked hurt. She was staring forward, as if in shock.

It was seeing people who behaved just as she did back in junior high that had led me to decipher a pattern to their way of thinking. They were the sort of people, I was sure, who believed only in their own logic, thinking everyone else around them who could not understand them stupid. And so, I was surprised to not see her express the sort of displeasure that such types of people typically did when they were denied.

I had no interest in getting involved in this, but her face certainly piqued my interest. However, this interest was nothing more than what one might feel at hearing a strange melody when walking down the street, and by the time the bell rang, I had already forgotten all about it.

I handed in my copy of the brief feedback survey we had been provided with in order to confirm attendance and stood up from my seat. I did not have any classes scheduled for fourth period on Mondays, so I decided to head to the cafeteria to take a late lunch.

At a university, there were always people in the cafeteria no matter how odd the hour. With nowhere to really situate myself in this environment I was not yet used to, I loaded one of the day's meal sets onto my tray and then settled myself at a four-person table by the window, clapping my hands together and bringing my miso soup to my mouth.

"This seat taken?"

A voice from a conversation that had nothing to do with me emerged from the sea of sounds around me. I obviously was certain that the voice could not be speaking to me of all people, so I just chomped down on my fried fish. A sudden poke to my shoulder shocked me into dropping the half-eaten fish to my plate with a satisfying *crunch*.

I looked up, chopsticks still in hand, and was doubly surprised. The girl who had been sitting beside me in the lecture hall was standing there with a tray full of katsu curry. For some reason, I kept looking back and forth between her and the curry.

"This seat taken?" she asked again, which is when I realized that the voice I had heard before had been most certainly directed towards me.

"Oh, no, it's not."

I had no idea why she was speaking to me. However, I had no reason to lie, so I simply shook my head. She flashed me a grin, face beaming, and sat her tray down, taking the seat opposite mine.

"I was next to you in class earlier. Mind if I eat with you? Since you're alone too."

Seriously? I thought. Not only was she the type to blab her own opinions in the middle of class, but she was undeservedly self-confident. It made me cringe. The only reason I did not refuse her was that, as per my own personal philosophies, I placed more weight on not contradicting others' opinions than on distancing myself from them because that was merely the sort of mood I was in that day. There was no other reason.

"C-certainly," I said politely as it suddenly occurred to me that she might be an upperclassman. The fact that she thought it natural to speak so casually with me led me to assume that she considered me, who had been in a lecture hall full of freshman, her junior. That she had so suddenly decided to share lunch with a stranger like it was nothing was perhaps not a mark of how annoying she was but merely that she was an upperclassman with too much time on her hands.

"Loosen up there, I'm just a freshman."

"Wha...?"

"Wait, are *you* actually my senpai?"

I really should have fled from this conversation—just the way she was goggling at me with her huge eyes was enough to inform me that this was a vexing person. Still, there was no reason for me to lie, so I just shook my head.

"I'm a freshman too."

"Oh! Thank goodness! I was kind of freaking out there! Thought I might've ruined my university reputation right from the get-go."

She put a hand to her chest, breathing a huge, exaggerated sigh of relief. *Didn't you ruin your reputation already with that act you put on in class?* I thought.

"Anyway, sorry to impose on you out of the blue like this. I still don't know anyone else here, but just when I was starting to get antsy, I saw you! We were sitting next to each other in class, so I just thought I'd talk to you. Sorry, was that rude of me?"

It was.

"Nah, it's fine."

"Oh, sweet! Um, I'm Akiyoshi Hisano." How truly bold of her to presume I cared. "I'm majoring in political science. You?"

"Business, actually."

"I see. Could I ask your name?"

The way she asked that really left no room for refusal.

"Sure. Tabata."

"Well, I know we've just met, but pleased to meetcha, Tabata-kun."

Akiyoshi bowed her head. Her bluntly cut shoulder-length hair swayed. I politely bowed my head in return. In most cases, when an unplanned event occurred, it was typically most advantageous just to play along.

"So, Tabata-kun, could I ask your first name?"

"...Uh."

I faltered. It was an incredibly ordinary question, one which she was at no fault for asking. Though it was more or less a personal problem, the fact was that I hated my name. If I were some kind of supermodel, maybe I would have been proud of how flowery my name was. Or, on the other hand, if I were super burly and the direct opposite of the impression my name gave, that contradiction might have been a source of comedy. However, it was the fact that I was wholly nondescript and neither of those things that made me hesitate to share it.

But then again, I was not the sort of person who was brave enough to ignore someone's question.

"...Kaede..."

Of course, one's own complexes meant *nothing* to others.

"Tabata Kaede-kun..." she sounded out. "*Ta* as in *tanbo* and *hata* as in *hatake*?" she asked, trying to pin down the kanji for my name.

"Oh, no, *hata* like in *hashikko*."

Akiyoshi pulled her cell phone out of her bag, tapped at it in a practiced fashion, and then tucked it back away. The strap of the bag dug into her shoulder.

"Note taken!"

Grinning, with eyes narrowed and teeth bared, she lifted her spoon and took a bite of her katsu curry as though it were some long-awaited treat. Realizing I had, for some reason, watched this entire sequence of actions, I averted my eyes and once more took a bite of the fried fish atop my own plate.

"Gosh, I was hungry. My stomach was growling all the way through class! You hear it?"

"No, I didn't." I was not paying attention to such things whatsoever.

"Well, that's good. I've always got a pretty healthy appetite. Don't judge me if I end up eating more than you, 'kay?"

"Good metabolism, huh?"

"Old habit from when I played soccer for a bit in high school. I probably need to start eating less, though."

A bit, I noted, which led me to the independent conclusion that she probably had not attended some kind of powerhouse school that was all about winning. The fact that she needed to cut back also meant that she probably had no intention to continue playing through college.

"You play any sports, Tabata-kun? Er, sorry... I'm asking a lot of questions."

Apparently, she did have *some* tentative measure of consideration. I had assumed from her display in class that she was the sort of person who would step all over others' personal boundaries. At least she apparently had the courtesy to take off her shoes before doing so.

"It's fine. I didn't really do any physical activities in high school."

"Oh, more of the artsy type?"

"I was part of the go-home club."

"No plans to do anything in college, either?"

"Not really, currently. Oh, what about you, Akiyoshi-san?"

"I was thinking I'd join something, but when I looked into all the groups on campus, including the unofficial ones, there were just way too many options. Sort of interested in the Model UN or something, though."

"Mottle Yuen?" I parroted.

"Yeah, it sounds really cool!" she said, taking the opportunity to immediately launch into an explanation of the group. To simplify Akiyoshi's exposition, this club was apparently one where students interested in international affairs took on the roles of different nations and carried on mock sessions of the United Nations. Of course. I was starting to form a more solid internal picture of her.

"How's something like that sound to you, Tabata-kun?"

"Sounds like an overly complicated TTRPG game."

I had no reason to either criticize or laud the model UN concept, so I simply voiced one of my opinions on the matter that did not lean either way. This time, Akiyoshi was the one to parrot, *"Tee tea are peegee?"* Given the way that the conversation was going, it would be odd of me not to take my turn at explaining. I gave her a brief, simple, and objective as possible explanation of what a TTRPG, or tabletop roleplaying game, was.

"So, yeah, it's also the kind of game where you play different roles, I think."

"Whoa! That's so cool! I would definitely want to play some type of hero!"

She held her still curry-covered spoon out in front of her face, perhaps attempting to mime the wielding of a sword. Seeing this joyful reaction got a surprising stir out of me.

"I guess the model UN really is kind of the same. Wanna go check it out with me? If you're up to it."

"Oh, ah...no, I can't."

Whenever I had to refuse an invitation that came my way, I hated having any looks of disappointment cast on me, or having to do the same, or even someone being disappointed about it at all. Thus, though refusing this casual invitation of Akiyoshi's conflicted slightly with my own philosophies, Akiyoshi, who had no idea that I was this way and smiled, clasping her hands in front of her chest with a, "No, it's cool! Sorry for imposing on you so suddenly." The fact that she seemed to realize that there were some drawbacks to her own personality gave me a slightly more favorable impression of her.

Just slightly.

"Oh, no, it's okay, I really don't mind it," I said.

"Really? I'm glad. I know that I can be a bit much sometimes."

So I had gathered. I had assumed from her bubbly nature that she was not capable of such self-awareness, so I was surprised at this newfound calm of hers. It made me wonder if she was the sort of person who really only thrived within a small, close-knit group.

I have no idea whether telling her that I didn't mind had merely encouraged her, but her barrage of questions continued. I answered them as well as I could and learned more about her in return. She was born in Ibaraki, currently enrolled in school, lived alone, and had applied for a part-time job at a cram school. She liked shonen manga and was a fan of *Asian Kung-Fu Generation*. Based solely on this information, she should have seemed like a perfectly normal person, but unfortunately, I was hearing all of this through the lens of my first impressions of her in class and through the filter of my view of her as an irritating person. I saw no reason to amend my perception now. There was no need to do so.

"Catch you later then!" she said, standing from her seat. The building that her next class was in apparently rather far away.

I waved a hand at her, replying, "Sure, later then," but, in fact, I did not assume that there would be a "later." This was not me being coldhearted, though. People like Akiyoshi, who could have conversations with anyone, soon found better people to talk to, forgetting the acquaintances they had made along the way. I had been the subject of this many times before and understood by now that such things were inevitable.

So, just as I did not think there would be any "laters" to come, I did not feel that there was any reason why I should need to fully comprehend Akiyoshi.

However.

I did not even have to wait until the following Monday. That Friday during fourth period, when Akiyoshi, who was sitting boldly in the front of our fifty-person classroom, saw me enter through the front door, she waved at me. When I took my seat in the farthest row to the back, by the window, she picked up her things and moved to sit next to me.

"Morning! Been a while, eh, Tabata-kun?"

"Oh, y-yeah. You in this class too?"

"Yeah! Didn't realize you were too." I had taken a seat farther away from her, assuming she had come with friends, but I suppose it was a good thing that she relocated. There had been no point in such serious, careful consideration on my part.

Just as she was cheerfully telling me about how she had gotten the cram school job, the bell rang. It did not seem that there was anyone else around that she was acquainted with.

The moment class started, she clammed up right away, looking dutifully ahead. I was not quite so dutiful, but I faced forward anyway, lending my ear to the lecture, quietly, dazedly pondering the fact that Akiyoshi's "later" had in fact come to be. However, I need not have been so fixated on this. About an hour into class, I was made aware of what was perhaps the most important fact about her of many.

There came a voice.

"Pardon me. Can I ask a question?"

Once more, there was no need for me to search for the source of this voice. *Seriously?* I thought. Once again, she was right beside me, only this time, I knew her voice. I looked over to see her hand yet again boldly raised.

The lecturer this time was far kinder to her.

"Oh, sure. You're paying tuition after all, might as well participate in the class. What's up?" said the teacher, permitting her to speak.

"Thank you," she said. I already had some prediction about

what it was she was going to ask, but when that prediction came true, I regretted having thought it. Once more, her voice resounded throughout the room with a statement of childlike opinion, disguised as a question.

This time I did not silently belittle her—I was merely stunned. That time in the cafeteria, I had come to believe she was at least *somewhat* of a normal person. However, my bewilderment was a little premature. From elsewhere, I heard words of disbelief.

"Again?"

I understood the sentiment, one hundred percent.

It was time for me to revise my opinion about Akiyoshi. Akiyoshi was not just annoying—she was dangerous. She was not someone to associate with.

I pretended to focus on the lesson, taking care not to glance even *once* at this dangerous person sitting beside me. I understood now; this was why no one approached her, why she would even bother to remember me and strike up such a friendly conversation. Apparently, other people's senses of danger were even more finely honed than mine.

There was, perhaps, still time to get out of this.

While I half-watched as, like before, the lecturer rebutted Akiyoshi with a grimace, I began contemplating some evasive maneuvers. For now, all I could do was simply run. The moment class ended, I stood up, handed in the impression survey that I had already filled out during class, and left the room, not once looking Akiyoshi's way. That would afford me at least a momentary measure of peace. When it came to next Monday's lecture, when we would cross paths yet again, I would simply wait until the very last moment to enter and take my seat; same with the class we had just finished. Then, sooner or later, Akiyoshi would forget about me. There were tons of other people at this school.

There was no reason that it had to be *me*.

And so, I could not even begin to understand why it was that, just then, she came running up to me.

"Oh God, *why*?"

"Why what?"

"...Uh, nothing. I was just thinking about something."

Without me ever determining the reason why, somehow, before I knew it, two months had passed since our first meeting. Already I had resigned myself to spending every Monday fourth period, and the late lunch after, with her. Due to my own shortcomings, I was unable to push away someone so clingy, and so I had kept up the pretense of her acquaintance.

I started to pick up the fried whitefish that I always seemed to be eating, before placing it back down on my plate. "You know," I said, "you really need to stop attention-grabbing so much attention during lectures."

"I don't know how many times I have to tell you, Tabata-kun, but I'm not attention-grabbing! I just want to be certain about the facts."

"Yeah, but all it does is make you stand out."

I had come to realize that, surprisingly, there was no real harm in just keeping on as her conversation partner.

"Well...I mean, I think it helps the lesson if the professor realizes that there are students with opinions that differ from what they're teaching in the lecture. During our lecture just before, I was thinking, 'Idealism isn't the same as an ideal.' An ideal is something that you should strive for, but idealism sneers in the face of that. Peace clearly isn't built on the back of war, it's built on the back of *more peace*. At least, that's what I think."

There was no real harm in it, but there was no mistaking that being deemed her *friend* was an incredibly vexing thing. Partly as a means of silently arguing against her, I once more picked up my fried fish. If I were to voice an opinion now or do anything that might imply I was invested in this conversation, she would just argue herself blue in the face until we were both in accord. It wasn't out of a desire to beat her opponent down so much as sincerely wishing to understand the thoughts of people with differing opinions from her own and amend her own opinion if necessary.

I *really* hated that part of her. It was this vexing part of her that kept her so clearly ostracized from the people around her. Plenty of times when Akiyoshi was not around I had overheard disparaging whispers about her.

"An ideal is something that you should chase until you can seize it."

As always, I kept quiet under the unerring gaze from those big, round eyes of hers, poking at my salad as a diversion. Thinking about it now, those eyes were perhaps the very reason that I had not managed to shake Akiyoshi at all during those two months. At some point or other, within the many times each week that I would make her acquaintance, I had come to discover a certain purity to her, beyond all that vexing naiveté. It was a purity that was certain that the things she believed in could be brought to fruition with effort and that with the power of that belief, they *would* come true.

However, I believe the reason this so pained me to see was that I could recall, in some small way, having thought similar things myself in the past, which meant that my opinion of her was based somewhat on my embarrassment at my own past self. Looking at her from afar, one would take her for a simple idiot. However, when faced directly with that purity, it was difficult for me, at the very least, to completely write her off.

Had I cut all ties with her at that moment, she would not have had any particularly sour feelings toward me, but it still would give me a bit more freedom than the times when others thought it was best to cut off ties with me and treat *me* as a stranger. Rather than hate that about me, Akiyoshi accepted me. As a result, within those two months, the whispers surrounding her had begun to spread to me as well.

This was not the university life I had hoped for.

"That reminds me, what was the Study of International Relations club like?"

"Mm, I dropped in on one of their meetings, but I didn't really vibe with it," Akiyoshi said, laughing it off, but the truth was all over her face. More than likely, there had been those present who had already come to the conclusion that they did not care for Akiyoshi. At least once, I had seen an upperclassman directly express their disdain for how often she interrupted class. I got the impression that something had happened with the aforementioned Model UN as well.

"Gonna go check out any other ones later?"

"Well, by the time we're juniors we're going to end up pretty busy with classwork, and I get the feeling that the first two years are going to be pretty focused on self-directed studies..." she trailed off, but there was obvious disappointment on her face.

"If you really want to join an activity, maybe you should start something up yourself," I consoled, halfway joking.

"Mmm!" Akiyoshi suddenly shouted through a mouth full of hamburger steak.

"...What?"

"That's a *great* idea!"

She swallowed the bite that was already in her mouth and stared at me with her usual intense eyes. I knew in that moment that I made a mistake.

"A club... That's it. *I* could start one! Why did *I* never think of that?!" She took out a memo pad and started scribbling something on the paper. "Waiting around to find somewhere that'll accept me is a waste of time. I don't know how I never realized that. Thanks for the advice!"

Her cheeks pinked in elation.

"No, uh, that's...not what I was getting at."

"How many people do you think we need to apply for a charter? Five, maybe? I'd need to officially confirm that, but there's already two of us here, so I think we just need three more."

"Wait, are you including me in that number?"

"Well, I mean, it was your idea, Kaede! And we're friends, aren't we?!"

We had already reached the point where Akiyoshi sometimes called me by my first name. I assumed it was to lessen the awkwardness of asking favors or thanking me.

I hardened my face just enough to not overtly dampen her enthusiasm.

"That seems like a lot of work..."

"I mean, we'll start off with activities that won't be boring with just the two of us. You don't have to do anything that makes you unhappy. We can leave the range of activities pretty wide open, though. Oh, we'll have to make sure we stick to our principles, so we don't just seem like some weird adults."

Her vision was expanding outward infinitely with no destination in sight, and I had a front row seat.

"Um, a mission statement such as...?"

"Becoming our ideal selves within four years."

"Ah."

She really is chock-full of embarrassing quips, I thought. I felt such strong secondhand embarrassment that I nearly let out an awkward laugh myself but did not. I still had my principles.

That said, I got the feeling I was about to be swept up into some strange organization just because I sympathized with my hypothetical friend's sorrows. So I asked a question that was somewhat belittling, with a nuance that suggested it wasn't.

"You know, I always have to wonder how it is that you can live your life thinking about such overambitious ideas." What I hoped to imply was that I was not capable of the same, so I would not be participating.

"It's not overambitious, it's what's inside my heart! But, I mean, trying to become the person that you want to be is something that everyone thinks about, right?"

Not really.

Obviously, you had to think about what you were going to do after college. I, at the very least, did not spend my days pondering my ideal self the way Akiyoshi seemed to.

"Hm, I mean, I'm not really that much of a positive thinker."

"Is that being positive? Honestly, if I had to put a label on it, I'd say that seeing your current self in a less favorable light is more like negative thinking. If I was to become the sort of adult that I never wanted to be, some sort of authoritarian people pleaser who always cared about what other people thought, I'd rather be *dead*."

As her so-called friend, it occurred to me that things would be a lot easier for Akiyoshi if she *were* to become that sort of person.

"Also, I guess that becoming your ideal self might be overambitious if you imagined yourself as an *ally of justice* or something silly like that. But much smaller dreams are just as valid. Like living by a personal code!"

"A personal code?"

"Yeah. The sort of thing that you can never discard. It's that important. You must have at least one principle like that."

I closed my mouth and averted my eyes, to evade her steadfast gaze.

A personal code.

The philosophies by which I lived my life were something deeply engrained within me. However, I was unsure if that was something safe to voice. The only thing that gave me push was the simple fact that I realized that all I'd lose here by facing her criticism was the time spent listening to her lectures. So, I decided to try telling her about my personal code.

"I'm not sure it counts as my personal *code*, but I always try to be careful not to get too close to others or to directly contradict anyone's opinions, I guess. As long as I do that, it reduces the chances of me hurting others, and as a side effect, protects me as well."

I remember Akiyoshi's face clearly after she heard this short and dry little spiel of mine. Her eyes were wide open, her mouth tightly shut. I was certain that this philosophy was one that Akiyoshi, who always loudly voiced her opinions in the pursuit of becoming the person she wanted to be, could never agree with. It was only natural that she would be lost for words, I was sure.

However, instead she said, "Wow, that's really nice of you." Her eyes were still open wide. "That means that you don't want to hurt anyone, right? I had no idea you thought about stuff like that. Like, what the heck? You're a really nice guy, Kaede."

"I don't really think that's nice, per se."

"No, it's super nice! Wow... Honestly, that's an amazing way of thinking." She nodded profusely, huffing through her nose.

Not once had anyone ever affirmed me in that way. Again, she looked at me with those eyes of hers. Whenever she did that,

I could not dismiss her opinion. It's embarrassing to admit, but I suddenly realized that somewhere, in some corner of my heart, some small amount of kindness might actually exist in there.

"C'mon, you have to do this with me." Her gaze burned brighter.

"...I really hate standing out, though."

"Well then, in secret. If it'll get you to agree to it. It can be a secret society."

"A secret society?" I uttered reflexively, hearing this childish proposal come flying out of her mouth.

As though this in fact embarrassed Akiyoshi as well, she averted her eyes, waving her hands in front of her face with a, "Well, something like that..." I couldn't help but smile at seeing her so uncharacteristically flustered.

"Well, I'll think about it."

"Okay."

"So, what's the name of this secret society?" I said, half-teasing.

Akiyoshi jutted out her lip and then pointed at my T-shirt, saying, "Something for which there's no confirmed theory about its purpose or function."

"A moai?"

On the front of my T-shirt, which I had just happened to pick up somewhere or other, was a caricature of a moai statue in profile. Not wanting to orient myself strongly in any particular direction, this vagueness put me at ease.

I suppose that was the day it all began. I started getting together with Akiyoshi more than I ever had before, and it was perhaps then that the *pretense* of our shared friendship truly vanished. It was not the university life that I had hoped for from the outset, but from there on out, an exhilarating time began. No matter how quiet or passive I remained, Akiyoshi always had something new and exciting to bring.

And then, one day...

"Kaede!"

"Hm?"

"Say cheese!"

As I sat beside Akiyoshi in the usual lecture hall, she suddenly called my name and grabbed me by the shoulder, taking a selfie of us both with a digital camera before I could comprehend what was happening.

"Huh? What's with the photo?"

"I just bought this camera. Pretty cool, huh? I'll send you the pic later!"

"Test shot?"

"Yep. I can take pics anytime I like now, so it's best to get some practice in."

When I finally got the file for the picture from my sharp-tongued friend, I saw myself looking at Akiyoshi in confusion, and Akiyoshi with a wide smile upon her face. From then on, taking photos became part and parcel of our Moai activities, but thinking about it now, that was the only time that the two of us ever took a picture together.

Then, another time...

"It's ready!"

"What is this?"

I took the item that was offered to me, finding myself holding a plastic keychain. It depicted a cartoon moai head.

"Awesome, right? We can hang it on our bags, as a mark of our membership."

"Uh...but aren't secret societies supposed to *not* stand out?"

"Jeez, you still on about that? It's fine, Kaede! I'll be the one to wear it. You just keep yours somewhere safe." By that point, Akiyoshi was always calling me by my given name. I eventually ended up putting my keys on the keychain, though I never told her that.

Then, another time.

And another time.

And *another* time.

I came to realize that Akiyoshi was spending the majority of her time at university with me, and so just once, I had to ask.

"Shouldn't you be hanging out with other girls sometimes?"

"I prefer hanging out with guys. You don't have to worry about stuff as much."

It had occurred to me that Akiyoshi probably had very few people she could call friends, and I understood that life in feminine society must be difficult for a person like her.

There were plenty of times when she did not smile. Her face hardened when she read the news, and when she grew angry at someone's opinion, she cut them with a sneer. By the time I realized that though, I was already well beyond thinking that she was someone to be avoided. I recognized this, and I understood her.

The embarrassing behavior, the naiveté that she possessed, always chasing after her ideals, after the truth, were things that I did not share.

"By the way, Kaede. Thank you for accepting me," she said suddenly one day, sometime after our first meeting, I believe when we were on the way back from some museum we had visited.

"What do you mean?"

"Well, I mean, you once told me that you try to avoid getting close to people, so that you can avoid hurting them just by living. So, I'm glad that you accepted me as your friend when you could have just turned me away the first time I ever spoke to you. Without you, I'd be really lonely at school."

By then, I was already beyond thinking what an embarrassing thing that was of her to say. Akiyoshi was the sort of friend who could think those things and say them aloud.

"Woooooow, awkward. What's with this all of a sudden?"

"That's *so* rude! I'm opening my heart up here!"

I still remember the way we laughed that day.

Even though Akiyoshi's laughter is no longer part of this world.

FROM THE MOMENT I opened my eyes in the morning, all I could think about was the bothersome tasks I would have to attend to all day. As a testament to my displeasure, upon merely raising myself up from my futon, I heaved a sigh as though it had already taken up all of my energy for the day to do so.

Regardless, I changed dutifully into my interview suit, picked up my bag, and stepped out of the house, wondering all the while exactly what it was that I was moving my body for. I suppose social sensibilities, or some vague sense of unease.

I grabbed some bread on the way to the station to fill my stomach and stepped onto the train along with all of the salarymen who were running late. The suited figures on the car seemed to be collectively carrying baggage far heavier than the large parcel in my arms.

The train arrived at a station in the business district, one which I had disembarked at many times before in the past few months. At this point, there was no excusing ever letting my facial muscles start to atrophy, so I put on as lively an expression as I could, one that would be, objectively, societally acceptable.

As I exited the turnstile, I took out my smartphone, confirming the location of the business I was visiting today, as well as the name of said business and what their industry was. I crammed information about so many different companies in my head every day that I often forgot which one was which. Basically, I only ever got a strong enough impression from each of these places for them to be totally forgettable, but as long as I prepared suitable enough questions and answers, they would never know that; or at the very least, even if I did fumble, I could show them that I had the chops to cover that up.

I navigated my walking route via a map, arriving properly at the office building in question ten minutes before the appointed time. I wondered what the adults who worked here felt when they showed up for duty at this towering building every day. Perhaps it at least helped them feel as though they were maintaining some measure of self-respect.

I straightened my spine, put on a casual smile, and plunged into the enemy stronghold. I passed through the automatic sliding doors and headed for the spacious elevator lobby, finding two people already waiting there. There was a grinning man who looked to be in his later twenties and a woman similarly clad in interview attire. One could tell at a glance that they were a recruiter and a job hunter. I had a fundamental dislike of job hunters, so I kept my distance. Still, I was able to overhear much of their conversation while waiting for the elevator to arrive. The recruiter seemed overly familiar with the woman, the woman speaking in an oddly flirtatious fashion. Just as I was quietly wondering whether she might not be aiming to sleep her way into a job, the elevator arrived, and I stepped in.

I assumed the pair might board the elevator together, but as I waited inside, the woman bowed her head, said a thanks and some parting words to the recruiter, and then the man stepped through the open doors alone. It seemed their interview or whatever had concluded. The pair continued chatting until just before the doors closed, and I wondered whether I should go ahead and push the "door close" button, when at the very tail end of the conversation, I heard some unforgettable words from the recruiter.

"All right, see you at the Moai meet."

Though there was no way I was going to let the businessman beside me see my reaction, internally, my mood immediately soured. So that girl went to my school, then.

The recruiter disembarked at the third floor, leaving me alone for the rest of the ride up to the ninth floor. I took the opportunity to heave a sigh and then steadied my breath, once more straightening up my spine and fixing my expression.

There was a reception desk immediately outside of the ninth-floor elevators. I approached with a smile and gave my name.

"Hello, my name is Tabata Kaede. I have an appointment

for an interview," I said with an award-winning smile. The receptionist showed me to the waiting room, where there were two other students with the same smiles on their faces—smiles that looked as though our faces had been permanently frozen in place.

It was enough to assure me of how desperately unnerving the creatures known as job hunters were.

Though I had not physically exhausted myself whatsoever, by the time I returned home I was exhausted nonetheless.

After my arrival that morning, I had attended one interview and one information seminar. I collapsed the moment I made it to my living room, loosening the necktie that I was expected to wear on a daily basis but could never truly get used to. I would probably wrinkle my interview suit that way, but I couldn't bring myself to care. I was supposed to have used my last three years as a grace period to recharge my batteries, but instead I was about to hit rock bottom. Going through the motions of job hunting in earnest had thoroughly exhausted me.

Thus, it was probably good that I received the call when I did. I waited dutifully until the third ring and then picked up.

"Tabata Kaede of XX University speaking. Yes, oh no, thank you so much for taking the time out of your busy schedule to speak with me. Yes. Of course. Oh, thank you very much! Yes, I understand. Yes. Thank—oh, yes, thank you so much. Yes, well then, mm-hmm, I will talk to you later. Yes, thank you very much. Goodbye for now."

I hung up the phone, suddenly noticing that I had at some point started kneeling seiza-style. All of the tension then flooded from my body, and I fell back onto the floor. There was no point in me even worrying about wrinkles anymore.

The call had been from the last company I had spoken with today. The call's contents? "We would be absolutely thrilled to hire you, Tabata-san."

In other words, I was in the home stretch.

"All *right*..."

I looked up at the ceiling just above me, speaking tentative words of triumph, but there was no joy behind those sounds. The problem was not that this company was not my first choice. It was a large corporation and there were no unsavory rumors about it, so I should have been thrilled. I was also relieved not to have to go through the interview process again. However, I was immediately stricken with a feeling of anxiety. In an instant, I had become a full-fledged member of society. I had only spoken any words of joy because I knew that while this decision was only still tentative, this was a joyful thing as far as my position in society.

It was just that my emotions did not actually agree.

I got it in mind that I might go to sleep right then and there, enjoying the warm May weather, but I realized that there were still some things I needed to do and stood up. I changed into some sweatpants and took out a *happoshu* from the refrigerator in the kitchen on the other side of the doorway, heading for my computer desk. I tapped away on the keyboard (which was short one Shift key) and logged into my Hotmail account. I had to e-mail the HR departments of all of the companies I was interviewing at, including the one I had just interviewed at today, and let them know that I had accepted an offer and would no longer be continuing the interview process.

I pried up the pull tab on the can, taking a sip of the *happoshu*. I tried to imagine how it might feel to be a personnel manager turned down by a hopeful student. It probably just meant that it narrowed down the pool of people they had to reject. Thinking about it that way made this a little easier.

Just as I had finished draining the can, my vision began to swim. I could feel the alcohol buzzing in my skull. I did not even have to wonder if it was because I was tired. I leaned back into the chair and again looked up to the ceiling.

The ceiling was still clean and white. I had once tried smoking a cigarette, but I found it didn't suit me.

The thought suddenly occurring to me, I picked up my phone and sent Tousuke a text letting him know about my offer. Immediately, I got a reply of, "'Gratz!" and was relieved to know that there was at least someone I could be myself around.

I tossed my phone onto the desk and dazedly returned to the grind.

Thinking about it, job hunting was all about pretending over and over again not to be yourself. That's why I was so tired.

However, I doubted that was merely an issue restricted only to job hunting. It was sure to continue into my professional life, and I would need to be even more cautious. I had tried to get some practice with this working part-time jobs, but it was nowhere on the same level.

No one gets to live by their own principles once you become a working adult. Everyone has to suppress their true selves.

Thus, that simple "'Gratz!" from Tousuke was a sign to me that I had cleared the first hurdle—and that even more formidable obstacles awaited me ahead. I wondered if I should even be thankful for it.

I emptied the can and retrieved another from the fridge. On the short trip back to the office, the overly chilled beer in hand, I staggered, slipping on a badly written CV that had fallen onto the floor.

I picked up the CV that had attempted to wound me. It was distressingly smooth to the touch. I thought for a moment of throwing it away but instead returned to my desk and sat down, the book still in hand. I read over the tidy self-introduction and personal statement that had been written in ballpoint pen.

Find meaning in your life by being helpful to every single person you meet, not just some theoretical individual.

Be ambitious in your hopes and dreams, but don't just stare into the far distance.

Cherish every step of the journey.

There is joy in seeking common ground in every conversation.

It was lies. All lies.

But that was to be expected. I was by no means such an upstanding person.

It was idiotic, but I also did not care to give up the lie. It was my ability to survive that had gotten me this job offer after all. I had obtained the means to live. I was not wrong in this.

It was fine if you had the ability and the looks and the means to live however you wanted, but that was not me.

And that was fine.

Living life as someone other than yourself.

I wasn't wrong. I couldn't be wrong.

I...was simply not wrong.

...Was I?

Perhaps it was both the power of the alcohol and my own sense of relief from the job offer that lowered my defenses. Those sort of thoughts that I would never usually care to think began drifting through my head.

By not being myself, I had gotten results. However, that did not feel like my own success.

From here on out, I was going to have to live half my life with something that I had obtained by disguising my own self. A stifling life, one that deep down I could not fully consent to.

So then, what had the twenty-one years I had lived up until now all been for?

Was there even any point to the past three years I had lived? My head swirled with the knowledge that that wasn't the problem, that that was not what was wrong here. This was all because of the alcohol and because of the job offer.

What if I could live without worrying about my abilities and my looks and my surroundings—without having to make those calculations every day?

If only I could just be an idealist.

What if there had been something I had wished more strongly to obtain by my own hands? I shook my head.

No such thing existed.

So that I could rid myself of these pointless thoughts, I drained the second can in one go. However, once I had begun sinking into the bog of these booze-muddled ponderings, all I could do was sink in deeper. By the time I rested the weight of my fevered head onto the desk, stacking a fourth can along the edge of it, I had lost not only all my defenses but my reasoning.

And then, I realized it.

It was not a distant memory. It was there, stark.

I lifted my hot and heavy head and rested my fingers on the mouse. I moved the arrow-shaped cursor down to the lower left, hovering it over a folder. I double-clicked, finding only a single image file inside. My fingers were trembling solely because of the alcohol. I steeled myself and once more double-clicked with unnecessary speed.

The image that opened was a photo, taken three years prior. I regarded the photo through eyes swimming in a swaying skull. The price of my haircut aside, I had not changed one bit. In the line of my surprised gaze in the photo was a smile that was no longer in this world.

A sigh slipped from my lips all on its own.

"Hey, Akiyoshi."

My own voice was much higher than I thought it would be.

"I've got a question."

I could feel my own thoughts curdling in my mouth.

"What did *you* want to be...?" I asked, though I knew I would never receive an answer to that question. Still, I wanted to know, more than anything, what it was that Akiyoshi was thinking back then. I wished someone could at least impart that much knowledge to me, someone who could accomplish nothing as himself.

"It was all a lie in the end..."

The words that we exchanged. Mine...and Akiyoshi's.

I remembered how we were back as freshmen. I tried not to remember, but the seams of the barrel burst, and the memories came flooding out.

When I first met Akiyoshi, I thought she was nothing more than a troublesome person, but I accepted the way she was, and we became friends. Akiyoshi was always spouting her ideals, and under her influence, at some point I began to have dreams of my own. I even thought that within those four years I might find it, that ideal self of mine that Akiyoshi spoke of.

But it was too late for that. There was no going back now.

Now, I was alone.

"Maybe things would've been different if you were here," I called to her, but of course there was no reply. She could no longer speak to me.

And so my life as a university student had come to an end—exhausted from job hunting, grumbling into my beer cans, unable to do a single thing.

I could not become the person I wished to be; I had no idea who that person even was in the first place. Four years were going to pass me by without me so much as receiving a sign that those ideals of Akiyoshi's were ever going to become a reality—even if there were still ten months left.

"The world could change tomorrow."

Akiyoshi had said that once. I heard those words in my head as clearly as if they had been spoken yesterday. My own mind was slipping, taunting me.

"If there was a reason for everyone to put down their guns as one, then all wars would end tomorrow."

You did say that, huh?

Stupid. These stupid, stupid, *stupid* ideals.

"So, there's nothing that will ever be too late to change."

Stop it.

It hurt. It hurt so badly.

The pit of my chest ached.

"...Are you saying that there's still time?"

These last three years of mine... Could I still make them mean something? If I could still make it in time, like Akiyoshi said.

Maybe I did want to change something. Maybe there was something I wanted to change about myself.

I no longer knew who it was that I wanted to become. Without Akiyoshi, I had no idea.

You can't change the things that you don't understand.

So then, what could I change?

In the photo, Akiyoshi was smiling. A smile all her own, utterly unlike the one that I or the other job hunters who had been present in that office had worn.

Suddenly, the scene I had witnessed just before boarding the elevator that morning flashed before my eyes. I saw again that girl from my university, who was accomplishing all that I had in three years just by flattering a salaryman.

"That girl was part of Moai," I told Akiyoshi, but she did not reply. She was gone, after all. Never in all this time had that fact been as clear to me as it was right now. If the Akiyoshi in that photo had heard what I was presently saying, she would have been shocked. She might have been disappointed, or even angry.

However, all we have is reality. Reality is what's here with us right now, and the end result of all that Akiyoshi had left behind was the job hunter I had seen today. Thus, in the end, Akiyoshi had ended up a liar.

Even now, it still aches me somewhat to think that she would ever be deemed that way.

...Something I wanted to change.

"Like...making that lie Aki...yoshi told...into a reality..."

If only.

As I spoke my slurred words with my clumsy tongue, though I had no real goal or concrete plan or means, I felt a flame burning in my aching chest. It was not a raging fire, just a quiet, smoldering, little ember.

It was around then that I blacked out.

The next morning when I came to, I found myself curled up on the floor beside the office chair that I should have been sitting in. The flooring beneath me was sticky. Before I even moved, just as I was registering what sort of a position I was in, I realized that the flame inside my chest was still burning.

—✶—

When we first formed Moai, we went out to all sorts of places under the pretense of the activities of our secret society. More succinctly, we went to photo galleries of investigative journalism from around the world and lectures given by authors who spoke out against hate speech and the like.

Naturally, it was always Akiyoshi who strong-armed me into these adventures. That day, the two of us had gone to see a war documentary. It was as we had stopped in at a café along the way home afterwards, sharing our impressions on the film, and it was beginning to seem that one or the other of us was looking to part ways that I suddenly asked Akiyoshi, "So, we went to see a movie today, but what really is your ultimate goal here?"

I needed to know. If I was to be involved from here on out, I needed to know what destination was in store for the future of Moai.

Last time, we went to a photo gallery, this time, a movie. I had no objections with going on these excursions, but to be honest with myself, I wasn't keen on the idea of doing volunteer work or anything. However, as she was very much wont to, Akiyoshi completely misinterpreted my question.

"Hmm. Well, my *ultimate* goal is to achieve global peace..."

"...Mm, no I mean like, not *your* overarching goals. I'm

wondering what it is we're supposed to be doing in Moai over these four years," I corrected. She looked at me a bit dumbfounded and then with a timid smile that could almost be construed as self-conscious.

"Aha, I gotcha. But I mean, I think it's the same for Moai."

"The same for Moai... You mean world peace?" I said with an unintentional smirk. Akiyoshi did not share my wry smile.

"If we could, yeah. I'd like to ease the suffering of the people of the world, only if it's just a little. That's why I think it's really important to watch these films and such to increase awareness. Because we learned about these things today, perhaps you or I could do something about this stuff one day, Kaede," she said, completely earnestly.

Akiyoshi had misunderstood me—but at the same time, I had misunderstood her. I don't think I understood what it truly meant to have an "ideal." There were no limits or bounds to Akiyoshi's ideals. It didn't matter if we were just students, if we were only two people. She would never even voice such an excuse.

I'm sure that, at that time, Akiyoshi truly believed that she could bring peace to the world with her own two hands. I had no idea just how wide the world was in Akiyoshi's eyes.

"W-well, one day, maybe."

"One day means it could happen *any* day. That's what I think. You could die any day, and you never know when it's going to happen. You've got to leave at least a little something behind."

In that moment, I felt that, unlike myself, there was no way that Akiyoshi was not going to leave something behind in this world when she died. She was going to live an accomplished, fulfilled life.

Or so I hoped, anyway.

"That's why, should anything ever happen to me, I want you to carry on my and Moai's mission, Kaede."

"Don't say ominous stuff like that."

"You never know! Nothing in this world is certain. But doesn't that just mean that we have to live every day to its fullest?" She looked me straight in the eye, and I averted my gaze, unable to voice any further opinion on the matter.

And yet, even now, in my fourth year, I had yet to live up to this important role that Akiyoshi had thrust upon me.

—*—

All that said, despite this new impulse of mine, I was currently without any direction, unsure of what I should do, what I *could* do. So, for now, I just decided to hit up my buddy Tousuke. He had received a job offer one step ahead of me, having devoted himself to job hunting since the end of his third year, previously having mainly busied himself with part-time work and seminars. I figured that if there was anyone I could consult, it would be Tousuke, who had far more activities, more opportunities than me, who at least ostensibly did not avoid people or loathe to set foot in new environments. I also just wanted to tell him face-to-face about the end of my job hunt.

We decided to meet up at a karaoke place, which I was convinced was only doing so well at the moment because of the amount of money we students dropped there. The location was my idea. Tousuke had previously suggested that we go to karaoke to celebrate the job offers, so I decided to piggyback off of that.

We would be meeting up that evening after my last class of the day was over. Typically, students took a lot fewer classes in their senior year, but as I had had no particular plans for the first three years of my university career, I had now cracked down on my studies, finding myself in classes alongside mostly underclassmen. It would be no laughing matter if I ended up having to stay on another term because I was short a few credits despite already having a solid job offer, so I was pretty serious about things.

In classes that had group activities, I had assumed that I would have trouble keeping my head held high among all these younger students, but it turned out that there were a handful of other wayward seniors in the mix as well, which made things a lot easier to handle emotionally. Presently, we were all huddled together, drudging our way through our lessons.

As always, I greeted my fellow group members and quietly took my seat, waiting for yet another class period to march on by. However, just before class began, a breeze stoked the flames burning within me.

From the group of juniors sitting nearby, there was a voice that could be heard clearly throughout the classroom, a loud "What?!" from a girl who I had independently decided must have a strong sense of responsibility. It was a different volume from those voices that were normally so indistinct within the din of classrooms in all their varying sizes.

I turned only my ears to her, half assuming the usual stance of a lackadaisical senior uninterested in the underclassmen I was taking class alongside, half-unable to contain my curiosity. The girl who had shouted sounded as though she was angry at someone.

From what I could gather, one of their group members had been assigned an important task but had gotten busy with club activities and neglected to complete it. Moreover, said member had sent an e-mail boldly informing them of this, as well as notifying them that they would be skipping class today, which had gotten this girl, the group leader, quite vexed. Come to think of it, we did have some small group presentations to give that day.

One of the other girls noted that person had an important part of the presentation, along with the fact that they had sent that e-mail and refused to answer any calls. *Man, that sucks,* I thought, fiddling with my phone, when right on time, the group leader roared indignantly, "We're in big trouble!"

How did people get their voices to echo that loud? I wondered.

"Is it not enough for them to just sit around hogging up the whole cafeteria all day?!"

"A-all right, calm down there."

"I can't stand those Moai *creeps*!"

After an indistinct moment of silence, just then, luckily for all of us, the bell rang. The collective sigh of relief from everyone but the group leader could be felt from every corner of the classroom.

Unsurprisingly, the group that was missing their materials was not able to give their presentation during that class period. When the group leader explained the situation to our instructor, an associate professor, she was met with a reply of, "Well, they're probably pretty busy right now," in support of the student who had skipped. The girl's shoulders trembled.

After class, I was a bit peckish, so I picked up a bread roll from a kiosk and ate it. I had a bit of time to kill before our scheduled meet-up, so I sent messages to my parents and the manager of my former part-time job informing them I had accepted a job offer.

I arrived at the karaoke bar about three minutes after we had agreed to meet. Tousuke was standing out front, poking idly at his phone.

"'Sup," I called casually. Tousuke looked up, pursing his lips dramatically.

"Well, if it isn't the man who's just run away from a life of endless, infinite possibilities!"

"Like I ever had those to begin with."

We continued our vapid conversation as we entered the bar, finding in fact several groups of students from our university inside. Thankfully though, there was no one who I recognized. We stood in line, checked in, collected some drinks from the bar, and moved up to our allotted booth on the second floor. A faint smell of tobacco wafted out as we opened the door. I should have just taken a seat on the sofa and struck up the conversation right away, but we had come here for karaoke after all, so I decided I may as well sing a few songs first and not think about anything.

Both Tousuke and I sang whatever songs we liked in whatever way we liked, regardless of whether we both knew them or whether our own choices would get the other pumped up. Every once in a while, one of us would find the song the other was singing catchy, and we would make a note of it in our phones' memos so that we could look it up online later.

This was the proper way to enjoy karaoke.

After we had had a little bit of fun, Tousuke stood from his seat for the umpteenth time, saying he was going to get more drinks and asked me what I wanted; I asked for a melon soda.

I watched him go but thought it would be weird to sing something without him and so just scrolled on my phone in the meantime. It would take him a little while since the only bars were on the first and third floors. Melon soda was only available on the third floor, incidentally.

I finished checking over my feeds on some social networks I had joined just to lurk, and started to feel a strange curiosity and discomfort when Tousuke returned, making a show of furrowing his brow and sighing through his nostrils. I knew from experience that this was a face he made when he was trying to disguise actual irritation.

"Thanks. Something happen?"

"Oh, caught on, did you? Gonna ask about it?"

"What is it?"

He took a swig of the Calpis he had bought himself, glancing outside of the windowed booth door. I followed his gaze but saw nothing and no one there.

"Hm, maybe I was mistaken."

"Could be."

"Listen. Ugh, I hate seeing people have that much fun."

"Well, aren't you a piece of work," I snarked.

But Tousuke shook his head in a joking matter with a, *"Non, non."* He continued. "It would've been fine if it was more upstanding young students such as ourselves or a group of cute girls, but there are two types of gatherings I absolutely cannot stand. One, couples."

"And two?"

"Big, noisy groups."

"I mean, I get that." I nodded, the portrait of unparalleled virtue.

"Right?" said Tousuke, pointing back at me for no particular reason.

Then, he said something that was incredibly relevant to me.

"What I hate the worst, though, are those lame people who walk around like they own the whole place, on campus and off. They act like they're the representatives of our school or something, making a mess everywhere they go. It makes outsiders doubt the character of even upstanding guys like us."

"...Yeah."

I nodded in understanding. I understood immediately who it was that Tousuke was regarding with such contempt, these "lame" characters who acted like they owned the place. He was always taking any opportunity he could to badmouth them, after all.

Most crucially though, I knew who he meant, because I resented them as well, more than Tousuke, more than even the group leader who had been so incensed during class. So as not to be distracted by that last fact, I scrunched up my face and asked, "Let me guess, Moai?"

"Yep. They were swarming all around the party room on the third floor. They're so annoying. I should've gone down to the first floor."

What an utterly fortuitous topic of conversation.

"Off by a factor of two," I teased.

Tousuke sullenly put in a new song, so I granted him a reprieve. It was the latest track from his newest band, which put him in a good mood.

Normally, I would have felt the same.

Normally, I would have been irritated to know that those people were at the same establishment as us, just like Tousuke was. Having to cross paths with the Moai folks during my university life was inexcusable.

Today, however, was different. You could perhaps even call this convenient. I had decided on something, after all.

I would talk to Tousuke. I would tell him that there was something I planned to do—something that I *had* to do, in order to give the last three years of my life any measure of meaning. Before anything else could happen, I decided to confide in my dear friend.

In order to do so, first, I would have to tell him all about them. I had to tell him about the Moai that we had originally built, and the Moai that Tousuke so loathed.

After much loud protest and resistance, Tousuke set down the mic, and I took the opportunity to strike up the conversation. "Okay, listen."

Tousuke's only reply was to look back at me, wide-eyed and questioning.

"Can I talk to you about something a little serious?"

"My, how *rare*! It's one thing to come from me, the honors student, but to think that even Kaede would have something serious to say! What ever could that be?"

I gave him the expected retort of, "I don't see any honors students here," before once more starting, angling myself slightly away from him so as not to make the conversation seem too intense.

"So those Moai guys, the ones you hate."

"They oughta go back home to Easter Island!"

"Yeah, so about them."

In my twenty-one years, I had become quite skilled at forming a troubled smile.

"I started that group."

"You can't be serious! No way you'd put together a bunch of stick-in-their-ass creeps like that! I thought that you were more low-key and just wanted to have fun and relax every day, but I guess I misjudged you!"

"No, I really am serious."

Tousuke's face, which had twisted in mock rage, now twitched, his crossed arms unfolding.

"D-don't worry, even if you really were the evil commander of that wicked group, I would never stop being your friend. I would bury you in the name of justice, with my own two hands—okay, what's with *that* face?"

"I'm serious."

"...Wha?"

"I'm being serious here. Me and a friend who's no longer around actually started that group."

"...What are you saying?"

He was staring at me slack-jawed, his eyes wider than I'd ever seen them. I got the feeling that if I looked back at him for too long he would start thinking I was joking, so I averted my gaze slightly.

"There's a little more to that, though."

"...Well, okay, let's hear it then, I guess," said Tousuke, making it obvious that though he was listening, he was still skeptical. Despite all his posturing, though, I knew that Tousuke was a good person deep down and would listen carefully to what I had to say.

Without any reservations, I told him about my connections with Moai.

This was the first time I had ever told this whole story to anyone. Because this was the first time, I decided to tell the story simply, starting out with just the important points.

First, I explained the current state of Moai.

As far as I was aware, all of the founding members of the Moai that Akiyoshi and I had founded were now all gone. However, the Moai that had persisted afterward was *not* the Moai that we had founded.

Our founding ideals of "becoming the people we wished to be," and the idea that we would only act in the way that represented all of our members' interests, had already faded. I didn't know the details of it, but the group had completely changed form from the original organization, expanding into an immense group that had spread to every corner of the campus.

How could this have happened?

Moai, the group that had been founded on a promise between just two people. Two people concerned only with our own opinions, going to museums, attending lectures, and volunteering—doing idealistic things that would result in no profit at all.

There were a number of causes behind the group's transformation.

Others saw us doing these activities, things which on the surface looked as though we were just having fun, and grew interested, and our membership grew. The university began to see some value in what we were doing, at some unexpected juncture.

However, the greatest reason was neither of those. It was that our unparalleled, idealistic leader and her lofty notions were lost to the sands of time. There was nothing more crucial than this.

Without its captain at the helm, the organization grew weaker than I ever could have imagined, gradually warping and twisting, eating into its own flesh. It metamorphized into a group that sought profit over ideals.

Finally, there was someone who was expelled from the group: me. This new form of Moai had no use for me and my lingering, lofty ideals. And so, I distanced myself from the group. Laying this all out before me, that was all there was to it.

"At least, I assumed that was all there was to it, so I haven't really bothered worrying about it, until now." I heaved a sigh. "But now I have a job, and my future is secured, like you've said, so I've been rethinking the things I've done up until now. I started thinking about when we founded Moai. And since we got on the topic of Moai, I figured I should tell you," I explained, even though I'd actually been working up the courage to bring this up since morning.

Tousuke listened quietly, dutifully to my story, not giving away what he was thinking. From the next room I could hear a song from a band that was popular when we were in high school.

"Sorry for not saying anything until now," I apologized. Tousuke scratched his head awkwardly.

"No...I get it." He looked truly troubled. "Seriously though, I hate that I've been sitting here badmouthing something that you created... Or, well, I'm sure it sucked more for you to have to sit there and listen to all that." Tousuke gave a cautious, bitter smile before his face cramped again. "Yeah, it must be worse for you."

"Ah, yeah, really though, if you're angry about things, I'm sorry."

"I'm not. It's just, well...hearing all that, I think it just makes me hate them more. It's a group that you, my friend, put together, but I just can't bring myself to like them in the slightest."

I found myself grinning at this earnest, yet considerate, admission. I waved a hand at him.

"It's fine, I really don't mind. I'm not involved with them at all right now, so I don't care if you love them or hate them."

"You sure?"

"Really, I'm sure."

"You aren't angry at those guys? I mean, all those guys who are in Moai right now pushed you out!"

Put simply, I understood what Tousuke was saying, that I would be justified in disliking the people who had done this to me. Given how well I understood this, I chose my words carefully.

"Hm, I can't say that I'm angry, per se. Thinking about it now, I've never *really* been angry with them. After I left, I was kind of just disappointed, so honestly, I wrote the whole thing off, and I've just found their behavior since then shocking."

"And the friend you built that group with is now..." Tousuke struggled to complete the sentence.

"She's no longer in this world," I confirmed, smiling to make this topic as light as possible.

"Sorry," he muttered. Tousuke really was a good guy.

"No, it's all right. And actually, there's one more reason why I brought this up just now. I was wondering if there was something I could do for my friend, and I was hoping to pick your brain about it. I'm done with job hunting and I've got some time now, and as for my thesis, well...as long as I graduate, I'll be happy. I was thinking I should use the last of my university days to do something for someone else."

"Well, that's awful thoughtful of you."

"Isn't it? Wonder if there's anything I can do."

"Hmm," Tousuke sighed, looking deep in thought. However, I realized at length that he was not coming up with ideas. He was thinking about what he should say to me. I laughed at my own imaginings.

"I'm guessing if you were in my position, you'd just rip all those Moai guys a new one," I said, and his face twisted, as though he had been scheming something wicked, before he leaned in close to me.

"Well, if it were *me* and these guys had not only pushed me out but disrespected my long-lost friend, I would want to settle this at graduation."

"Settle this?"

"I dunno how, I just know it'd be pretty hard to take the group back at this point."

He was right. Wresting back control would be impossible. Warped and stained by self-interest or no, at this point in time, it had grown into quite a large organization. It was no longer just some small recreational club. Taking Moai back by conspiring to steal it away with words would mean trying to make the entire organization my own. Trying to overthrow all of the current leadership and get the sudden unconditional backing of the whole membership would be difficult.

I thought for a moment, then looked firmly into Tousuke's eyes.

"So, what then, do I just try to tear the whole thing down? That's impossible."

"...Mm, well you said so yourself, didn't you? It's a fragile organization. There might be some way to do that."

"Some way… I mean, all I've really thought about is how I'd do Moai over again. It seems like all that would do is make things messier, though."

"I gotcha. Well, I mean, you could just take them down and then form a new Moai. Reform it with someone who would have the backing of the underclassmen. Oh, but who supports the original ideals, of course."

I wondered if I could do that, if I could cure Akiyoshi's words of their falsehood.

"I could even be a secretary or something."

"Oh, no, man, I don't want to get you caught up in this."

"You really gotta rely on your friends."

"You ready for a fight?"

"Well, I mean, it's all up to you, but if you're down, then I'm down to help."

Destroying the current Moai and building a new one; I gave the proposal some serious consideration. Erasing that twisted organization, so removed from its ideals, from existence and rebuilding it upon its origins. It would be founded around someone who had the same sort of ideals as Akiyoshi.

That would be the sort of conflict that she would have relished.

That said, at some point, the scales within my heart had begun to tip in favor of my own will. I had begun to think that it might not be so bad to put my friend's words behind me and try living my university life again as I chose. I wondered if I hadn't simply grown tired of living as someone else.

I was struck by a naive sort of feeling, just like a certain someone who called the nonsensical pattern that she wrote into the future with her own feelings "ideals."

"I...I guess so."

"Hm?"

"...I think...I might do it. Try fighting Moai," I said tentatively.

"Well, all right then!"

"...I don't want to do anything that's gonna mess with our job offers or anything like that, though. And obviously this all has to stay within the bounds of the law."

"We're going to be a secret society battling an evil organization! That's kind of cool."

Seeing how thoroughly Tousuke was on board with this, I felt a renewed regret about having broached the topic of Moai in the first place.

"If you get uncomfortable, you can bail at any time."

"Sure. I've got plenty of time though, and honestly, this is totally my jam. I've always wanted to be part of some underdog team taking on a huge organization. It's just like the *20th Century Boys*."

I half-wondered if he was saying this just so that I would not worry, but seeing the genuine excitement in his smile, I realized he might actually be serious about this.

Battles are decided by force, but we could not take on the Moai head-on, so first we needed to gather more intel on our enemy. Ever since I left, I had had no connection with them, and in fact, had only a hazy awareness of the group. I would need to do more concrete research into their current activities and their internal organization. To that end, Tousuke tagged along to my place after we left the karaoke bar.

First, we decided to check their homepage. Upon seeing the overly simplistic lettering and images that appeared on the screen, Tousuke, who had kept his distance from the group purely because he hated them, let out an "Ugh" behind me. Given his displeasure, I took over the task of checking the page.

Displayed in large lettering atop their streamlined front page was a summary of the group's major activities. I had already had some idea about them having become a job-hunting organization, but it also seemed that the scope of their activities had become a lot more solidified than when I was part of the group. I continued reading the fine print.

Moai, at present, was chiefly a networking group. Naturally, that was a separate activity from the horsing around Tousuke had seen them doing in the rented party room at the karaoke bar that evening. Clearly, that had been a gathering of all the self-centered job seekers who had come together under the group's banner to celebrate their shared victories under the guise of a meet-up. These meet-ups, which consisted of Moai members, university alumni, and the professionals they were affiliated with, were billed as an exchange of knowledge and creativity. Apparently, students and professionals would be put into groups together to discuss such big ideas as "true independence" and "dealing with differences," but judging by the fact that they had posted up the personal histories and companies of those professionals, as well as students' intended career paths, the important part here was the connections.

"So basically, they're all just trying to network with people for their own gain," Tousuke sighed bitterly behind me. Apparently, this so-called meet-up was an incredibly popular, large event that brought together fifty or more Moai members, and as many working adults. The home page was covered in images of an unnecessarily large event hall and students putting on serious faces while listening to other people talk. Here and there I glimpsed faces of people that even I, with my immensely narrow school social circles, was familiar with. I looked at the upcoming events to see that they intended to book the hall again for another such meeting the week after next.

If you're wondering how I felt about this, all I can really say was that I was sure that this was not what "becoming your ideal self" meant. I also felt bewilderment that such a drastic shift in philosophy could happen in just a few years.

There were apparently a number of small discussion groups and lectures that were held more frequently than the mixers, but there were very few pictures of these gatherings, as though perhaps they were really more of an afterthought.

I returned to the front page and looked at the menu. Following from there, I was able to read about their group philosophies, and the companies that graduates were headed for employment at and so forth—but none of this was particularly valuable information to me. Perhaps aware of the fact that no one was interested in the individual members, there was no specific information about them.

"Hmm, guess an evil organization would never hand over the intel you want that easily," said Tousuke as he peered at the screen, crunching into an *umaibo* stick he had purchased. "Hey, what's that? A blog?"

"No pointing snacks at the screen," I chided, but then I looked at the corner of the screen he had indicated. There was a banner with the label "Moai Diary." I clicked on it, wondering why it was called a diary and not a newsletter, and was greeted by a page with an overly florid look, accented with a background of an image of the blue sky, which I supposed *would* be a bit much for a newsletter.

I scrolled down and read the latest post.

"Howdy, Ten-san here!"

As I read that line, I heard Tousuke mutter, "Wonder if that guy's in our department."

"You know them? I'm assuming Ten is a nickname."

"Ah, yeah. There's an underclassman I know pretty well who's in the group. Not sure if I've heard of him or not though."

"I see."

I was somehow relieved to know that Tousuke didn't hate the players as much he hated the game, though perhaps that was not the most apt metaphor.

I continued reading the blog, skimming an article that seemed to be alluding to the launch of some kind of event or something, spelled out in emoji. *Well, that's charming,* I started to think, a weary Tousuke reading my mind and sighing, "Charming. They really stole your Moai away."

"Well, I'm sure they don't think of it like that."

"So the victim feels like bullying was going on, but not the offenders. How pleasant."

"Aha..." I nodded in agreement and scrolled further down the blog, finding that several people seemed to be taking turns keeping it up to date, but all that was written was a bunch of miscellaneous info. No useful intel at all—neither for our purposes, nor for anyone who even might have come here seeking information on Moai for innocent reasons.

"Wait, so you mentioned having a kouhai who was in Moai. Do you not hate them too?"

"Well, y'know," he replied. "She's a good kid. Pon-chan, from Ehime."

"Pretty auspicious nickname there. You know, 'the Pon in Pon Juice is the Pon of Nippon,'" I quipped, referencing the slogan of a popular drink from Ehime.

"Really?! Thought it was like a *ponkan* orange."

I was surprised at the fact that he'd be caught by a joke like that at this juncture.

"Anyway, I don't see anything from *that* Pon-chan here on this blog."

"Ah, she said that she's only involved with Moai because she's got a friend in the group. I think she just joined because she thought it'd be an easy way to meet alumni. To be honest, I don't usually respect half-assed decisions like that, but other than that, she's a pretty swell gal."

"You're really talking her up here. You got your eye on her or something?"

"No way! Apparently, she's got some boyfriend she's been with since high school, anyway. Cute girls are always already taken when you meet them," he sighed mournfully, and then, as though overtaken by some impulse, started chugging a bottle of lemon tea.

I continued on for a while looking for information on Moai, eventually having checked every corner of the group's home page. Having gotten little results, I decided to open up YouTube, when Tousuke, who had been messing around on his phone, suddenly offered, "Oh, hey, you wanna meet her? Pon, that is. We might be able to ask her about the members."

"Ah, yes, the girl who was taken."

"Shut up! She's a good kid, and she just sent me a message about a seminar. I guess her supplemental lesson ran long."

"Oho."

I decided to press a bit more about this proposal. "If we meet her and tell her that we're looking to overthrow Moai, won't the jig be up?"

"It should be fine. I don't think she's all that invested in Moai, and we don't have to go into it acting like Moai is our objective. We just let it come up during the course of our conversation."

"I see..." The sense of worldliness that I had cultivated over the past three years had somehow managed to overtake my own personal philosophies. "That makes sense. Sure, wanna set it up, then?"

"Can-deedily-do."

I left the arrangements to my reliable pal, who set us up to meet sometime on the following Monday. Tousuke's social circles were so much wider than mine; thanks to him, we had a shortcut right into Moai that I never would have found on my own. I really had to thank him.

While my buddy set up the meeting, I searched Moai on social media. I found a number of accounts indicating, in their display names, that the owners belonged to Moai, cringing again as I peeked at some of the feeds, full of nothing but photos and comments that would give the impression that they were living their university years with some kind of noble-mindedness. Moai's activities were not supposed to be the sort of thing you'd want to show off to others.

I continued my search, finding some posts that spoke out against Moai as well. Most of them were from students from our university, but a few of them even seemed to be from working adults. It felt like the wind was blowing in my favor.

Tousuke and I had already vaguely discussed after karaoke the notion of how an individual might take on an organization. The swiftest ideas we came up with were a scandal or a scorched earth attack. There were plenty of stories of groups going up in flames after a single tawdry exposure, and it was easy to conceal the source of that spark. What was crucial here, I realized, was that there were enough people around to keep pouring oil on the flames—but what I was seeing might do the trick. These were the thoughts I had as I looked on, unable to distinguish what about the organization that I myself had founded was a lie and what was the truth.

Though, the badmouthing did start to get to me, ever so slightly.

Regardless, I had decided my course of action. Tousuke and I played some games for a while until we grew bored, and then Tousuke went home.

Then, the following week.

I entered a coffee shop a short walk from the university to the sound of a ringing bell that imparted a peculiar sense of nostalgia, finding Tousuke seated at the very back. I could only see the back of her head from where I was, but there was a short girl seated across from him. That had to be Pon-chan.

I had come to this shop many times before at Tousuke's invitation. It was a regular haunt of his, and the sort of place that suited perfectly both Tousuke's surprising fascination with the Showa era and my own desire to run into other students from our school as infrequently as possible. It was, incidentally, also close to where Pon-chan lived.

I held a hand up, approaching them. Tousuke waved back. I have no idea whether or not it was rude of me to think that I suddenly understood why Tousuke thought her name was the "pon" of a *ponkan* orange when she noticed this and turned around, looking at me through big, round eyes in an oval, child-like face.

"Sorry I'm late," I said.

"No worries! Here, Pon, this is Kaede, the scoundrel who saw you on campus and fell in love at first sight."

"Whaaaaaaaaat?! Oh jeez, I guess I really am popular with older men!" said Pon-chan, slapping her palms against her cheeks and tilting her head, laughing merrily. I could tell simply by her expression, and the fact that she had gone along with Tousuke's joke, that she was a good person.

I had not been so jovial in my twenty-one years, so I jabbed at Tousuke, "What're you saying?" observing her expression afterward.

Still smiling, Pon-chan bowed her head to me, saying, "Ha ha ha, sorry about that. Nice to meet you!"

"You too. I'm Tabata. Anyway, I'm the one who should be apologizing, dragging you out here to help with my thesis when we don't even know each other."

"Oh, no, if it'll help, I'm happy to answer any survey questions you have!"

That had been the excuse we had come up with when I was discussing this with Tousuke. I suddenly felt a little guilty; she had actually seriously believed us and come into this meeting looking to be helpful.

I ordered an iced coffee and then decided to at least preface the main topic. In other words, breaking the ice with Pon-chan, ribbing at Tousuke, and asking about their seminars. She backed me up in bullying Tousuke and gladly told me about the amazing professor who was teaching the seminar she had started this spring. I could tell, at the least from this, that she truly was a really lovely girl.

Once there was an opening, I spread out the official-looking materials we had prepared over the weekend. Even if it was all a ruse, proper preparation was key. I took out a memo pad and asked Pon-chan a number of questions that seemed suitable for a business studies thesis, which of course she answered earnestly—totally unaware that I was interested in something other than her innocent face, or how oddly prominent her chest was for her short height.

"All right, that's all I've got! Thank you. Oh, and feel free to order another drink or some dessert if you like, my treat."

"Well then, I guess I better take you up on that and have some cake!"

"Go right ahead."

I watched as Tousuke looked at Pon-chan now and then, eyes soft, and thought that this must be what it was like to actually dote on an underclassman, to be liked by them. Once Pon-chan's cheesecake and the second coffee I ordered had been delivered, Tousuke moved in to broach the main topic of today's conversation.

"By the way, Pon, you been going to that club of yours lately?"

"Nah..." As she peeled off the film wrapper around her cheesecake, she continued, "It's a ghost town in there...which would be perfect if I'd joined a paranormal research club or something. They're all so busy with their seminars and part-time jobs, and now this year, they have to think about job-seeking, and—*Oh!* If you seniors have any connections, please introduce me to them!" Her face twisted up into an eerie expression that was wholly at odds with her babyface.

"Er, I mean, if you're talking about *us*, you'd definitely be better off looking elsewhere. Maybe you should make use of that one group, the one you were part of for a bit," Tousuke prompted. Pon-chan's face twitched.

"*Ugh*, Moai? They're all ghosts too, but...hmm." She paused. "I guess there's some event coming up. Hmm, it's kind of awkward though. Their interests are all different from mine, but I guess it would be useful to make use of those guys."

"Different interests?" I asked, avoiding fading into thin air and leaving everything to Tousuke. I also needed to see clearly for myself exactly what this distaste upon Pon-chan's face was directed towards. If I stepped out of bounds in questioning or criticizing Moai, I might end up offending her.

I was no Tousuke-senpai, but she prefaced it in the same way.

"I went once or twice to mingle, but I wasn't really into it."

"Yeah, I think I get what you mean, but...how come?"

"Oh, good. Yeah, I mean, it's just kind of trashy, don't you think?"

It was convenient to find that Pon-chan already had a negative opinion of Moai. It meant that she would tell me, without reservation, the things she knew about the group. That aside, the fact that her opinion was different from what I imagined piqued my interest.

"What's so trashy about it?"

"I mean, holding events like *that* in the name of becoming your 'best self' like they say they're all about. That's a pretty respectable goal, but when I went to one of those events, it was nothing but just people chatting and fawning over businesspeople. That alone was enough to give me a pretty good impression of trashiness, but *also*, I got the feeling that I simply was not going to become my ideal self at that rate, as Moai puts it. So, like, I dunno if it's wrong to deny those people though, but…well, I do kinda get it." Grimacing, she continued, "Maybe I should still go, though." For the sake of job hunting, she probably meant.

Being someone who already rejected "those people" outright, I had already come to grips with what it was that we were trying to do here. There was something that I *had* to do. And so, I pressed on.

"Did you think you were going to be attending those events when you first joined?"

Pon-chan shook her head twice, her mouth full of cheesecake. "I just went there at first because this girl I'm good friends with invited me. That friend and I are both dead now as far as Moai is concerned."

"Friendly ghosts," said Tousuke, amused.

Pon-chan grinned and exclaimed with a saucy wink, "A funny guy! I like that in a senpai!" I was glad to see the pair got along so well, but it suddenly occurred to me what a painful exchange this must be if Tousuke really was into her in that way somewhere deep down. I prayed that was not the case.

"Wonder what kind of folks are in there from our year," I said, half to myself. Pon-chan took the bait.

"Well, from your year, there's the leader, someone named Hiro. I sometimes see lots of girls flocking around her in the cafeteria and whatever."

"Got a harem, huh?" Tousuke interjected emptily.

"What, you jealous?" Pon-chan shot back. "Apparently," she continued, "she's a pretty sharp character with lots of leadership qualities. I dunno if it's true or not, but supposedly, she remembers things about each and every member."

A sharp character, huh? I guess everyone had their own impressions.

"I've never even said so much as a hello to her, though."

"Guessing you don't know much about the other members then, either?"

"Well, I know there's someone named Ten-san who's in charge of most of the event coordination and is good enough at communicating to handle that stuff. He's the one who was our guide when I went to check the group out. I think he's got a pretty high-ranking position in Moai."

"Seems like the group ranks are pretty codified. Doubt someone like me or Kaede would *ever* get promoted."

"So totally true," Pon-chan said with a sneer, ribbing her interrupting senpai. "I mean, I have no idea if that's what you'd actually want, but it does seem like if that group got any bigger, the power struggle would be explosive! Must be nice for you to be in such a tight-knit little seminar group."

"But you have one too."

As the two of them chattered, I began to piece together some conclusions from what she was telling us. In some ways, it was because of that power struggle that I had been forced out of the group. No such thing had ever occurred when we were a more intimate group.

"Oh, but also, I mean, not thinking of anyone in particular, but there seem to be a lot of fanatics in that group, which isn't really my vibe, so it kind of made me want to stop hanging around them."

"Fanatic? In what way?"

"Well, it was pretty obvious that there were a lot of people who basically worship Hiro-senpai. It'd be one thing to just rely on her, but they're practically intoxicated by her, it's creepy. Also, speaking of creepy, I guess this doesn't really have to do with those people, but when I went to check out the group, they were showing a movie about how *great and wonderful* Moai was," Pon-chan said, cringing.

"I mean, that is creepy," Tousuke agreed. "On *that* note though, how do you feel about me, Pon? You intoxicated?"

I knew by the way that Pon-chan went along with every bit of Tousuke's ribbing that she really was a nice girl.

Someone making unreasonable demands of people who were intoxicated with them seemed like the sort of thing you'd hear about with larger organizations. Someone would be elevated to the status of a god or an idol—and sooner or later begin to develop a warped world view.

"That's really awful. Oh, but hey! What if I was to help you out as your senpai in your job hunt? Help you protect your dignity and all. I could even go to those Moai events with you as your backup."

Despite all the wisecracking Tousuke had been doing, this was a surprisingly decent proposal from my buddy. I had rudely thought that he might throw things off, but it turned out to be useful to have him here.

"Oh, that'd be nice. If you're there with me then I should be able to avoid some of the awkwardness. Then again, I get enough awkwardness from you already."

"He *is* pretty annoying," I cut in. Pon-chan laughed.

"Ha ha! That's just how things are with me and Tousuke. It probably would be pretty useful if you came with me, though. It won't interfere with your thesis or anything, will it? And also, don't you hate Moai?"

"If my thesis was so weak that I'd be thrown off by missing just one day of work at this point, then it would be worthless no matter what I did. Also, I'd already decided I hate those people without even seeing what they're about, so I may as well have well-informed hatred."

"See, this is what I respect about you."

"Alrighty then, time to see if I intoxicate *you* by the time I graduate, Pon."

"If that ever happens, please end me, Tabata-senpai," she said to me, her face serious. I let out a laugh. It really felt to me that the relationship between the two of them went far deeper than just senpai and kouhai. I have no idea what that meant to Tousuke, but it made me rather jealous.

Jealous of the fact that he still had a dear friend in this world.

I shouldn't have been getting so sentimental here, but I couldn't help it.

And thus, this was how Pon-chan, the one who would guide our ship into the sea of Moai, joined the party.

—*—

That day, I had been sitting on the floor in Akiyoshi's home, eating tomato-flavored Pretz sticks.

The primary reason I was there was because we had realized that despite us both taking Chinese in different time slots, we had the exact same class exercises—but I soon grew bored of that and started snacking. Incidentally, we had ended up here because I wasn't looking forward to the idea of cleaning up my own place and because Akiyoshi had asked, "You wanna come over?"

"...Okay, so first off, we need to discuss how we get more members in Moai."

Akiyoshi, who had been sitting across from me on the other side of the table silently reading her textbook, suddenly declared the start of a group meeting. Apparently, she was also quite finished with study time.

"Still haven't given up on that?"

"I'd at least like to have enough members to be officially recognized by the school." She stuck her hand out, and I passed over the box of Pretz. "Thanks!! I don't actually mind it being just the two of us, though. It might get annoying if we got people whose way of thinking was too different."

I gave a half-hearted nod and a "Guess so," as I stared at my textbook, unable to shake the anxious question of what I might do if more people with as radical of ideals as Akiyoshi began to show up. "Wouldn't that be tough for you?" I added. "You'd have a lot of responsibilities as a leader..."

"Mm, you're right. If we were a big club, I guess we'd have to select a representative. I mean, you could do it too, though."

She wasn't kidding, I realized.

"No thanks, I'm too irresponsible."

"I don't think it needs to be either of us, though, if we get someone else with a strong sense of responsibility to join. Long as they aren't too strict."

I took back the Pretz that were sitting in front of her.

"A leader who doesn't care if all we do is eat snacks."

"Yeah, something like that."

It was such a silly, fruitless conversation, but even then, I'm sure that I knew that Akiyoshi was the only person who could possibly lead Moai.

—*—

I'll handle the disguises, Tousuke had told me confidentially—and so, the day of the networking event, I found myself in a jacket, stole, cap, and some fashion glasses.

"Lookin' sharp, Kaede! Could see you hangin' out with all the cool cats in Shimokitazawa."

"Is that supposed to be a compliment...?" Tousuke, in his sharp suit, laughed and clapped me on the shoulder. I got the feeling it was *not* a compliment.

Today was a momentous occasion—our very first concrete steps in Operation Moai. We were infiltrating the enemy to see for ourselves just how unjust, how corrupt they were, and what faults they had.

That said, it was actually Tousuke and Pon-chan who would

be actively going in. My duty would be to sit outside the venue, eavesdropping on the participants traveling in and out, as there was a chance that my face might still be familiar to some of the members. I had agreed to do this because we felt I might be able to get some valuable information from the unguarded conversations of the Moai members, but Tousuke had playfully insisted that I would also need to wear clothing that I would normally never wear in order to disguise myself, lest I be found out.

The stole I had wrapped around my neck was *particularly* miserable.

We had only told Pon-chan that Tousuke would be joining her today. I was going to pretend to meet up with them by chance later, but the thought of her seeing me like this made me uneasy. Incidentally, Tousuke would be sending me play by play updates about what was happening inside of the room.

The assembly today was being held in a hall on campus. The meeting would take place from one to five in the afternoon, after which there would be a follow-up dinner, so Tousuke, who was not a member of the group, would only be able to participate in part of the day's activities. We had gotten the rundown about this from Pon-chan at our previous meeting.

"They really do seem pretty fired up about this, though," Tousuke muttered as we looked over some materials at a MOS Burger some distance from campus. He was currently reading a pamphlet that Moai had distributed for participants of today's event. The pamphlet was in full color and neatly bound—it was easy to surmise from the quality that this was not a student production.

"That thing looks pretty pricey."

"Looks like they have some spots in here where people can buy ads, like Pon mentioned. Oh, yep! Here's some business names on the back. I'm assuming there was nothing like that when you were with Moai?"

"I mean, who the hell would spend their sponsorship money on a group of *two*?"

"Good point."

I was sure that was probably one of the facets of self-improvement that the current Moai espoused, through exchanging and negotiating with professionals, but honestly, at this point it was just a group that existed to produce more professional workers.

That wasn't Moai.

"I'm sorry to push all this work onto you though."

"It's fine. It's for my kouhai too, and I'm not about to give up over something like this, especially after I was the one to raise the battle flag."

Tousuke was always saying dramatic things like that.

"I mean, I guess it'd be good if Pon can network with some alumni separately from our agenda here."

"That's true. I know that I need to protect her from any malicious working folks, but, well...I hope that I'd be able to distinguish them from the actually helpful professionals."

"I don't think there even is such a thing. Just keep an eye on her."

I still was not yet a working professional myself, so I did not truly know that much of their ways, but I suspected they were neither good nor bad so much as trapped in an endless cycle of depersonalization.

"Okay, I better get going!" said Tousuke as he stood, checking his wristwatch just like a professional. I checked the time as well, seeing that it was, in fact, right around when he and Pon-chan were supposed to be meeting up.

"I'll text you when we get in. See you later."

"All right, take care."

"Don't get *too* excited now."

Grinning, Tousuke picked up his bag and left the burger shop. I headed for the vicinity of the hall shortly after so that no one would make the connection between us. The weather outside was lovely, so much so that it hardly felt like a day where I was disguised and on my way to vanquish a group of evildoers.

Alone now, I sat sipping my vanilla shake as I swiped on my phone. The cold, sweet drink that was sliding down my throat had been Akiyoshi's favorite. She always wanted to swing by MOS Burger, and whenever we did, she always got a vanilla shake. Before I knew it, I found this cold, sweet drink giving me courage.

I was taking back my ideals.

For Akiyoshi's sake. I would strengthen my own resolve.

I waited for a while, when suddenly I heard some girls behind me saying, "Well, *he's* got a look about him, doesn't he?" The thought that they might be making fun of me shook some of that newfound resolve, but just then I got a text from Tousuke. It seemed he had met up with Pon-chan, and the two of them had safely made it to the hall. The event would be kicking off in fifteen minutes. All of the Moai movers and shakers would have already been inside, so I decided to wait around outside the hall until then.

In all actuality, there would be hardly any members who knew me, as I was still an enrolled student. It was the professionals who had already graduated and would have been invited to this meeting that I was looking to avoid—the ones who imparted most of the value to this newly enlarged Moai. Cover blown or no, I simply did not wish to speak with them.

Though I realized that it was only the ridiculing from those girls that was making me overly self-conscious, this wasn't the time to go letting my nerves be shot by random things like that. So I put my iPod earbuds into my ears and let the music play, blocking out the outside world. My personal philosophies of keeping away from others did not simply mean maintaining an emotional and physical distance. It was also important not to be influenced by others or influence them myself. That was the only way to protect both myself and everyone else.

Around the third track, when I had already lost myself to the music, my phone vibrated.

"About to start. A lot more people here than I thought."

I laughed a little at the thought of Tousuke trembling, Pon-chan placing herself in front of him when she noticed.

"Gotcha. I'll start headin' over."

I stood up, my out-of-character jacket swaying listlessly. The hat, which I would not normally wear, turned out to come in handy for the unusually bright spring sunlight as I stepped outside. Tousuke had taken a moped to the hall. I should have ridden my bike, but in addition to the ache in my feet from the unfamiliar shoes, it just seemed like a hassle, so I just took the two train stops there.

The station I disembarked at was on a line I did not normally take. The assembly was being held in a hall on campus, but it was a fair distance from the buildings that I normally had classes in, so the nearest stop was different as well. More succinctly, it was a part of campus I had never actually once set foot in at all. It made sense though—this was a university campus, so I only visited the parts of it that I needed to. When I first enrolled, I had probably felt as though this whole place was my oyster, but in actuality, I don't think I was making use of any more campus area than I had during my time in high school.

It was largely empty within the train car, and when I arrived at the station, the only people I saw who looked like students were all wearing sports jerseys and appeared to be on their way to club activities. Though there were a number of college courses that ran even on the weekends, hardly anyone attended those willingly.

I left the station and walked through the school gates, careful to avoid the suited professionals who were probably late to popping in at the assembly. I pulled the brim of the hat further down over my eyes and walked towards the hall. I stopped by a vending machine along the way and bought a can of coffee. There were a few students around when I got to the campus proper, which probably gave me some cover, but just in case, I pretended to sip my coffee so as to hide my face.

This was all just a contingency anyway. I had no idea if any of them would even remember me.

I got just close enough to see the hall, when I spotted a signboard advertising the meeting. I stared at it for a few seconds, before a girl who was nearby called out to me, "Will you be joining us?" She was wearing a suit and holding a clipboard and pamphlets, and was probably there as a docent for latecomers. I politely told her something to the effect of I had come there for some other reason, to which she replied, "Oh, sorry about that. Our group is called Moai, though. This is the event we're holding, so, if you have any interest?" Naturally, I politely declined the absurd invitation as well.

Despite my polite declination, however, I moved to a nearby shaded rest area and took a seat on a bench. I thought that I might keep an eye on this docent girl. It was lucky that I had been able to pick out a Moai member this quickly.

I looked down at my phone. It was quiet around me, which made it easier to hear the conversations of students passing by. The docent called out occasionally to the suited adults who approached, some of them going along with her, some of them refusing her pamphlets.

It was around the time that I had finished drinking the canned coffee that I had initially purchased as a prop that I got another message from Tousuke.

"The first discussion session is over. There's a ten-minute break. I'm getting tired of hearing all the smug bragging from the professionals. Got some business cards. Gonna try to get in with some of the popular Moai kids for the next part."

"Nice work. I'm keeping watch on a Moai guide outside of the building."

Saying that I was "keeping watch" gave my current task something of a dutiful ring, but in truth, the fact that I was saying something like this without being the one to do the infiltrating just imparted me with a sense of guilt.

A few minutes after Tousuke's text, a number of students and suited figures came walking out of the hall. I lifted only my eyes up toward them, not turning my face. They seemed to all be people who needed to leave part way through—the whole group was heading towards the school gates. The students, probably Moai members, were chatting in pairs with the suited adults. The docent called out a, "Thank you for coming!" to each of them.

Just as I was wondering whether someone else might not step in to relieve the girl, a man approached, taking the clipboard and pamphlets from her. It was none of my business really, but I was glad that he had arrived before she totally wore herself out. Despite my relief, however, I realized that this was the first interaction I had seen today between two Moai members, so I frantically strained my ears to listen. However, what I overheard was a frankly meaningless conversation.

"All right, good luck out here."

"Honestly, this job's way easier. Those discussions were putting me to sleep."

"I'll bet. Can't wait to put on my best business face and collect all those business cards!"

Frankly, I was surprised at just how disappointed I found myself to overhear this pointless, disillusioned conversation, despite having already predicted such a thing. *I should have been happy about this,* I thought. Even those who had been trusted with the duty of being Moai's guides were less than thrilled with it. It's much easier to combat an enemy who is not a monolith.

Still, it was in that moment that my nonexistent hope that some of the original ideals of Moai might still have a hold on the group vanished. In the end, the second docent merely went about his task with some measure of diligence—nothing in particular really happening until I received another text from Tousuke.

"Second part's over. Got in a group with that Ten guy. He was way too cozy with the ladies. Pissed me off. Seems to be popular with professional women too. Was more like some kind of debate though, was more fun than the first part. Guess that's the elites for you."

"I'm gonna laugh at you if you end up turning into a Moai member yourself."

It seemed highly unlikely to me, but there was somehow an inherent impartiality behind Tousuke's extreme thinking, so I couldn't be entirely certain. I thought that Pon-chan might have just been being peevish when she said that just getting in with that group one time and getting a good look at them would be enough to make you hate them, but perhaps she had been serious. Still, even on the off chance that he *did* end up expressing some desire to join Moai, I wouldn't attack Tousuke over it. I would genuinely laugh at him.

"I would too," he replied. After receiving that message, I decided

to relocate. I wasn't going to get anything from just hounding the docents over here. I waited for them to switch places again, with a new girl coming in, then gave my legs a much-needed stretch and headed for the hall itself.

The fact that this meeting was being held on the weekend when there were fewer people around was most convenient for me while moving from place to place. If I were to brush shoulders with anyone at close range, I would have to stake my faith on Tousuke's powers of disguise, but with so few people around, it would be easier for me to spot any Moai-associated acquaintances at a distance. In such events, I would be able to distinguish such people by their hair, clothing, and a number of other factors, while they would be forced to try and recognize me through my completely atypical getup.

The entrance of the hall came into view. Outside, there were a number of suited men and women, most likely professionals or seniors, so I kept my distance as I passed them by. Ahead, there was a school-run café, which is where I decided to station myself next. The café was open all days of the week for students, and there was a gentle stream of air-conditioning running inside. There were a number of other customers there already, but thankfully, one of the window seats was open. Though this spot would not give me a direct view of the hall entrance, I could at least see the hallway junction where one of the paths away from the entrance ended. Additionally, just as I anticipated, there were four young women in the café who seemed to be participants on break from the assembly.

I purchased a coffee and took my seat, flipping open a book and gazing out the window. One of my ears was angled towards the seats at the table behind me, the other towards the incredibly self-conscious conversation of the four girls. Sadly, no matter how self-aware and idealistic their conversation might have seemed, in the end, it was nothing more than idle chatter—or so I had been convinced, when finally the topic turned to something that was advantageous to our cause.

"Hm... Man, you know I'm always wondering with Ten where he got all that self-assuredness from."

Ten. Ten, huh?

That was the guy who had been writing on that blog. Good, time for some *real* intel. I casually glanced over my shoulder to see the four girls. I did not recognize any of the formally dressed girls, but given that one of them had referred to Ten, a senior, without any honorific, one could surmise that she was probably a classmate of his.

"Maybe it's his clothes? Or do you think he's born with it?"

"If he were born with it, he wouldn't always be showing off and pandering for approval."

"Guess so. He never looks too pleased when Hiro gets mad at him, but he definitely strikes me as a very meticulously self-styled kinda guy."

"You really think he's that complicated? I've always just pictured him like a grasshopper!" One of the girls struck up an amusing smile.

"Him and that queen ant Hiro make a good pair."

"Even though he's just going to end up starving to death?"

The girls giggled at this. Apparently, this Ten was something of a ridiculous figure—or at least he was well liked because he accepted such a treatment. I could tell just by the fact that he had come up in such a conversation that they were fond of him. An *ant queen* though, huh?

Interesting.

"Good pair or no, I'd never hand Ten over to someone like that." They were slightly malicious words, but I felt no real malice from them.

"Hiro's more suited to like, you know, a nice old guy, with a fancy suit and a mustache. She's had a lot of men in her life. I'm sure that'd bring out her softer side."

"I mean that's just what *you're* into." Another bout of laughter. I started to wonder if I'd be better off training my eyes than my cars on this frivolous conversation, but it was best that I didn't. Then, the one more comparatively serious of the four took the helm of the conversation.

"Is this all right though? For us to not be in there cheering on the junior members?"

"That's not for us to say. I mean, Ten *did* say that we don't have to be in there if we're busy."

"Ah ha ha, are we really busy, though?" A fine retort.

"Suppose not. Guess we better get back in there!"

"We too must toil for the sake of the ant queen and the colony. That grasshopper can just perish!"

"Wow, *cold*." She seemed to be the designated comedian.

"Forget all those dudes who just come to these things to pick up girls, though."

"Oh yeah, speaking of, whatever happened with that lady he took home last time?"

"Mm, doesn't seem like they're together anymore."

"Seriously?"

"My research shows that statistically, men with a high degree of self-confidence like to follow trends and are bad at holding on to their possessions."

"Yeah, and when they're born with it, it's incurable. Ah well."

There was a loud rustling as one of the girls stood, followed by the sound of chair legs scraping across the floor. At length, I spotted through the window those same four girls, heading towards the three-way junction that led to the hall.

I watched the four of them walk away, stunned at my repeated good fortune. Their conversation was the sort of thing that typically I would have liked to drown out with music. I was both stunned and grateful at my own timing, so good it had almost seemed planned: that not only had the four of them been present in the café, but there had been a seat free nearby, and they had even conveniently brought up this Ten fellow in conversation. Though of course, I had planned none of this; I had merely gotten lucky.

It was only a small thing for now, but perhaps I had already found it—a possible backdoor into a scandal that could send Moai up in smoke.

I studied the grain of the tabletop through my fashion glasses as I pondered. For us to bring up the fact that there was someone who was supposedly part of Moai's leadership who was using the group for his own sexual gains would be dreadful, but we still might be able to make use of this somehow. If we were able to prove that even just one person was using these meetings as a hook-up spot and that the targets were the professionals who were being invited—and successfully wooed—and then being treated poorly, it might be enough to start raising opposition toward the group amongst the student body. Luckily for us, this Ten guy was a senior, and even part of Moai's management.

This could work.

Of course, exactly how could we get evidence of that? It would be ideal to catch him in the act, but obviously Tousuke and I could not tail him 24/7. So perhaps it would be best to hunt down one of these professionals who had been cast away by Ten. It was unlikely that such a person would attend another meeting—we obviously couldn't ask anyone who it was directly.

Getting an e-mail or a statement from such a person would be enough, but how?

I thought hard, utterly lost in my own ponderings. Thus, my focus on the hall outside of the window wavered. I did not notice that there was someone who I knew, and who knew me, fast approaching.

There was a sudden knock on the window, and I nearly jumped out of my own skin. I looked up to see someone standing there. However, for a moment I did not recognize them, but when I did, my stomach leapt into my throat. I inhaled sharply, choking on my own breath.

Standing there in his jeans and casual top, he either didn't notice or didn't care how badly I was shaken. Perhaps satisfied enough by the fact that I had noticed him, he waved at me with a soft smile that insinuated nothing less than placidity, then headed the opposite direction and disappeared down the hall.

I had been caught so utterly off-guard that for a few seconds I just sat there dumbfounded, unsure if I had even actually seen him. I had only the pounding of my own heart as proof that the encounter had been real.

Perhaps in order for something to be timed well, in exchange, something must be timed very poorly. I first took a moment to calm myself, taking a sip of my coffee and placing a hand to my chest, breathing deeply.

"Why now...?" I muttered unconsciously to myself.

I was stunned. I had seen him around, but I couldn't remember the last time we'd actually stood face-to-face. I was just glad he hadn't come into the café to try to start a conversation.

Seriously though, what was *he* doing here? If all had gone according to schedule, he should have finished his graduate studies back in March. Had he stayed on another year? I started to wonder if he was still sticking around the school just to look in on Moai, even after graduating, but then it occurred to me that he *was* exactly the sort of person who would do such a thing.

This former senpai, Wakisaka, was a vexing character, the sort of person who knew no concept of shame or pride, living only in whatever way best suited him—at least, that was the gist I got of him when he dropped in to Moai meetings.

It was when we were still freshmen. Wakisaka became fascinated with Akiyoshi, and despite not joining us, would keep an eye on Moai, popping up to give unsolicited advice and telling all sorts of people about our club. In other words, it was Wakisaka who set the stage for the shift in Moai's values that would later occur. He was not the one who put a definitive end to the Moai we knew, but nevertheless, I hated him just as much as I did the people who had taken charge of Moai now. I tried to make myself understand that it was not truly his fault, but there was a disconnect somewhere between my head and my heart.

Regardless, he had recognized me, even through my disguise. I wondered if I was a lot more conspicuous than I thought.

As I worked to settle my nerves, trying to stretch my coffee out all the way through the next discussion session, I got another message from Tousuke.

"All done. Next one's the last one. I'm getting a little tired, but Pon looks practically dead. I'm thinking I'll take her out for drinks, so you can join us there."

"OK. I'll bring some for Pon-chan. Would love to get more info on Ten if possible. Heard some rumors about him having inappropriate relationships with professionals."

"Roger that. I'll get in his group."

With that final message I stood from my seat. This was my last chance today to get some information. I figured I would linger around the outskirts of the hall for a bit, then make my way off campus before the event was over.

I placed my coffee cup and tray on the return counter, bowed my head in reply to the greeting from the cashier, and headed outside. Somehow the day had progressed from noon to evening without my noticing. The sunlight was waning, the wind growing colder.

I headed for the T-junction. A number of professionals and students had begun filtering out of the hall, perhaps being called back to their offices and part-time jobs. With my previous mistake of being spotted by Wakisaka still in mind, I kept my eyes down as I walked. All I needed to do was try and take in more conversations and not run into anyone. I lowered my gaze, so that no one would spot me.

It occurred to me as I did this that this was more or less the way I had been living my life for the past three years. There had been a few brilliant months where I had a friend who shone brightly enough to illuminate even someone like me, but that had been all. After she was gone, I led a quiet life, suffocating my own self—though perhaps it would be imprudent to phrase it so violently.

The only person I could proudly call a friend who I had met since then was Tousuke. However, that had not occurred of my own power; it was thanks only to the kindness of Tousuke, who was fair to everyone, whom I often had overlapping shifts with at the part-time job I had during my sophomore year. We both ended up quitting that job within a few months of that, but somehow, we managed to stick with one another and now were even co-conspirators.

I suddenly started to feel like it was wrong of me to be stealing away Tousuke's time, making Tousuke, who had so many friends, spend his weekend in a place like this. I would have to check in again with him later to see if he was really okay with this.

My feet carried me to just before the T-junction. Just then, I noticed a rather lively group making their way out of the hall. I glanced up to look at them.

I'm not sure if my timing then was good or bad, or both, but there she was. I realized that, had I looked up even a second sooner, our eyes would have met, and I would have been spotted.

She and her followers had just rounded the junction that I had been looking at and turned towards the path I had come from. My feet stopped in place all on their own. I hadn't learned at all.

Once more my wits had abandoned me.

I only learned later the contents of the frantic message from Tousuke that had arrived on my phone, still in my pocket.

"The leader's heading out!"

It had been so long since I had seen her. My body registered her presence before my brain even did.

I felt a strange coldness, goosebumps rising on my skin. I was cold, but a trail of sweat ran down my spine. My hands curled into fists, fingernails digging so hard into my palms that they were sure to leave a mark. I felt nauseated. Finally, the anomalies made it to my brain, and I panicked all at once. I had no idea what this feeling was. And then, I understood. I knew that what I had felt towards Ten, towards Wakisaka, was only a facsimile of the real thing.

This was true hatred.

I realized then that the only reason I had been able to live my life so peacefully these past two years, pretending as though Moai did not even exist, was because I had averted my eyes from this fact.

There, several meters behind me, was the one who had been primarily responsible for stealing Moai away from us.

It is only when you acknowledge that something is real that you can embrace how it is that you truly feel about it.

She was the one in charge of Moai—the final boss, as far as Tousuke and I were concerned. The one who had been running Moai, a Moai without ideals, in its current twisted form. The current leader: Hiro.

Once more, I felt my flesh crawl. From this distance, it would be so easy to grab her by the shoulders and tell her off. However, I couldn't. My feelings towards the warped and twisted Moai were not something that could be quelled by such half-hearted measures.

It would look bad for me to just keep standing there. She knew who I was, after all. I wrenched myself from my fixation on Hiro and dragged my heavy feet in the opposite direction of her group. I passed by the path that led to the hall and walked to the bench where I had stationed myself earlier. I needed to better steel myself. I nodded my head at the polite, "Thanks for coming!" from the bespectacled, serious-looking girl who was currently stationed out front, practically crumbling the moment I reached the bench.

For a while, I did not move from that spot. Of course, this was partly because I could not risk going back towards the hall and running into Hiro, but that was not the whole reason. My spirit was being crushed under the weight of my own emotions.

I did no further investigation. I merely waited until my heart rate had slowed down to something resembling normal and then left the campus.

I loitered at the Saint Marc Café near Tousuke's place. About an hour after the first portion of the event was scheduled to end, I received a message.

Apparently, after the event Tousuke had gone with Pon-chan to celebrate a mission accomplished; this info was accompanied with information about the izakaya they had gone to. It was fairly close to the coffee house we had initially met Pon-chan at. In other words, it was near Pon-chan's place. *That makes sense,* I thought, starting to stand up. Just then, I received another text.

"Make sure you keep that getup on lmao"

Obviously, I was still wearing the same clothes—I didn't need to be told not to change my clothing—but I at least stowed the hat, glasses, and stole away in my tote bag before leaving the shop.

I had no bike with me, so I took the train, walking the last ten minutes to the shop. It was a chain izakaya with semi-private booths, one that Tousuke and I had visited different franchises of many times before. As a university student, it was important to have some awareness of menu prices when selecting a dining location.

I entered the restaurant, gave Tousuke's name, and was brought to him. It was Pon-chan who spotted me first, looking far more normal than I had earlier with just my jacket and tote bag, her chin resting on her hands.

"Ooh, Kaede-senpaaai! Good work todaaaaaay! You look good, goin' out on a date? Sounds fun!~"

I could see that her cheeks were already fairly rosy.

"Heya, buddy! Oh, wow, you really did keep your formalwear on!"

"Whaddya mean formalwear? Anyway, hope you had fun at the meeting today, you two."

We were still keeping the plan a secret from Pon-chan, so I chose my words carefully. I sat opposite her at the four-person table, beside Tousuke.

"So, how was it?" I asked.

Pon-chan swung her head heavily back and forth, flashing her neck—just as red as her cheeks—through the collar of the white dress shirt she had apparently chosen for the occasion.

"It was soooooooo long!" This much was emphatic. "It was soooooooooooo exhausting!" she continued. "Is job hunting always like this? I can't do it! I'm gonna crumble to dust before I even make it to my senior year!!!"

"Well, today was very much hard-mode, getting asked our opinions that many times."

"That settles it though. I can't stand those Moai jerks! Whenever I finally got to voice my opinion, they'd just be like, 'Oh, but what does that mean?' I already said my piece! Now it's your turn!!!"

Pon-chan, more fired up than I'd ever imagined her, took a gulp of what appeared to be some kind of highball. It was fortunate that the shop was bustling enough to drown out any one girl's passionate laments.

"*Seriously* though, listen, Kaede-senpai—Oh, wait, guess you'd wanna order first."

As heated as Pon-chan was getting, she still remembered her manners. At her prompting, I flagged down the grinning waiter who had been lingering nearby and ordered a draft beer. The drink was delivered to me promptly. I gave a little "Cheers" and told her, "Go ahead."

"Right! So..." she started, as though she had just remembered what it was she was going to say. I gathered she was fairly accustomed to talking to her seniors. "This guy! This guy *here*!" she shouted, pointing at Tousuke, who tilted his head theatrically. "He was acting like he was having *so much fun* talking to those Moai guys! What happened to you saying you'd back me up, huh?! They started getting all excited, and just because I was with you, they wanted to hear *my* opinions too!"

"Well, c'mon, I mean, if someone asks your opinion, you answer, right? That's just how a conversation works. Right, Kaede?"

I was not there, so I couldn't say, but I knew that Tousuke was a fairly erudite person. I was sure he truly enjoyed talking to people from all different walks, no matter what their differences.

"That is *not* true! You were going on about how to protect the labor force in rural areas, and the economic benefits of nuclear power, and all these other highbrow topics. What happened to the fun, laid-back senpai that I love?!"

Tousuke laughed giddily at his kouhai's disparaging. They were probably always like this. It was just like what Tousuke had said to me back at the karaoke bar.

"It's not *highbrow*. Those are just the sort of things that even I think about. Right, Kaede?"

"I dunno, Tousuke, sounds pretty highbrow to me," I said.

"Right! Ugh, he's been tainted! Before you know it, he's gonna turn into a Moai too!!!" she wailed.

"Will *not*!" Tousuke jabbed back. "Listen, if you're gonna take part in somethin', you gotta do it right, yeah?" There was no need for him to excuse himself—I already knew that Tousuke was that sort of person. However, that was not the entire issue here.

"Actually though, how was the event for you, Tousuke? Considering you never liked Moai." I was curious what he thought. He folded his arms and jutted out his lip.

Sorry, Tousuke, puppy dog looks don't work on me.

"Hmm, if I'm being honest?"

"Don't even hold back."

"Hm..." He seemed as though he was choosing his words carefully. "How do I put this... Well, I thought that it *would* be a pretty good event for anyone who has their own ambitions to satisfy."

"You seemed pretty satisfied yourself, Tousuke-senpai!!!" Pon-chan idly chided, snapping up a healthy portion of the rolled omelet that had finally arrived.

"Own ambitions?"

"Like, I think it's a good sort of thing for people with their own desires to fulfill, who don't really care what the event is actually about, to participate in."

"Hmm..." My sighed reply was largely for the sake of not

letting on to Pon-chan the sort of relationship that Moai and I shared. Perhaps catching on to this, Tousuke ignored me and continued speaking.

"There were way more people there who were actually actively seeking job connections than I expected, but even though they seemed fairly engaged in the discussions, they were way more engaged in making conversation with the various professionals afterwards during breaktime. It at least seemed kind of taboo to bring up company names and the like during discussions. You could have just mentioned what kind of industry you were in. I thought we would exchange business cards or something, but that was mostly during breaks. It might sound kind of awful to say this, but if you were a girl who's fairly confident in her appearance, you'd almost be better off just sitting around quietly during the discussions and making eyes at whichever guys appeared the flashiest."

"I haaaaaaaate girls like that."

I noticed just then that Pon-chan had divided the rolled omelet into portions for all three of us. I thanked her, to which she replied, "Well, when it comes time to really pull out the big guns, I'll leave it to you two senpai." How smooth of her.

"I'm not really big on them, either. Anyway, I just thought this sort of gathering is probably useful for folks who know exactly what it is that they want."

"That's a pretty Tousuke-like appraisal." Being able to distinguish his thoughts from his feelings, that was.

"Well, that is my appraisal. What Pon said earlier was right, though. It's not the same as 'becoming your ideal self,' so I don't think it'd be suitable for those who can't deal with that sort of dissonance. I think that's why she got fed up with it."

"What I just wanna know is why *you*, someone who supposedly hated Moai, had such a blast at the event that you're *still* acting like you enjoyed it," said Pon-chan.

"I mean it *was* pretty fun," Tousuke said, before glancing my way and whispering, "It does at least give me some new perspective on them." Though that much was already obvious from looking at him, I was glad that at least he did not lie to me about it.

"Still, I can't really speak on the whole of Moai, but the leadership seems to be pretty gung ho about their initiatives and the stuff they've got planned. I got particularly ticked off at all those haughty attitudes that the high-ranking guys had, but it did seem like *a lot* of work went into planning this event. So, ticked off or no, I can respect that these are guys who get the job done. You can really tell they're ready to graduate into real society." It was a very forthright opinion, which I couldn't help but acknowledge.

"Still, like, this is stuff that the university's employment office could take care of for you, and I don't like the idea of schmoozing with professionals as some kind of backdoor cheat code to getting a job. It would be a perfectly fine event without Moai focusing on all that. Even the discussion groups were mostly just professionals gloating about stuff."

"And then there was that old geezer who was probably just some underling who was forced to give up his weekend to come here and give some scripted talk. I wanted to wring his neck."

"Hah, that bad, huh?" I laughed at Pon-chan's complaint, but honestly, I was just relieved to hear Tousuke actually criticizing Moai.

"Well, it was at least useful for learning what companies *not* to work at. I'm assuming you got business cards from recruiters in your prospective field afterwards?"

"That's true. One sec." Pon-chan fished a hand into her breast pocket. It took her a bit longer than expected because she couldn't reach it with her opposing hand. It looked like it must be painful to have the buttons pulling at the fabric like that.

"Here we go! Takasaki Hirofumi-san. He was tall and pretty handsome. He didn't piss me off too much either because he seemed like he was actually successful."

"I get that."

"Man, he was suuuuuuch a nice person! Unlike *you*, Tousuke-senpai! You're so small and clingy...!!!"

I was glad that it at least appeared to have been a fruitful day for Pon-chan. It was for the sake of *our* plan that she had ended up attending, so I would have hated for her to come back with nothing but exhaustion.

I breathed a solitary sigh. At least the day's operations had concluded without any major slip-ups. The next course of action I would discuss with Tousuke at his place later, once we had wrapped up here. I thought about this as I moved some grated daikon atop my rolled omelet and took a bite, when suddenly Pon-chan offered up an unexpected fact.

"Oh, right, Tousuke-senpai. Didn't you exchange numbers with someone?"

"Oh yeah, that Ten guy!"

"Seriously?!" I asked in shock. Tousuke turned to me and gave an emphatic blink, which I could only assume was a failed wink. "I mean, are you seriously thinking about joining Moai, Tousuke?"

"That's what I was wondering," Pon-chan chided.

Tousuke, for some reason, shrugged and shook his head. "That's not it. We just ended up in the same group a bunch of times! I just happened to talk to him while Pon was collecting business cards. It turns out he also got an offer from the company that offered me a position, but he ended up settling on somewhere else and turned them down. He was just telling me we should go for drinks sometime, so we traded numbers."

Well, that certainly was something.

"You see there, Kaede-senpai? Those two fools had a deep, spiritual bond. I suppose we ought to live a more serious life too." I laughed at this.

However, I could feel a strange, slow dread beginning to crawl up my fingertips. I had no way of confirming these fears of mine there, as Pon-chan suggested we move the conversation to less dry topics. It did feel strange to be obsessing over Moai in a place like this, so we shifted gears and made idle conversation a while, drinking and enjoying the rich food.

Before we knew it, two hours had passed. Within the bustle of the restaurant, not even the loud sounds of laughter or glasses breaking was enough to rouse Pon-chan from her position where she had collapsed upon the table. She had had more than enough to drink and was likely already exhausted.

"Seriously though, thanks," I said, lifting my lemon sour. Tousuke, who had moved to beside Pon-chan after getting up to use the restroom, raised his glass to mine and clinked it. "Sorry to make you do most of the legwork. If there's anything I can do to help out with Pon-chan's job hunt, let me know."

"I'm sure she'd be happy to hear that, but seriously, I'm fine. I'm already done with my hunt, so I was mostly just watching over my kouhai from up on high."

"Really though... Also, that's some fancy footwork you must've done to get close enough to that guy to get his information." Without Tousuke, I would have never been able to get this far this quickly.

"I mean, I just approached him because of your text, and he was pretty pleasant to deal with. This guy doesn't seem to have any boundaries. Honestly, I was pretty stunned that he was the one to suggest exchanging information. I just was like, 'I don't really have any interest in joining Moai, though.' And he was like, 'That's a shame, but since you're already here...' so we did it. Those kinds of guys are unbelievable."

"Yeah. It's like they're from a completely different world."

"Right?" Tousuke laughed, as though he understood everything about me. "Anyway, what was that about some scandal about him?" I realized then that I had not yet explained that to him and regaled Tousuke with the encounter at the café that afternoon.

"I see," he muttered, once I was through.

"Was he doing anything like that there?"

"I mean, it's not like I saw him straight up feeling up some businesswoman's tits or anything."

"Well, if there was a guy like *that* in the leadership then we wouldn't even have to lift a finger to fight them."

"I mean that's true, but like, he did seem to get along pretty well with all the businesswomen who seemed like they had been there a bunch of times before, and he even had a lot of conversations with the first-timers, trying to make some sort of connections. By that extension, it wouldn't be all that surprising if he *was* doing that sort of stuff. He seems to be a smooth operator and attractive enough. Not *that* cool, but..."

But charming enough, I'm sure he wanted to say.

"You don't seem too fond of him."

"I mean, I definitely wouldn't have approached him if it wasn't my duty."

I could not say that I understood all that there was to Tousuke, so I just settled the matter with, "Seriously, thanks. Anyway, sorry to keep poking while you're tired, but mind if I make some proposals about our next moves?"

"You've got it, boss!"

"Right, gonna keep this simple and clean, but I feel like the most effective way to get this thing to blow up would be to get the man himself to slip up and say something or to catch him in the act. So, much as I hate to say it, I think we're gonna have to make friends with him."

"You're probably right. You say we, but he doesn't know you, does he?"

"I don't think so. We inhabit totally different worlds. And also, he wasn't there while I was still around."

In fact, I had no idea when he *had* gotten there. Regardless of when it was, though, if in fact he had joined merely to find hook-ups, to find someone to get off with, if he had managed to make it into the ranks of leadership while joining under those pretenses, then Ten's very existence was a symbol of all that was now wrong with Moai.

"Well then, I guess the first order of business would be to get in touch and actually take him up on those drinks. Oh, but if it turns out to be a mixer or something, I'd only be going for the sake of my duty, so don't say anything to this one," he said, gesturing to Pon-chan with his thumb. I got the feeling there might be more than one reason for this, but that was none of my concern. I could still hear her faint snoring.

"Got it, I won't tell her you've got the hots for her."

"Stop it!" It was charming the way he looked at Pon-chan, whispering the warning in a way that almost made me think he wasn't joking. I wonder if it's strange to be so endeared to someone your same age.

"Oh yeah, Kaede, so you saw their leader?"

I was sure he saw the way that my gentle smile faded when he asked me this.

"I did."

"How'd that go? Er, sorry, that's kind of weird to ask."

"It's fine. Hm."

How *had* it been? I had to sit and think. I thought about it and came up with the most straightforward way to convey this to Tousuke.

"It just made me think...I have to take them back. Not just Moai but our ideals."

"Yeah?"

"Yeah."

"Well, I mean, it's not every day I hear you get fired up and say something that embarrassing, so I'm all in."

I offered my wonderful friend a heartfelt, "Thanks."

He waved it off with a, "Stop thanking me, it's embarrassing."

For about the next thirty minutes, we drank, forgetting all the day's woes.

"Mm, well, think it's about time I get Pon back home. You can get changed over at my place. Oh, or if you like those clothes, you can borrow them?"

"I would in fact like to get out of them as quickly as possible, so I'll stop by."

"C'mon, didn't you tell Pon you were goin' on a date? Why not go out and find yourself a new girlfriend? Oh, wait, are you still hung up on that girl from work...?"

"I'm not like you were back in the day. I'll be fine. Just wake her up already."

As instructed, Tousuke called out to Pon-chan. When she did not stir, he poked her in the shoulder. She jolted, revealing her now reddened forehead.

"Oh, sorry...I wasn't slee...er..."

"Yeah you were."

"Yeah..."

I went and settled the tab, leaving the dazed Pon-chan to Tousuke. We left the shop and saw her home, heading to Tousuke's place with the intention of having an afterparty there, but at some point, the two of us just passed out on the floor.

For some reason, both Pon-chan and the girl from work I had dated and broken up with over a year before came to mind.

Now that I thought about it, just when was it that Pon-chan had started calling me Kaede-senpai? I wondered upon waking the next morning, for no reason in particular.

—*—

When Akiyoshi came down the stairs and noticed me walking down the hall, she signaled to me with her eyes. As she reached the floor I was on, she said a farewell to the older woman she was walking with. She turned her back on the woman, who was heading farther down to a different floor, planted herself before me, and said, "Yo! Heya, Kaede. Surprised to see you around here."

"Hey. I had to give a report in one of the classrooms above here."

"Oh, I gotcha. Headed to another class now?"

"Nah, I'm done for the day. You?"

"Done with classes now, but I've got to meet up with someone. Oh, hey, you wanna go grab something to eat?"

"Well, this is sudden."

It was rare, I thought, to see Akiyoshi actually having fun with someone, to hear about her meeting up with someone. I didn't get why she'd be asking me out to eat if she had someone to meet up with, though.

"So actually, I'm going to be meeting with someone who's interested in joining Moai. You saw that person I was with earlier? She's one of my professors, but when I was talking to her about Moai earlier, another girl in my class seemed to be pretty interested. Oh, but no worries if you're busy, or you just don't feel like it."

I, in fact, was not busy, and while meeting new people was not my favorite thing in the world, I did not outright hate it. I was just a little concerned.

"Is this some kind of initiation test? For our secret society."

"It's nothing *that* outrageous. We're not looking for 'special individuals.' We aren't Freemasons or something." She chuckled at her own joke. Even if it wasn't something that outrageous, this still seemed like it was probably some sort of interview.

What she said next confirmed my suspicions.

"But yeah, if she happens to say she wants to join, it'd suck if she was someone you don't like. There aren't many girls that I dislike, personally. My shyness sensors are kind of broken."

"Broken? I don't think you had any installed to begin with."

"What does *that* mean?!" she laughed, slapping my shoulder and adding, "I guess that is kind of a specialized skill."

Naturally, at that time, neither of us had any idea what the future had in store for us. Neither those who would vanish, those who would become corrupt, nor those who would take up the fight knew what would lie ahead.

Back then, Moai was still about nothing more than our ideals.

That day, at Akiyoshi's invitation, I headed to a nearby diner and met with this potential recruit. My initial impression, after talking to her for a short while, was that she was a different type. Given that she had interest in joining Moai, I had assumed I was about to have another person just as vexing as Akiyoshi on my hands, but this girl turned out to be a completely different type of person.

Her name was Tazunoki Mia. Half-Italian on her mother's side apparently, she had monolid eyes, thin lips, and a cold air about her. I could tell just by her looks that she was not the sort of person whose feelings you could tell right from their expression, like Akiyoshi was. What they did share was a conviction in the futures they saw before them—only she would be taking a different path to get there.

"Currently, I'm studying religions and economics. I want to know more about the structures that make the world work and the types of people that make that happen," Tazunoki confidently, quietly explained to us over a cup of coffee. Put simply, she was the sort of person who sought logical answers to things. Logic to her was what ideals were to Akiyoshi. Akiyoshi listened to what she had to say, this girl so different from her, with deep interest. It was not long after that Tazunoki became the third member of Moai.

Then, it was like the dam had broken, though in reality, the opposite was true. Nevertheless, now that the gates were open, there was no way that the surge of the no longer two-person Moai could be contained. Three members became four, four became five, and soon we were able to apply to the university as an official organization.

Akiyoshi seemed pleased about this, but it was around that time that we shared the following conversation.

"Since this was my idea, I went ahead and applied. However, this group is all of ours, and yours, Kaede. If you think I'm doing something wrong here, I want you to say so. I want this to be done with both our consent."

That was the shape of Akiyoshi's ideals. None of us ever believed that those ideals could ever be tarnished, that one day there would be no one left to strive towards them.

This was roughly two and a half years before Tousuke attended that meet-up.

—⁎—

Time passed. It was about a month after that meet-up.

"Oh, well if it isn't Kaede! Hey there!"

"Oh, hey there."

The temperature had gotten warmer and already the smell of summer had begun drifting along the breeze. I was in the cafeteria eating some *zarusoba* when Ten happened to pass by, a girl at his side and a giddy smile on his face.

"Being too sociable is just as bad as not being sociable at all," said Pon-chan, who I had happened to run into early and was now eating with, dull and ominously.

If it could be said for some that shyness was a strength; then there were also those for whom being communicative was a weakness. Though it may sound odd to say, you never know when you're going to have a change of heart in terms of your own values. That was probably why Moai had changed from back then and why I decided to proactively embrace the fact that it was not an impossibility that we might someday change as well.

One month from the start of things, I was still working hard on the plans we had laid.

Things had been going well. We had since gotten in touch with Ten and had managed to forge a bond over food and drinks. It worked out for us that Ten rarely rejected those who approached him, nor chased after those who left him. By his philosophy—that once you got to know someone, you were already friends—I suppose you could even call us friends. As Tousuke had accurately predicted, he was very different from me, and the sort of person I did not usually get on with, but there was no direct harm in dealing with him. Though I did, of course, have to be careful never to approach him when he was with any members of Moai that I knew.

"Wearing a jacket in this heat... Is he out of his mind?" said Pon-chan, who was wearing a short-sleeved jacket herself, about Ten. In the month since, her feelings of hatred towards Moai had only intensified, but I could not exactly call this a problem, for our purposes.

The problem lies, specifically, elsewhere. Unlike Pon-chan, Ten rarely spoke about people who were not present. While this had the inverse advantage of making it unlikely that he would ever reveal anything about us to others, it also meant that he never actively spoke about any of the women who might potentially be involved in a scandal with him. Thus, the only course of action would be instead for us to bring up the topic of women, but in the end, it just seemed too forced and unnatural.

Presently, we were struggling to come up with ways to make this happen.

To sidetrack for a moment, let me talk about this jacket of Ten's which Pon-chan mentioned. When I had overheard the Moai members in the café a month ago, I was waiting in talking about Ten, I had thought it a lucky coincidence, but I now doubt that was the case. As it would turn out, the disguise I had been wearing at that time bore a striking resemblance to the sort of clothing Ten usually wore. I must have reminded one of those girls of him, which is why he came up in conversation. Though unintended, this had been yet another smart move on Tousuke's part.

Apparently, there really was a reason for all things.

After lunch, I parted ways with Pon-chan, sat through my last class of the day, and then headed to work. For a change of pace from the Moai developments that had been occurring during that month, I had picked up a new part-time job. Well, I say "new," but the fact was that when I had informed my manager from my previous part-time position about my job offer, I had been asked if I would come back to work. My Moai plans were important, but I did need money to live.

I rode my bike ten minutes from the university and stopped behind a large drugstore. When I took the familiar back entrance into the locker room, I came face-to-face with Kawahara-san, a girl who I had been privately referring to as "Miss Yankee," and whom I now often shared shifts with following my return. She greeted me with a, "Morn,'" to which I returned a, "G'morn.'" She was a freshman at my university, so at least in terms of school she was distinctly my kouhai. However, if you counted the time *after* I had come back to work here, I was *her* kouhai. But if you counted the time *before* I left, I was her senpai, so we had spent the past month struggling to decide on how exactly we were to address one another in terms of formality, eventually settling on a mutually relaxed register. Luckily, we had yet to encounter one another on campus.

Working here at the drugstore was easy. I was mainly in charge of stocking and manning the register and other odd jobs, and because it was located in a residential district, there were few troublesome customers. Even if they did show up, I could just have them speak to a certain other employee on staff. Only once did I have to deal with a customer demanding a particularly unreasonable return; the "Come again?" that Kawahara-san gave them sent a shiver down my spine. Since then, she had privately earned from me the moniker of "Miss Yankee" as per the thuggish impression I got from her. She was also easily distinguished by the sparkly silver earrings that peeked out from behind her hair that hung over her ears.

I guess I couldn't be as carefree as Pon-chan was. I diligently did my work, not making much conversation with Kawahara-san, as it grew steadily darker outside the shop, and soon night had come. We got few customers at that hour, so we mostly swapped positions between one of us tidying up the store while the other stood at the register staring off into space.

I mopped mindlessly around the register, letting the music from the store radio drift into my ears. Kawahara-san stood nearby, idle. The interior of the shop was the same as always. We had passed many days like this.

It was just as I was passing in front of the register that Kawahara-san suddenly called, "Tabata-san!"

"Huh?" I replied at this rare address, perhaps sounding a little jumpy. Kawahara-san glanced upward, as though trying to think of what to say, and then looked back at me.

"I went to check out that Moai thing, the one you were talking about before."

"Wait, *seriously*?"

"Yeah." She nodded, her lips moving ever so slightly.

"They had an info session, so I went."

"Well, that's some initiative..."

"And then I joined."

"Wait, really? Oh, I mean, uh..."

"Well, I've got some spare time."

Kawahara had just confessed to me that she had joined Moai simply because she was bored, as casually as if she were buying manga. I was completely taken aback.

If I was being honest, though, I should have expected in these last few days that this might happen. This was not pure coincidence. What I was shocked at was my own cowardice.

As part of my anti-Moai plans that I had launched a month before, I had been considering sending in a spy. It could not be an outsider like Tousuke, who was not actually part of the group, nor someone like Pon-chan, who took part in group activities despite actually hating them. No, I needed a spy who would join the group legitimately of their own accord, who would be willing to divulge what they had seen and heard inside as gossip, unawares. Of course, I had no such existing person on the inside, and I had given up on the plan as unrealistic—but when Kawahara had asked me recently, "There any interesting clubs around?" I had recommended Moai to her as a group that seemed rather high-minded, saying, "Might be kind of cool."

Naturally, I had suggested this to her because I thought it might be easier for me to get information if she were to join, but I had never thought that she would act that quickly, nor that she would tell me she had joined, which was where my surprise came in. I felt quite guilty, as well.

"Had no idea you'd be that interested."

"It's not that I'm interested in that stuff, but I'm not big on athletics, and if I were into cultural studies stuff I could just do that on my own. That's why I joined up."

"I see."

"What? Do those guys actually suck or somethin'? They some kind of *cult* or somethin'?"

Though you probably could call the club's foundation

something akin to a cult, I was aware that was not the question that Kawahara-san was asking, so I shook my head and said, "Oh no, it's nothing like that."

"Well, that's good. I could tell that those Moai folks were pretty gung ho about their stuff. With other groups I was invited to, you could practically smell the cynicism. I like people who are kind of into themselves, though."

Once again, it seemed that I had orchestrated an arrangement that suited both of our needs perfectly. However, I could not let her know that—rather, I could not say that it did not seem to me that a group of people who were drunk on their own ideals were much different from the cults Kawahara was so worried about, so I chose my words carefully.

"I don't know much about it, but it seems there's a lot of rumors about them, so just be careful, and let me know what kind of stuff they get up to."

"Why, you interested?"

"Only as far as hearing anything juicy."

"Gotcha."

And with that, our conversation was over—we noticed a customer approaching the register. I turned my back, returning to my mopping. Behind me, I heard Kawahara-san give a "Welcome" without raising the corners of her mouth so much as a millimeter.

Two hours later, both of our shifts ended. Kawahara-san hurriedly changed out of her uniform and left the locker room. I have no idea why, but for some reason she always left the locker room a little before I did. When I got outside, I would find her waiting for me atop her scooter, helmet already equipped. "See you later," she said curtly, before riding off into the night. This was always the pattern.

Maybe it was because of the sort of people she hung around that she was very strict about hierarchy, I mused as I unlocked my bike, glancing down at my phone to find a text from Tousuke.

"Apparently Ten's gotten a businesswoman girlfriend."

To the untrained eye, this would be nothing more than a meaningless update on a male friend's love life, but for us, this was the opportunity we had been waiting for.

"Looks like everything's falling into place," said Tousuke, leaning against the door of the crowded subway car, with some surprise, when I later told him about Kawahara-san and how she had apparently become a legitimate member of Moai. It was the weekend, and no seats were empty in the car. As we slipped past the tall buildings that surrounded the train tracks, the bright sunlight pierced through, glinting off of Tousuke's gaudy fashion glasses.

"We've still got a lot of work ahead of us, though it seems like she'd made a friend."

I recalled how sincere Kawahara-san had been at work the day before when she told me, "I'm going to hang out with someone." *I guess you've got a friend already, huh?* I had rudely wondered, but of course I had not asked.

As I gazed at the scenery rushing by outside, I suddenly noticed that Tousuke was facing somewhere behind me and waving.

I turned cautiously to look, thinking he must have spotted a friend or something. I was relieved to see he was just returning the greeting from a little girl who was waving our way.

The train, packed with couples and families, carried everyone on to their intended destinations. Most of the passengers were probably headed for the amusement park at the end of the line. As for Tousuke and me, we were headed solemnly to a station near a certain park—we had been invited there, after all.

"A barbecue club?"

"Yeah. Ten invited me. Said there would be girls there so I should come. Apparently, you just sign up with your e-mail address and as long as you pay the membership fee, anyone can attend. Guess that's a fairly common setup, though."

"Only a hipster of a college student like you could say that something that inscrutable is *commonplace*."

"No, no, no. I'm just talking about these kinds of events where you have no idea who's hosting them. Also, according to Ten, he didn't invite any Moai members, so no need to worry about any of them showing up. I mean, I suppose any of them might still have some other connection that brings them there, but at least the risk is low, so I figured I would check it out. How about you, Kaede?"

Thus, gone was the conversation four days prior. In the end, I had decided it would be bad of me to leave everything to Tousuke, so I decided to go with him—so that I could collect intel from Ten in a more laid-back setting. This would be my first time going undercover with Tousuke.

Tousuke, who had suggested going undercover to eliminate as many points of worry as possible, seemed oddly fired up over this operation again.

"I knew you'd be a natural at this, Kaede," he half-laughed.

"No way," I refused. "If anyone we know sees me, I'm going to swallow my own tongue."

"It'd really make it tough on the investigators if you died in a getup as ridiculous as that," he cackled.

I took a moment to really look at what it was I was wearing. I had on a chartreuse Hawaiian shirt over a white T-shirt, with yellow shorts and stark white slip-on shoes. For accessories, a white straw hat and a necklace. Surely, from afar, no one would ever be able to tell it was me, but it was still incredibly embarrassing—I looked like I was on my way to a *resort* or something. Conversely, Tousuke's more modest attire of a polo shirt and fashion glasses was just as bad.

"There's no reason for you to be disguised too, though. What's with the fake glasses?"

"Listen, don't knock the glasses. They're the easiest way to up a dude's hotness factor."

"Pretty sure actual vision-impaired people would take umbrage with that..."

Tousuke chuckled again. He was always rather spirited, but perhaps it was the bright sunlight that had him in even higher spirits than usual. Or perhaps it was just the prospect of meeting some girls.

We should have invited Pon-chan too, I realized as the train gradually slowed to a stop. Tousuke stepped away from the door he had been leaning against, which presently opened. We stepped resolutely out from the feeble air-conditioning of the train car into the muggy outdoors.

"Hot out here!"

"And we're gonna be grilling meat out in this..."

It was not that I particularly disliked the outdoors, but it was only June, and my heart was not yet ready to handle this sort of heat. The thought of charcoal flames sapped the life right out of me.

As we exited the gates, I noticed a group of young people in picnicking attire headed to the intersection that led to the park entrance. It was unclear whether they were headed for the same destination as us, but just in case, I scanned the faces of everyone around us to make sure there was no one I recognized.

"Oh, there's Ten," said Tousuke from beside me. Instinctively, my body tensed up. "Yo!" he called out without even stopping to warn me, waving his hand. I looked up, and sure enough there was Ten, crossing a crosswalk with a bag from a convenience store in one hand and his phone in the other. Ten looked up, waving back with a smile, and waited for us on the other side of the crosswalk.

"Morning, Tousuke. Oh, hey, Kaede, that's a new look for you. Guessing you're pretty fired up! Love to see it."

"You know, ha ha ha." I laughed it off, though of course that was the opposite of how I felt. Ten, by contrast, seemed to be full of vigor, with his wide hat, matching shirt, and silver jewelry glittering on his fingers. Though for all I knew, this was just a normal weekend for him.

After a few rounds of pointless conversational back and forth, Ten showed us to the event site. We had purposely arrived a little bit after the starting time so as not to draw attention when there were still few attendees around, but we were told that only about half the attendees were there yet—little shock for a college student gathering. This left me faced with the nerve-racking task of having to keep an eye on everyone else who came later to make sure that there was no one who I knew.

As we moved into the barbecue pavilion, a number of groups already appeared to be setting up camp. When we asked Ten what sort of people would be coming to the function, he led us to a group that had occupied one fairly spacious corner of the site. As we approached, I was shocked—by the number of people. There were enough people there to make up a full high school class, and this was supposedly only half of them. Just what sort of a group was this?

Blessedly, we did not have to introduce ourselves to everyone. Hitches in our plans aside, I just hated having the attention of that many people at once. We were led to the man who was acting as coordinator and paid our fees, before Ten introduced us to a few acquaintances of his.

"Oh, so they go to the same school as you, Amano-kun? They must be pretty sharp! Anyway, let's get some drinks!"

Hearing these sorts of things from the whole group, something occurred to me. Though it wasn't a matter of whether this was good or bad, these people were all so carefree that I could see how it was that I had managed to go my whole university career without knowing about these sorts of gatherings.

As we each took a beer out from the cooler at someone's urging, Ten, who was standing nearby to keep an eye on us, put his phone to his ear. Judging by what he was saying, someone else he had invited had gotten lost along the way.

"Sorry, guys, gotta go find one of my friends. Go find someone to hang out with." He gave us a charming smile and jogged off in the direction we had just come from. Sure had a lot on his plate. Suddenly abandoned, Tousuke and I looked at one another, pulled the tabs on our beer cans, and clinked them.

Here beneath the sunlight, the first sip tasted of guilt.

As I sighed, glancing around us unsure of what to do, I suddenly heard an "Oh!" from beside me. I looked up to see Tousuke waving to a man across from us who was grilling meat. Before I could even ask, "Who's that?" Tousuke explained, "I'm going to be working with him next year." In other words, a future coworker at the company Tousuke would be joining.

"I'm gonna go say hey to him," he said, heading for the grills, leaving me all alone. Just to give my hands something to do, I took another sip of beer. At times like these, it occurred to me that if I were the sort of person who could make conversation with strangers all on my own, I would have already known that these sorts of events existed.

After spending some time blankly watching Tousuke chattering with his coworker, I realized someone was standing beside me. Before I could turn to look, someone spoke my name.

"What're you up to, Tabata-san?"

Just as my name was spoken, I turned and nearly jumped out of my skin. A bit of beer splashed out of my can.

"K-Kawahara-san?" I asked dubiously, but surely enough, there was Miss Yankee herself. I was sure that I had gotten a good look at the faces of everyone who had been present when I arrived. She had not been there previously. I was the one who should have been asking what *she* was doing.

"Howdy," she replied. "Didn't know you liked this kinda thing."

"Uh, w...well."

"Just a sec." She glanced me over from head to toe. "Interesting style."

Welp, time to swallow my tongue.

"Well, uh, I kind of think my friend was just messing with me..."

"It suits you."

"Um, thanks...I suppose." I *assumed* it was a compliment, but her tone now was even more lax than it was at the store. As per usual, her clothes were mainly black. More casual than normal, she wore a T-shirt and jeans.

"Same to you though, what are you doing...er." No matter how surprised I was to see her, I was there too, so it would be wrong of me to speak as though I was questioning her right to be there. "D-didn't know you were into this kind of thing either. Or wait, was this what you were talking about when you mentioned hanging out?"

"Yep. Came with a friend."

I followed her gaze and saw a cheery-looking girl bowing to a man, probably the senpai who had invited her.

"Who d'you know here, Tabata-san? Someone just as fashionable?"

Apparently, she did not honestly believe that my outfit had been a prank on my friend's part, so I had to explain myself.

"Er, no, you know Ten, from Moai? I think he's a pretty big deal or something, but my friend Tousuke, the one with the glasses over there, he's friends with Ten. That's why I'm here."

I was aware of how rushed and unnatural my explanation sounded. I was worried that Kawahara-san might think this odd, but instead she nodded, and said, "I haven't talked to Ten-san, but I know about him." The conversation trailed off there, a brief silence falling.

We had never spoken much about our private lives to one another, and neither of us was the especially chatty sort. I was starting to wonder if I had made things awkward, but before I could get a sense of that, thankfully Tousuke reappeared. When Tousuke spotted me, he signaled toward Kawahara-san with his eyes, silently asking who she was.

"Oh, Tousuke, um, let m…ah, this is K-Kawahara-san. She's a freshman at our school, we work together." It was not her name I had stumbled over, so much as wondering just how humble I ought to be in introducing her.

I pointed to Tousuke, saying, "This is my friend."

Kawahara-san gave a polite bow and said plainly, "Hello, I'm Kawahara." At times like these, I would have immediately slipped into a more polite register upon meeting someone for the first time, but judging by how he interacted with Pon-chan, Tousuke was accustomed to dealing with his juniors.

"Oh, nice to meet you! I'm Kaede's friend. You all work together, huh? I'm sure Kaede's always causing all sorts of trouble for you. Please forgive him!"

"You've never once visited me at work," I jabbed back like usual, suddenly wondering if Kawahara-san would find that charming. In fact, the corners of her mouth pricked up slightly.

"No, he's always looking after me, actually."

"Oh, no, I'm the one always relying on you," I replied, not remembering a time when I had ever been much use to her. Perhaps the phrase "looking after" had given Tousuke the wrong impression, because he looked at me with the sort of eyes he would about ten seconds before bullying someone. I changed the subject.

"So the friend you came with, is she connected to Moai somehow?"

"Yeah. I'll introduce you when she gets back."

Just as she said this, her friend walked over and introduced herself. It was surprising that Kawahara-san would make friends with someone who seemed like a bottomless ray of sunshine, but then, that was just the way, wasn't it? Often in friendships, each party would make up for something that the other lacked.

Now, it was Kawahara-san's turn to go greet her friend's

senpai. Speaking as her senior, at least at the university, I joked, "Don't worry about us, go have fun," to which she replied, "You too, Tabata-san." That was not something I could do, in fact, but I graciously accepted the overture.

Once we were alone again, as I had predicted, Tousuke grinned and elbowed me.

"Going after young coworkers again, eh, Tabata-senpai?"

"No. Way. Maybe I should tell Pon-chan you went to a barbecue to pick up chicks."

"That is *not* true! Well, whatever, you gotta be careful about acquaintances popping up like that."

That was very true. I had to be more vigilant from here on out to keep an eye on every new person who arrived.

"She still recognized me right away even through all this. I wanna change."

"What? But I mean, she didn't say it looked weird or anything, right?"

"She said it was flashy."

I didn't tell Tousuke that she had meant it as a compliment.

After some time, Ten returned, a graceful lady on his arm. Several people piped up when they saw her; apparently, she knew quite a few attendees at this event.

"Well, she's cute," said Tousuke.

Maybe I will *tell Pon-chan,* I thought briefly.

Of course, we had not come here to feast our eyes on pretty girls, nor were we here to sample food, drink, and vices under the blazing sun.

We had a mission to accomplish.

Basically, what we needed was for Ten to disclose his indiscretions with women of his own volition. We needed to hear a tawdry saga of Ten using Moai as a hook-up spot and sinking his claws into professional women, throwing them away when he was through with them. From there we could sort out the facts and expose Moai's evildoings. I, in fact, had a voice recorder in my breast pocket as we spoke, which would be recording all of the conversations around us. I'd considered posting Ten's confessions to the web unedited, but I decided not to, as we would need the identity of the informant to remain anonymous.

Our team was but a select few. We had to do things aboveboard.

We would first need to make conversation with Ten's group, but I was personally ill-suited to that sort of thing. Approaching someone and addressing them was a high-level skill. It was not as though I *couldn't* do it, but doing so felt highly unnatural. Thankfully, Tousuke made up for what I lacked there. He could make targeted conversation much more smoothly.

Perhaps because he was so close with the organizers, Ten was frequently called by name, asked where drinks could be found, and asked to grill meat. Though he grinned and griped each time, he completed his duties swiftly and efficiently—perhaps a hallmark of someone who would have risen to the top ranks of an organization. No one would ever follow someone who was only ever flippant.

Without making any declaration about the start of the battle,

Tousuke took point, saying, "Well, since we're here, may as well eat something," as he headed toward the smell of smoke and meat. I followed after him.

"Yo, Ten, can I grab some of these?"

"Whatever you need!"

Tousuke picked up two sets of plates and chopsticks and handed one of each to me, then approached Ten once again.

"Now, some meat, please!"

"I swear, all of you think I'm some kind of grilling machine! Just a minute!"

Tousuke grinned at Ten, who acted annoyed but actually seemed to be enjoying himself, and said, "Well, everyone's been asking you for meat, so I just assumed you were the expert!" The other guys around Ten, who all seemed to be of his ilk, laughed and prodded Ten for meat as well. Seeing this, the nearby girls laughed too. Watching this all from Tousuke's side, I gave a thin smile as well.

It was not unusual for us to keep loitering in the area, as we were waiting for our meat to be grilled. Tousuke informed the others around that he attended the same university as Ten and had gotten to know him this year. The others, who had known Ten for far longer, took the opportunity to bully Ten with facts that Tousuke was probably unaware of. Playing along, Tousuke responded, "Well, this is a side of Ten I've *never* seen!" which gave them a sense of superiority in their already standing closeness, and the friendly ribbing only increased. I watched this with a smile.

Naturally, the conversation eventually shifted to where the two had met. Both out of tact and technique, Tousuke prompted, "Well, about that…" looking to Ten, who followed up with, "Tousuke came to a Moai event." And thus, we were able to get him to broach the subject of the group without us forcing his hand.

There did not appear to be any particularly outstanding reactions to this amongst the others. In fact, everyone laughed at the mention of Moai's name, one of them quipping, "What, you still vying for world peace, Amano?" It was this impression of Moai they apparently had that they were laughing at.

"Yeah, yeah, yeah. I keep telling you guys though, I'm not some kind of hero or something." Ten's obvious sincerity in this just drew more laughter from the others.

"Well, aren't you somethin' special?"

"No way… Well, I suppose I *am* contributing more to society than you guys," Ten said haughtily.

"Like *what*?!" they jeered back.

Just then, the girl who Ten had brought with him earlier returned with drink in hand.

"The leader's always relying on him."

Ten gushed at this.

"Seriously, no way. She snaps at me every time I slip up, and we're always fighting. Oh, I mean Hiro *is* technically the leader, but really, she's so annoying. She even asked me if you were my mother!"

Here was the first time I had ever seen such loquaciousness from Ten, who rarely spoke about others.

"A girl? Is she cute?"

"Everyone here is *way* cuter." Very conveniently for our cause, all the girls laughed at Ten's joking compliment, one bespectacled girl saying, "You better stop saying that to everyone before you get yourself dumped." We had been hoping for a discussion of Ten's love life.

Yes, this was the moment we had been waiting for. To be honest though, it didn't feel right hearing about this. My sense of advantage lay somewhere, completely separate from my emotions.

Still, this was odd even for me. Though I had assumed that I would find a Moai that worshipped its current leader like a religion distasteful, I was in fact all the more upset and enraged to see even the management criticizing their leader. To think that this had become an organization where even the upper brass would talk behind each other's backs...

I knew that I could not let my emotions get the better of me. I would just have to listen quietly.

Now that I thought back, the girl with the glasses had said "*Get* dumped," rather than "dump." Perhaps that was the view that everyone had of him.

The girl who Tousuke had previously deemed to be cute tipped up her canned chuhai and hummed a "Mmm..." as though she was thinking. "I'm pretty sure that leader girl is into you, Amano-kun."

"No, like I said, we're always fighting."

"That's just how girls are!" she said as though she were a spokesperson for all women, an assuredness that perhaps only stemmed from her confidence in her own appearance and strength.

"You all go to the same school, what do you think?"

Normally I would have cringed at the sudden question, but luckily, I had been keeping on my toes and was able to answer more quickly than Tousuke.

"Well, we don't really know much about this leader, right?"

"Yeah," Tousuke agreed, "At least, when I saw her at that one event, I couldn't get any real sense from her."

Whether that was not the response she had been hoping for, or whether she simply had no interest in us in the first place, the woman turned her gaze right back to Ten and said, unrelated to the previous flow of conversation, "You just seem so in love right now."

I wouldn't be able to live my life if I started to believe that I had no interest in these sorts of things. Plus, she was an unexpected assistance to us.

"Oh yeah, didn't you get a new girlfriend?" asked one of the guys. Everyone bubbled with excitement. At this, even more people, who had previously not been part of the circle, began to gather around. Amongst the species known as university students, there are a certain subset who become quite uneasy if there's some excitement going on that they aren't part of—it would seem we had such people among us today.

"C'mon, enough of that," Ten said, taking a sip of the chuhai he was holding. It was not lost on me that the smile he had on his face until now was missing. I wondered if he was suddenly feeling the weight of his own infidelity. Perhaps these were not the sort of "friends" who would simply laugh and accept such a revelation without offering reproach.

Or perhaps he simply could not reveal such a thing in front of so many girls.

"Wait, seriously? Congrats! What's she like?"

"Don't tell me it's another businesswoman?"

"We gotta celebrate! Maybe next time?"

It was not unusual in these situations to hear more words of teasing than of congratulations, but I noticed that there was a tone of concern mixed in with some of these utterances. Ten tentatively accepted their congratulations, jutting his lip theatrically, before clacking together the tongs he had been using to wrest back attention from everyone and saying plainly, "I'm not seeing anyone."

Tousuke and I exchanged glances.

"What the hell? Was that faulty intel? What's the deal?!"

One bleached blond fellow looked back and forth between the man who had originally brought up the subject and Ten. I kept watch on Ten, keeping the can to my lips so that he would not notice my staring.

"I didn't really want to talk about it. It's pretty tacky." He lowered his eyebrows, giving a self-deprecating smile. That expression must be his power, how he survives day to day in society, I realized.

"I manage the contact registrar for Moai, so naturally, I have to give them my contact info too, but sometimes people I talk to at the events invite me out for dinner."

"You been hitting on them?"

"I have not! It's usually more like they want to show appreciation for my hard work. After all, I have a dedicated e-mail address. Mm...though I mean, it's true that sometimes when the conditions are right, after events they'll message me, very clearly with the intention of inviting me on a date."

"You're *shameless*!" one of the girls cackled.

"No way!" Ten said, shaking his head. "Listen, it's not like I'm some kind of player. If any of these guys got an invitation like that, they'd definitely take it." He pointed down the line at each of us men.

Thankfully, one of the other men, with an almost comically meek smile on his face, agreed, "If a hot older woman asked me out, I'd go!"

"I'd never turn down an invitation from an attractive older person," the woman who had been acting as a representative for the other girls chimed in turn, perhaps in order to give off a certain impression of herself to someone. Her comment was completely unnecessary to the flow of the conversation, but it did get the girls more fired up, which in turn fueled Ten's story forward. I wanted to hear more of what he had to say immediately.

So, the women had asked him out?

"Right? So, I mean, it's not terrible of me to go out on a date if someone asks me out, right? Of course, if things do turn that way once I've gone, and we meet up a few more times, well that's where it starts getting dicey." Trying to abate some of that diceyness by showing self-awareness of it was not a Ten-exclusive technique. Anyone would do the same.

"As it turns out though, I was the only one who thought we were in a relationship. She apparently did not feel the same way at all. Here, let me take a survey!"

"Ha! That's a group leader for you!" someone jabbed back,

eliciting a laugh. Even the current twisted Moai would never put out such a survey.

"Okay, so which of these scenarios sounds more likely to you: Two people have met up countless times, and even held hands. Are they not dating? Or are they just dating without explicitly saying so?"

Which of those sounded more plausible would depend on one's own level of experience, so I doubted that Ten would get the response he was seeking here. But he asked for a show of hands, so Tousuke and I raised our hands in the manner that would most tacitly reaffirm our acquaintanceship. In other words, we were on Ten's side.

With us included, the results were nearly fifty-fifty. However, it was Ten's personality that concerned more than those results.

"*Seriously?* You're telling me that some of you guys could hold hands with a girl you aren't even dating? You're even more shameless than me!" Ten turned to the girls who had voted on his side, who offered a kind, equivocal laughter.

I tried my best to give the benefit of the doubt and take his words at face value. Ten was not the sort of man who would hold hands with someone he was not dating. If this claim was to be believed, was there really nothing more than that?

"Well, guess you're purer than you look, Amano. Guess you've still got the heart of a virgin."

"*Who* does?!"

Apparently, the topic of virginity was something that got these men particularly fired up. After a bit of pointless rowdiness, someone seemed to decide it was finally time to let up and patted Ten on the shoulder. "Well, just glad that you figured out what kind of person she was before things got too serious. Next one'll be better."

"That's true. I'm glad too. You were way more depressed last time."

"I just wish I could do something about my love of older women."

I got the sense that trying to ask Ten, who was probably trying to make people laugh, what had happened in his previous relationship would not be the right thing to do right now—at least not in this situation. However, there are quite a few people in this world who have no sense of tact.

"Did something happen last time?" asked a girl with a fluffy white outfit and sloped eyes. She had been smiling along with the rest in the circle and rather gave the impression that she was only there as someone's plus-one.

For a moment, the air grew cold. Ten was skilled at bending the atmosphere around him to his will.

"Oh man, oh man, no! It was nothing! It was just at some point she found a better guy than me!" Ten waved his hands ridiculously over his head as if to downplay the truth. The men around him jumped in with "Stop it! You're gonna make him cry!" and "Don't beat yourself up, man!" The chill in the air dissipated in an instant, the sly girl looking purposely surprised.

The topic of Ten's love life gradually petered out from there on and within ten minutes had been replaced with another topic entirely. Tousuke and I lingered by this group, hoping that either Ten or one of the others would divulge some other useful information, but by the time we ate some meat, drank the drinks that were offered to us, and were cajoled into talking about the job offers we had gotten, suddenly it was time to clean up the barbecue.

As we walked, garbage bags in hand, Tousuke paused to make sure no one else was around us, then said to me, "Looks like maybe we were wrong."

I wondered for a moment if I was supposed to nod at this.

"Hard to tell still. Maybe Ten was just lying."

"It didn't seem like he was lying."

Again, I wondered if I should nod at this, but in the end, we simply disposed of the trash, exchanging no more words. Only our own breathing remained on the voice recorder as a mark of our disappointment.

About three weeks later, something that appeared to be the truth came out from an unexpected source: Kawahara-san.

"That Ten-san guy is really somethin'," she began during a shift one day, immediately getting my hopes up. "Friend of yours, isn't he?"

"I mean, I wouldn't say all that, but why? Something happen?"

"No, well... See, I always just figured he was some kinda pretty playboy, but I went for drinks with him the other day."

Remembering my own time as a freshman, I couldn't bring myself to say something boorish like, *Shouldn't you be focusing on your classes?*

"He's kind of a dandy."

That wasn't a word you hear very often.

"That, he's a…uh…what do you mean exactly?"

"When I joined Moai, people told me to watch out for him because he was a big-time player. So, I figured when he was drunk enough, I'd ask him about it."

That's a wild thing to ask about…though I didn't say that. This was incredibly valuable intel for us, anyway.

"Seems like he's dated a lot of businesswomen, and, well…to put it harshly, he's been dumped by a lot of them. He doesn't want to make them seem like the bad guy, so he always tells the folks at Moai that he was the one doing the dumping. Of course, I mean, that wasn't exactly how he put it, but that's more or less the gist of it. But, whatever."

Though her tone did not change, I could tell just by how talkative she was being that Kawahara-san was getting a little worked up. I had thought it surprising that she would be into guys with attitude, but it seemed that was not actually the case.

"He is really into himself!"

"…I said this already, but you sure you're all right with that?"

She nodded firmly.

"People who are drunk on themselves can intoxicate others too. It seemed like he wasn't sure if he was actually popular or just a target for more adept older people."

Putting aside the fact that I could certainly see her falling victim to such a person in the future, I carefully chewed up this information, swallowed it, and found myself disappointed at the bitter taste. Apparently, both we and those girls at the café had gotten a completely wrong impression of Ten.

When I called Tousuke after work to relay this to him, he simply said, "I see." Though Tousuke had done plenty of poking fun at Ten in his own way, it really did not seem that Ten was the one playing with these older women's hearts. Additionally, according to Ten, there were still people who worked with those women who had led him on who had ties to Moai. If Ten were entirely at fault, such a thing would be unlikely.

We talked for a bit and finally decided we would not be pursuing that method of disrupting Moai. It did not seem as though we would achieve any particularly useful result.

Our plans had ended in failure.

—*—

I had been sufficiently surprised to learn that Akiyoshi was seeing someone.

"Well, I mean that happens sometimes, right?"

"My bad."

She had prefaced this by saying she was a little embarrassed to tell me, and thus she seemed rather dissatisfied that this news of hers, which she had worked up the courage to share, had not resonated with me. Her face was flushed, whether in anger or embarrassment. I was shocked as well to learn that this someone was a person whom I knew through Moai, but there was something more than that.

"Wow, to think even someone like you has interest in things like that..."

"And just what the hell do you take me for, Kaede?"

"I take you for Akiyoshi Hisano."

As a college student, it was inevitable that I would have to deal with this sort of thing at some point, and it wasn't as though things were going to change much between us just because Akiyoshi had gotten a boyfriend. Even prior to this, the time we were spending together had begun to decrease.

Around this time, Moai was growing as an organization, with increasing membership and increased recognition around campus.

As Moai began to organize volunteer and disaster relief activities, this growing membership included not only new members but older adults who offered their backing. With this newfound support, Akiyoshi herself began to be recognized in a new light around campus. A female lecturer invited her to a seminar, she was giving advice to other organizational managers, and one page of a pamphlet that was being distributed around campus even heralded her as a "new kind of leader."

Additionally, a graduate student group that had been active on campus for some time and existed to encourage students to make proactive career choices, far from holding any sort of disdain for Akiyoshi, said that they would be honored if Moai were to be their successors and could even put them in touch with alumni who could offer their support, financially and otherwise. This of course further accelerated Moai's growth. Thinking back on it now, the social events that present-day Moai often held were probably based on the events that this group once held on a much smaller scale as part of their activities.

It was in this way that, all at once, Moai grew into a large group with dozens of members. I was flummoxed. It was amazing that so many things could come together with such convenient timing. Though, convenient for who...I'm still not sure.

Many times, Akiyoshi had asked me if it was okay for things to keep moving in this direction and if I was unhappy about this. As long as the organization continued supporting Akiyoshi's ideals, I thought it was fine. Thus, I had no complaints to offer.

Now that we were able to operate on a larger scale, Akiyoshi seemed to be busy all the time. She may have had support from every direction, but she was still just a freshman. I wonder how much pressure she felt she was under. How much responsibility did she feel she had to take on? I had seen the bitter expressions on Akiyoshi's face when she had failed to accomplish something or when an activity itself began to seem pointless.

Still, I wondered if she still held those ideals when we parted. I prayed that the faintest sliver of them still existed, somewhere deep down in her heart.

So, I'm sure it was good that she had someone to support her from the inside during this time when Moai was so in flux. I realized now that I should have been happier for her at the time, but it's far too late for that.

—*—

After our plan to expose Ten's scandalous behavior had ended in failure, we were left at a standstill. We were only university students after all; with no backing or support, we were limited in what we could do. The next meet-up was still a ways off as well. With not much time left before graduation, we began to attempt a lot of smaller tactics, figuring that we may as well do all we could manage for the time being.

First, we created several fake social media accounts. Posing as various fictitious university students and professionals, we began tweeting various slanderous and defamatory statements about Moai, in addition to believable posts about our everyday lives. Naturally, this had no real detrimental effect on Moai, but it was still better than doing nothing, so Tousuke and I always had our eyes glued to our phone screens.

We also began scouting new members for our rebellion amongst the social networks. If there were any people who had felt alienated amongst the Moai members, we might be able to recruit them to our cause. As it turned out, there were a surprising number of students who felt compelled to bad mouth Moai on social media, without even having the sort of motives we did. We observed their daily postings to determine if they were members of Moai or not.

Thinking about it though, it was obvious that if even proper members of Moai were already slandering the organization, there was little damage that someone like Pon-chan, who was only on the fringes of Moai, could accomplish. But naturally, no one who could actually deal a mortal wound to Moai, such as Ten, was posting anything that would be disadvantageous to Moai on Twitter or Facebook or the like, despite being active there.

Other than this, the only thing we could do with our smartphones and limited intel was to copy down and proliferate statements by people who had been harmed by Moai that we found on social media and send them directly to the accounts of Moai members. We sent Hiro and Ten the tirade of a professional who had ended up in a different industry than they intended because of the connections they made at the networking events, and the lamentations of a boy whose girlfriend was stolen from him by a working man, and other potential half-truths. Inspired by our actions, some of the accounts that seemed to belong to people who were already dissatisfied with Moai joined in with us.

Hiro and Ten more or less stayed silent on the matter, but some other Moai members began to message us in objection. However, since the "people" who were sending them these messages did not exist to begin with, it was little skin off of our backs.

What *did* make me cringe was when Kawahara-san suddenly brought up the subject.

"Those idiots are trash, laughing from behind the safety of their screens!"

I had worried that Kawahara-san might be on to us, but it turned out she was only making conversation. Ever since we had encountered one another at the barbecue, she had been talking to me much more often than before. Perhaps she felt that the event had given her a pass to.

The fact that she was bringing this up to me meant that it had probably started to become a topic of conversation amongst Moai proper. To see if we could add some fuel to this flame, Tousuke and I decided to try making some posters and posting them around.

Tousuke was the sort of student who was really enthusiastic about cultural festivals. When I suggested the poster idea, he went all out in Word and showed up later at my place with a copy of a poster that looked akin to a murderer's warning note, the letters in all different sizes and fonts.

"I suppose there are other questions I should be asking, but you really have a lot of time on your hands, don't you?"

"This was *your* idea!"

Even after our mission had dissolved, it seemed that Tousuke had still carried on his friendship with Ten.

"We got dinner together the other night. What sucks is that he's actually a pretty great guy."

I was struck again at how good and upstanding a guy *Tousuke* was, unlike me, who had long since withdrawn from that front—never mind that he was still helping me out this much. He declined to post any posters in his own dorm, given how many friends he had there, but I was grateful at least that he had taken the time to make them.

While I was busy sending the data stored in our file-sharing server to my barely functional printer and watching it spit out a large stack of posters, Tousuke sipped a probiotic drink and said to me something along the lines of, "Pon's been wanting to see you."

"Oh yeah, guess I haven't seen her around school much lately." I was sure he was exaggerating about her wanting to see me, so I did not react to the insinuation.

"We should get drinks again sometime, all *three* of us."

"Sure, I'm free any day that I'm not working, so just coordinate something with Pon-chan." I had just said that as a half-hearted response, but it turned out that our schedules aligned sooner than I expected. I was a little put out by this, though I didn't really mind it.

Three days later, we all met for drinks. This time, we met up at Tousuke's place. This was both to save on money and because Tousuke had purchased a takoyaki maker. It seemed like kind of a random investment, but apparently all the time he had to kill after receiving his job offer had been spent on hunting Moai and improving his cooking skills.

We decided to get started a bit early, around 6 PM, so as not to miss the last trains. While it was still light outside, the two of us had gone shopping for ingredients, which Tousuke was now prepping in the kitchen while I minced the rest on the small table in the living room. Just then, the bell rang. Tousuke went to the entrance, and I overheard a small squabble before finally Pon-chan burst into the room.

"Long time no see, Kaede-senpai! How've you been?"

"Pretty good, all told."

"Glad to hear it!" Pon-chan was as chipper as ever. Her two healthy-looking arms peeked out from the summery outfit she was wearing. She held a bag in her hand.

"Tousuke-senpai, I brought some cake! Hope you like it!"

"Oh, thanks. Could you put that in the fridge?"

After greeting her, Tousuke went right back to mincing the octopus, while Pon-chan, as directed, opened the fridge in an apparently familiar fashion. Even from behind, there was something very feminine in the way that she slid the cake box into an open spot in the fridge.

"Pon-chan, have you been here before?" I asked as I chopped up a green onion, while she neatly folded up the bag that the cake had come in.

"We have our drinking parties here for our seminars. I mean, look at this place, it's huge!!!"

Surely enough, Tousuke's living room alone was at least 150 square feet and very well organized—incredibly spacious for a university student's dorm.

"So, what should I do?" Pon-chan asked after washing her hands in the restroom, looking to the owner of the home.

"There's two tupperware containers in the fridge. Put those out on the table," Tousuke said, tossing all of the takoyaki ingredients together. After pulling said tupperware out, Pon-chan sat down in front of me as I minced the red ginger and then opened them. One had diced cucumber, the other a caprese salad.

"Oho!~" she cheered, pinching some cucumber and chomping down on it. "This is *good*! Want some, Kaede-senpai?"

"Oh yeah, I do! I'll grab some after though," I said, showing her my now red hands. At this, she grabbed a bundle of disposable chopsticks that were poking out from a bag on the floor, extracted and snapped a pair, grabbed some cucumber, and held it out to me.

"Open up!"

I could not ignore the cucumber that was being held right in front of my face, and I realized that it would be all the more embarrassing to act embarrassed at this, so instead I played dumb and accepted my fate. The cucumber seemed to be lightly seasoned with soy sauce and chili oil. It had retained a nice crunch and was quite delicious.

Eventually, Tousuke set up the takoyaki grill, heaping the ingredients on the table, and finally it was time for our takoyaki party to begin. Before we started grilling, we shared a toast. We all sipped our drinks as we waited for the iron plate to heat up, when suddenly, someone's phone started vibrating. All of us simultaneously looked down at our phones, very much children of our generation, Tousuke finally exclaiming, "Oh, that's me! Oh, sorry, just gonna step out for a second. Once that's heated up, go ahead and pour in the batter and whatever fillings you want."

"Alrighty!" said Pon-chan dutifully, poking idly at her own phone, an antithesis of my own preoccupation on what the call might be about. Maybe it was about his job offer or something, I wondered rather seriously.

We started grilling, as directed, when finally, we heard the front door open again, followed by a, "I'm back!" and for some reason a, "Thanks for having me."

The door that led in from the hallway opened, and we looked up to see Tousuke, followed by Kawahara-san, still dressed in her black work shirt. I nearly spat out the *happoshu* that was in my mouth.

"Oh G—*wha*?! Uh, K-Kawahara-san?" Recalling her sudden appearance at the barbecue, I just barely stopped myself from shouting, *Oh God, there she is again!* but I managed to rein it in in the nick of time, along with my *happoshu*.

"Good to see you," she said, bowing as always with only a polite bend of her neck.

"Oh, Kawahara-san, nice to meet you! I'm one of Tousuke-senpai and Kaede-senpai's juniors. You can call me Pon-chan!"

"Nice to meet you. I'm Kawahara."

After the two of them made introductions, Kawahara-san vanished into the restroom at Tousuke's invitation. I looked as suspiciously as I could at Tousuke, who now stood alone in the living room.

"Yo, what the hell?"

"Hmm?"

Tousuke was grinning widely. I could tell by his smile that he was scheming something annoying, and what that something was, but what I found peculiar was that he'd been in contact at all with Kawahara-san. I hadn't seen them exchange information at the barbecue.

When Kawahara-san returned, Tousuke invited her to sit, and she took the open spot beside me. I suddenly wondered if even Tousuke leaving that place open had been intentional. Kawahara-san was encouraged to have some drinks and introduce herself, telling us her school department and where she was from, as though nothing was going on. This was the first time I was made clearly aware that she was from Kansai. Apparently, her intended department and the subject matter of the exams had been a large factor in her deciding to move here. Though it was perhaps a bit rude of me, what I was more concerned about was why she was here, which Tousuke thankfully explained after another toast.

"So actually, I went by the drugstore the other night to come and heckle you, Kaede. I didn't say anything because I wanted it to be a surprise. But when I got there, you weren't there. Kawahara-san was there though, and I told her we'd be having a takoyaki party soon and asked her if she wanted to come. She said she would, so I invited her."

"So you did."

"I'm glad that Kaede gets to work alongside such an agreeable kouhai."

After nodding fervently at his own statements, Tousuke drank some *happoshu*. "Pretty smooth senpai move, just casually talking to a cute girl," Pon-chan teased. For the second time now, I was surprised to see such an agreeable side of Kawahara-san. Then, it occurred to me once more that this might in fact be her *actual* nature.

I suppose the problem here was whether or not I could be objective about the fact that Kawahara-san had arrived—she was here whether I liked it or not, so I had to just deal with it. It wasn't as if I could just tell her to go home, so I made up my mind to simply go on with my evening. Such was my primary way of living.

As we dryly explained the connection between Tousuke

and myself then Tousuke and Pon-chan to Kawahara-san, the takoyaki batter began to bubble, finally firming up. We each took our turns turning them over with skewers. Kawahara-san and Tousuke did quite well, Pon-chan and I so-so. Sadly, we were not quite bad enough to be laugh-worthy, so it was lacking in entertainment value.

We passed around the takoyaki sauce and mayo and tasted them. It turned out to be pretty good for amateur work.

The first round vanished with surprising quickness. We snacked on the side dishes Tousuke had made and the junk food Kawahara-san had brought with her until the next round was ready. After a while of vapid conversation, Pon-chan started asking about Kawahara-san's university experiences.

"Has the drugstore been your only part-time job?"

"So far, yeah."

Then, naturally, the conversation eventually trended *that* way.

"In any clubs?" Pon-chan asked.

Kawahara-san answered plainly and immediately, "I joined this one called Moai."

"Seriously?! Me too!"

Kawahara-san's slitted eyes opened wider as she let out a, "Oh. really?"

"I mean I don't really attend meetings, so I'm not surprised we haven't run into each other."

"Ah, that makes sense."

Kawahara-san, who took this at face value, did not expand on the topic further. Perhaps anticipating this, Pon-chan pressed,

"Do you go a lot?" I recalled having mentally compared the two of them before. Where Pon-chan was shrewd, Kawahara-san was not quite so much. Still, the Moai-centric conversation between the two did not make me nervous. I could not imagine the shrewd Pon-chan ever saying anything disparaging in front of an active Moai member like Kawahara-san.

"I go to a lot of the meetings, even the smaller ones. I like hearing what people have to say."

"Oh yeah? What kind of stuff do they talk about?"

I had to thank Pon-chan for broaching the topic for us. Kawahara-san hummed in thought, looking up into the air.

"Lately there's been a lot of talk about the business of war. The other day, we had an alumnus from the architecture department come in and talk about revivals and the architecture industry."

"Have any fun?"

"It's fun, especially when there's a lot of passionate people there."

Kawahara-san was a passionate person where Pon-chan was not. A simple question came to mind.

"I assume there's some less passionate people at those smaller meetings too?"

"Well, I say small, but there's usually about a dozen people, so there's definitely people who show up just to hang out and get lunch afterwards. Not that I think that's a bad thing, though."

Kawahara-san was a lot more laid-back in philosophy than I assumed her to be. I wondered why then it was that she was not better at dealing with unruly customers, but of course I could not ask her that. Thankfully, she herself explained it.

"Of course, every once in a while some guy shows up who is so obvious about just being there to assess the girls that I wanna kill him."

"Oh? How would you do it?"

"Well, if the only thing I had on me at the time was a pen, I'd just jab it in his eye, like this," Kawahara-san said, jabbing a skewer straight into the middle of a takoyaki to demonstrate. Of course, that was the Miss Yankee I knew and loved. No need to show flexibility towards someone she had deemed an enemy. Even if it was violent and extreme.

"I'd assume it's pretty easy for people to hook up at these sorts of things though, right? If there's someone there who shares their philosophies, then even if they don't have any sort of romantic feelings at the start. I'm sure they'd be able to find some extra time for each other."

"That's very true," Kawahara-san said, her expression ambiguous, as though she found the idea abhorrent but did not wish to criticize it.

"I'm guessing you don't have any interest in that sort of thing though, right, Kawahara-san?"

For some reason, Pon-chan seemed intent on needling Kawahara-san.

"Yer right. I always say everything I'm thinkin' while I'm at the meeting."

"Oh, no I mean, I'm guessing that you're not interested in any of the Moai boys."

Kawahara-san smirked and shook her head. "Absolutely not."

"Well then, anyone you've got your sights set on?"

"Nah, I mean...not really."

For the smallest fraction of a second, such that I was sure she had purposely done it so that only I would notice, I saw Pon-chan glance at me. Okay, yep, I got it now. The two of them had been colluding to set me up.

Naturally, though I would not let it show on my face, one part of me was about ready to laugh the whole thing off, though another part of me was suddenly not feeling so well.

I wondered if Kawahara-san would be annoyed. Thus, feeling slightly malicious, I decided to toss a pickoff pitch.

"Pon-chan, you've had a boyfriend since high school, haven't you?"

"*Wha?!* Hey, Tousuke-senpai, *what* have you been telling them?!"

She pointed a skewered takoyaki at him, Tousuke laughing and warning, "Hey, careful with that thing!" followed by, "Well, it's fine, since it's true."

"Since high school, huh? That's a long time, Pon-chan-senpai," said Kawahara-san.

"Pon-chan-senpai?! That's totes adorbs!" Pon-chan chuckled.

Kawahara-san replied and said, "It suits you." It occurred to me then that perhaps she actually was not shy—maybe just a bit more introverted than other people.

"Anyway, I don't really know anymore. We're long-distance right now, and it's been about a month since I last saw him," she sighed with a slightly dejected smile. I suddenly regretted bringing up the topic, wondering if things might be better for them if the circumstances were different.

"Oh, time to turn 'em" said Kawahara-san. I don't know if she was helping the conversation recover from my slip-up intentionally or if she had simply noticed that the takoyaki were done cooking. We cheerfully returned to rolling the takoyaki, as though the preceding conversation had never happened. I was able to manage it better that time. Kawahara-san's timing was perhaps even superb. I regretted that the topic of Moai had gotten away from us, but if we pushed it too far, she would probably grow suspicious.

My mission was, of course, always foremost in my mind, but we were still normal college students as well. So you could bet that from that point on we drank like normal college students. We enjoyed our takoyaki and shared our frivolous conversation. There were not going to be any grand revelations about Moai tonight, so it was fine for us to get wasted.

One hour passed, then two.

I guess today we'll just be able to enjoy a nice drinking party—no real loss or gain, I thought. I enjoyed both the tranquility and the mild tension. I'm sure everyone else felt the same. The screws had been loosened. We wrapped up the party by devouring the cake that Pon-chan had brought. We had drank quite a bit by then. My vision was blurry, Pon-chan was turning red, Tousuke kept laughing, and Kawahara-san's head was swaying.

I wondered if Kawahara-san would be all right getting home, and asked her, "You gonna be okay?" to which she drawled, "Yeah, m'fine," which told me that she definitely wasn't.

Just before things wrapped up, Pon-chan suddenly leaned towards me.

"By the way, Kaede-senpai. How come you're always so formal with Kawahara-san?" she slurred. I wondered internally why she was asking such a sensitive thing at a time like this, but I did not let the concern show on my face. Her head was tilted, and when her eyes met mine, I felt the same way I once had when I was little and learned that the other children in the neighborhood had stopped calling their mothers "Mama."

"Um, well...at work, it isn't clear which of us is the senpai." I told her the simplest version of the truth. I glanced at Kawahara-san, only to notice that she was staring at me for some reason.

"What? But you're *totally* her senpai at school, so I don't see why you can't just be casual at least outside of work?"

I nearly looked at Kawahara-san again at this unexpected challenge from Pon-chan but stopped myself. I assumed it would be far too meaningful to Pon-chan if I were to look at her face right now. However, she didn't need any such meaningful actions from me. Her own drunken mind had already decided where this conversation was going to go.

"If you speak to her formally as her senpai, you're gonna make her feel like you're pushing her away."

"Pushing...?" I had to wonder how Pon-chon interpreted the noise that had slipped out of my mouth.

It was only natural that there should be some distance between us, I thought, as I would feel equally distant from anyone else. Whether it was Kawahara-san, or Pon-chan, or even Tousuke, it was all the same. However, there was no need to address it aloud and make that distance feel like rudeness.

"Hey, Kawahara-san," she said. Now that her name had been spoken, there was finally a reason for me to look Kawahara-san's way. Kawahara-san's brow was furrowed. I shuddered at the clear displeasure on her face.

"...I..."

I braced myself. I doubted she was going to say anything even along the lines of what Pon-chan was hoping for. I was sure she would just let her expression speak for itself. This was not a disparaging opinion, so much as that I merely recognized what sort of person she was.

"I..." she said again.

However, the stiffening of my body was all for nothing.

"...I'm going home, sorry, guys."

With that, she suddenly stood up, tottering once before regaining her balance, bowed her head at the three of us, and then headed for the front door without awaiting a response. As we watched in shock, she paused, then turned to Tousuke and said, "Sorry, I'll pay you back later..."

"No, whatever, don't worry about the money. More importantly, you gonna be all right? You should wait until you sober up a bit."

"Nah, I'm...fine. I'll...I'll give Tabata-san the money fer you later. See you."

She wobbled toward the front door, her arm planted against the wall. I looked to the other two. Pon-chan appeared to be even more dumbfounded than either of us, while Tousuke just looked at me, gesturing with both his finger and his eyes for me to follow her. I more or less agreed with him here, and stood up, chasing after her. I quickly caught up with her as she stood in the entry trying to put her shoes on, and said, "Kawahara-san... W-will you be okay getting home?"

"Yeah, m'fine. I'm walkin' home."

"Uh, that doesn't seem like a great idea... I think you should wait."

It was then that she turned around and looked me in the eye. Perhaps it might have been more romantic to call what I felt when I looked into her eyes sympathy or empathy or something like that. But short of that, I simply wondered how I would feel in her shoes and chose my words accordingly.

"You mind if I at least...walk with you...until I'm sure you're all right, then?"

"...Sure."

"I'm just worried something might happen to you, is all."

Kawahara-san nodded, resigned, then looked over my shoulder and said, "Thanks for having me," before putting her hand on the doorknob. It took her some time to open the door and leave, as though she could not muster the strength to do so, so I took the opportunity to return to the room and tell the other two that I was seeing her home. There were no complaints from either of them.

"I wonder if I made her mad..." Pon-chan worried, but I assured her that was not the case.

I followed after Kawahara-san and put my own shoes on, then the two of us stepped out, feeling the warm air blowing across us. We walked down the stairs to the first floor, careful not to slip, and exited through the automatic doors.

"Mind if I go get my bike?" I asked.

"Go 'head."

I collected my old faithful of a bike I had had since my freshman year from the bike racks, thinking that I would ride it back here after. I would have offered to let her ride on the back, but I had drunk a fair bit as well. It wouldn't be especially amusing if we both fell off it.

Given her house was only a twenty minutes' walk away, she had walked here as well. I walked beside her, pushing my bike along.

"Sorry about all this..." she said quietly, about three minutes down the main walk.

"No worries, I drank myself stupid plenty of times when I was a freshman."

"No, that's not..." she mumbled awkwardly. "I mean yeah, that, but also, sorry for running."

Running? I got the feeling I knew exactly what she meant by that, but I decided to play dumb.

"I didn't think you were running."

"No, what I mean is...I guess she just got to me." She did not look at me. "I hated it, but...I couldn't deny what she was saying, and I know she hadn't said anything wrong, but my head's not right enough right now to explain any of that, so I just...ran."

Her head drooped, her face a perfect portrait of the word repentance.

"I mean, I didn't see it that way. I don't think you need to worry so much about it."

I had followed her partly because I assumed she would say something like this, which I don't say as a means of belittling her. That was just the impression I had gotten back at the front door.

I looked into her eyes and saw the guilt, the desire to flee, that crops up in people in the face of having to make an emergency retreat. Somewhere deep down, I think I felt the same way.

"I'll apologize to the two of them properly later."

"At least as far as Tousuke goes, I'm sure he'll find the time to see you no matter when it is."

"Thank you."

Though her pace was sluggish, Kawahara-san kept her eyes on the road ahead. I was glad to know that she really did seem to be okay.

As we walked slowly towards her home, we came across a FamilyMart, glittering in the darkness like an RPG save point, and stopped in front of it. I bought her a bottle of water, which she chugged, spitting out self-effacing words. "I really drank too much..."

Again, we set off as I received countless words of thanks in exchange for this mere hundred-yen gift. Her steps were still unsteady and reaffirmed that I had not made the wrong choice in coming—even if perhaps she might have misunderstood me somewhere along the line.

I had to make things clear to her, I realized, hazily picturing the words in my mind as though written on the ground, when suddenly she started off, "Um..."

"What's up?" I sputtered.

"Um, sorry for saying that I hated what Pon-chan-senpai was saying."

"Oh, no, uh, it's fine."

"It's not a lie, but could I at least explain what it was I didn't like about it?"

"Oh, sure, go for it."

If it was the sudden intrusion into our rather complicated relationship that she hated, I definitely felt the same way, but it didn't seem right to bring that back up now. I wanted to know how she felt.

"Um, I guess, to put it simply, I think that the distance between people is something that's determined on a case-by-case basis."

"...Uh, I'm guessing that you aren't talking about the group here?"

"I mean, that too, but I'm just saying there's no sense in applying templates to things." She put her palm to her forehead as though trying to determine the right words to express what she was thinking, then shortly continued. "It's kind of embarrassing to say, but I'm drunk, so, forgive me. I do think Pon-chan was right. By all rights, you're my senpai, so it's fine for you to be more casual with me. But I mean, you can still be formal, if you want to."

She took in a breath. She still did not look at me.

"I mean, like, the sort of distance that you've decided you and I have, I feel like that's something more deserving of respect in society than it gets."

The importance of distance.

"I think distance is a separate value...mmm, doctrine? A separate doctrine from friendliness. Or...something like that. Sorry, I don't really have the words to make sense of this."

"No, I think I get what you mean."

That was something that I, who was always acutely aware of the distance between myself and others, who lived my life by those principles, could perfectly understand. What I could not understand, however, was what she said next.

"I think it's pretty amazing that you've decided for yourself what kind of distance you wanna have from others."

"...Huh?"

My question was delayed by several seconds while I ruminated on these words in my brain.

"Ah, I mean, I might be drunk, but I'm not usually the flatterin' type. I really think that. I like people who have a clear sense of values in the same way that I like people who are into themselves. It's the same way with distance."

I suppose she was not accustomed to giving praise. She took another swig of water before looking ahead, snorting an embarrassed laugh.

I was, again, stunned by these words. It had been a very long time since anyone had affirmed that I was not being too distant from others. I was not used to having anyone look me in the eye—well, figuratively speaking—and validate my values.

"Well, um...thank you for that."

I had no idea what other words I should offer in response, but Kawahara-san likewise seemed lost on how to continue, merely saying, "Sure thing."

I had no idea that she had taken this in such a positive way. I had thought of her as nothing more than some rough and tumble yankee—which I say in a past tense because by this point, having met her several times outside of work, I had gotten a broader impression of her. My impressions had not changed per se, but at least I had seen more sides of her. She was a curt but carefree Kansai girl, and somehow, somewhat like me—even in the most awkward ways.

Likewise, she was not the type of person to unnecessarily prolong a conversation.

After that, we walked along through the summer night without any particular need for conversation. The most meaningful words spoken were when we saw a cat along the way and Kawahara-san said, "Oh, a cat." I knew that she was fond of cats.

Finally, we arrived in front of a very typical student condo block. I waved off her words of gratitude before we shared some goodbyes and polite bows.

"Oh, right, I should clarify that the stuff I was saying about distance wasn't me telling you to keep being so polite with me. It's perfectly fine to be more casual."

"Thanks."

If I had been the sort of person who could then immediately say, "Well then, see ya," I probably would have had a lot more friends, and a far more troublesome university life.

"Guess I'll just do my best to catch you off guard then," I said, giving my best attempt at a joke. Kawahara-san laughed.

"Sure, I'll be waiting for that."

She thanked me one more time, then bowed her head again and headed into the building. I stood there for some time, waiting until I heard a door close on an upper floor, and then climbed onto my bike.

There were times when I had wondered how I ought to get back at Tousuke for saying things to me like, "It's not a bike you should've been riding then," but then, he had gotten me a pretty decent-paying one-off part-time position, so it was water under the bridge.

Before he started job hunting, Tousuke had put those communication skills of his to full use working as a tutor at a large cram school. I was never the type to make much use of cram schools, so I knew little about them. Still, I knew enough to know that a cram school tutor was absolutely the wrong type of job for me, as part of the position of tutor entailed having discussions with high school students. Using his connections there, however, he learned about an opening for a proctor for mock exams, which he shared with me. The pay was good enough that I could overlook his bawdy punchlines.

I put on my suit for the first time since job hunting and met up with him in front of the cram school in question early in the morning. After greeting each other, we headed to a room that the receptionist indicated, where we found a number of long tables with a number of suits already sitting at them, so we took our spot in the back. Eventually, as we sat there in silence, a young man showed up and explained the job to us. I'll spare you the details, but it was a simple job, which mostly entailed handing out test forms, watching over the test takers, and collecting the answer sheets at the end.

We looked over the materials and were each sent out to our respective classrooms. The room I was in charge of was a long lecture hall that could seat about a hundred. It no longer contained tables but individual desks. I spent the time waiting for the test takers to arrive tidying up the desks into straight rows. The sound of the desks scraping the floor resounded sharply.

Finally, the time arrived, and the test takers filed into the classroom. I turned to them and read out the rote warnings that were written on the front blackboard, confirmed the numbers on the exam stubs, and so on and so forth. Honestly, the students were mostly just reading the blackboard, so no one was listening very closely to what I was saying.

Easy-peasy.

At the appointed time, I handed out the exam forms and announced the start of the test. All I had to do from there was kick back in the folding chair at the front of the room until the test was done without somehow falling asleep, occasionally taking a cursory look around or strolling about the room.

After one lap around the classroom, I sat down with a sigh, staring at the tops of the students' lowered heads, all in neat rows. It reminded me of a nest of some kind of creature—though the studious creatures varied in color and length of their hair, in body shape and clothing, they all made the same, basic motions. If one were to assume that we job hunters looked the same way to real professionals, then working in HR must have been *quite* the daunting task. After all, they had to try and pick out a preferred candidate from a pool of people who all, more or less, looked and acted the same. There were resumes and personality tests and interviews and group discussions. If, despite them wading through all of that in search of the ideal candidate, someone like me still managed to deceive them, then I truly felt sorry for those saps.

The front page of the Moai website had featured a list of all the very impressive positions their members had been offered. However, even if their whole mission was to create the ideal candidate, I doubted that their membership attracted those with more aberrant personalities to begin with. Recently, incidental to my harassment campaign, I had been browsing various Moai-related accounts on social media. All of them, from the leaders to the fringiest of members were basically mass-produced university students, all desperately trying to hide who they really were, indicating no real interests.

What the current Moai taught was nothing more than the means of depersonalization, so that a bunch of mediocre people could survive job hunting. How to flatter and inflate your own image—it was the direct opposite of becoming your ideal self.

Of course, I could not totally disavow what they did. I had done the same myself. Being able to take a stance like that was a crucial part of living in society. However, that was not the original intent of Moai. That was not the organization that *she*, that one in a lecture hall of one hundred, had created with her ideals in mind.

That was what the Moai we created *should* have been: a group about finding a way to become a person who would survive while still keeping one's personal philosophies, one's ideals, intact. We never wanted to change ourselves.

Even though I knew that, I, the one who had helped found the group and yet abandoned it, had some responsibility to share in this. Thus, it was *my* responsibility to take it back as well. I would take us back to the past—even if it meant destroying the present.

Speaking of this, I needed to determine *how* I was going to crush Moai, and I needed to do so as quickly as possible. I could not go on just harassing them forever. I had until graduation. Time was going to slip by me before I realized. It had been a long time since I was left on my own, but now that there was a deadline, I was sure that time would fly by.

Perhaps I needed to broaden my thinking a bit. Thus far, my top goal had been to cease Moai operations, but perhaps I did not need to go all that far. Maybe it would be enough just to diminish confidence in the group until it weakened, or at least just in the management. It'd be best to make the current Moai into another group entirely. Then, better yet, create a new group with the true values of Moai at its core. The real Moai needed neither achievements nor acclaim—only ideals, pure and simple.

Just like it was back then.

As I pondered this, mentally lowering the hurdles to the degradation of Moai, the bell rang, signaling the end of the first hour of testing. I collected the answer sheets and informed the students when the next portion would be starting. All the tension left the air in the classroom in an instant, some of the students immediately bounding out into the hallway to chat with friends. I couldn't help but think of the days when I sat for mock exams like this. Back then, I believed that something as simple as the results of a university entrance exam could change my entire life. However, that was by no means true.

I knew at least that much, far better than these young hopefuls did. I wondered how they would change in the next few years. How could there possibly be professionals who were so confident in themselves they could prattle on about their own experiences as though they were valuable, could hold those kinds of events? Did they actually feel like they were making a difference to those students somehow?

When the second exam period started fifteen minutes later, my activities were unchanged. It was best to do as little as possible so that the test takers could concentrate. I was good at that. That was how I had always lived, especially since starting university.

I continued my previous train of thought. Perhaps these self-conscious professionals *did* come because they felt they had something valuable to impart to their juniors, but even if the knowledge they shared *was* of use, why would they bother wasting their time on people who had so little to do with them? Certainly, I had kouhai in my own seminars, but I had purposely kept a set distance from them and never once considered going out of my way to make myself useful to them. The only kouhai I had who I was close enough to talk about our daily lives together was Kawahara-san, but I would never purposely try to meddle in her affairs.

Tousuke did seem to be the type, though. When someone was in trouble, he swooped in to help—especially if that someone was Pon-chan. And I didn't just think that in terms of my joke about him wanting to date Pon-chan; Tousuke really just was an upstanding person. He would always lend a hand to Pon-chan or his other kouhai, just as he was helping me.

From my perspective, Tousuke and Pon-chan's relationship was a bizarre one. For someone like me, who had no idea how to make friends with a kouhai like that, even expecting me to overstep boundaries as far as walking someone home was an absurd idea, even though such a thing would have been simple for Tousuke.

As I pondered Tousuke's dating record, the second period came to an end. From there, it was another fifteen-minute break, and then a third period spent doing largely the same amount of nothing, and then a longer break for lunch. The test takers headed to the cafeteria and nearby convenience stores, while we were provided with bento sets and tea. We sat down in the room we had gathered in that morning, where the bento were set out, and ate. It felt like eating at a gas station.

Tousuke arrived a bit after, sitting down beside me. We congratulated each other on our hard work—which really hadn't been all that hard—and nibbled our soggy fried fish.

"This really takes me back. Watching those kids, all I could think was: Man I never wanna take those exams again!" Tousuke waxed poetic, while shoveling his much maligned umeboshi into my bento box.

"Better than job hunting, anyway."

"I'd rather do that."

I felt like we ought to take an opinion survey of all job hunters. As I ate one of my two umeboshi, Tousuke gave a sudden, "Ah," as though he had just realized something.

"That reminds me, the day before yesterday, I saw Kawahara-san and Pon eating together in the cafeteria."

"Whoa, really?"

Tousuke was probably only aware that I had given him that response to be polite. In my mind, I was simply glad that the aftershocks of that evening had not created a rift between two certain someones. I'm sure he could read exactly what I was thinking. He grinned, took a sip of tea, and pulled his phone out from his pocket...looked at the screen and then placed it down on the table, muttering, "More spam. Been getting a lot of that lately."

"You must've signed up to some weird website."

"I only use the *finest* of websites, my good sir."

Wondering exactly what sort of sites he was talking about, I yanked out my phone and looked at my own inbox. I didn't see any suspicious activity. I checked my social accounts and saw nothing there either.

"No spam here for an upstanding student like me."

"Check again, check again!"

Tousuke presented his phone screen to me. Sure enough, there were a number of messages from various unregistered e-mail addresses. I grabbed his phone and opened some of them to find that these so-called spam messages were in fact invitations to interviews from various job recruiters and notices about upcoming events—even if such information was of no use to either of us.

"I've been to these kind of info sessions before."

"Mm, but I haven't, so I've got no idea how they have my address. Could someone possibly be selling my, an upstanding student's, information on the black market?"

"Putting aside whether you are upstanding or not, they do know the name of your school." Surely enough, we had reaped the benefits of our academic backgrounds.

"Wonder how much my e-mail address goes for..."

"I mean, I'm sure they don't sell them individually. They probably have some registry of student information or...some...thing..."

I tilted my head as I realized what I was saying.

Something had struck a chord with me. It was as if my temples were prickling. What was going on?

It felt as though what I had just said recalled something from the past. Like I was trying to find an itch to scratch. I ignored Tousuke's, "What's up?" so that I would not lose track of this image, thinking back to recent events.

When I walked my mental steps backwards, I found it. It was right there, in my grasp.

"Tousuke, when did you start getting those spam messages?"

"Three, maybe four weeks ago."

"When, more specifically?"

Curiously, Tousuke swiped on his phone and then showed me a number of subject lines. "I think sometime around here."

I compared the date against the calendar hanging in the front of the room. It was exactly as I had suspected.

"This was the week after that weekend of the barbecue we went to with Ten."

"That's true, but..."

"There had to have been some trigger for this increase in junk mail, right?"

"Hm? Wha, you don't..."

Tousuke, savvy as ever, seemed to understand what I was trying to say. If what I was supposing was correct, if it was true...

Could this be the decisive blow?

"Just a minute," I interrupted Tousuke, who seemed like he wanted to say something. I pulled out my own phone and logged into one of my burner e-mail accounts. After a few moments of loading, my inbox appeared on the screen.

I felt goosebumps rise on my skin.

"Nailed it."

I showed Tousuke the screen. There, listed, were a number of e-mails, just like the ones Tousuke had been getting. The contents were probably the same as well.

"In other words...?"

I started to speak, gulping.

"Ten must be making money off of giving out the registry."

"...How can you tell?"

"This e-mail's a burner."

Tousuke furrowed his brow; I explained.

"It's a free account I signed up for, separate from my normal one. I always use burner accounts when I need to give out my e-mail to someone I don't trust so my real information doesn't get misused. I'm assuming you made a business address while you were job hunting?"

"No, I just use the same one for everything."

"Seriously? You must get a lot of mail, then."

"I do. That's why the spam is bugging me so much."

I found this surprising for someone as conscientious as Tousuke. Was he some kind of secret Luddite when it came to technology? If so, then this was likely something he was unaware of.

"Well, anyway, this burner account is one that I just made and started using recently. Which means..."

"Means what?"

"It's odd that even though I only gave this address to Ten, I'm getting all these e-mails from businesses."

"True. But that means it's not just going to Moai members but us too."

"I'm sure they're just filtering out information for students who attend our school and sending them out to businesses indiscriminately or something. I think he slipped up. Just like you did with handling your e-mail address when you're usually so diligent about things."

As I spoke, I gave a shudder. I thought to myself. Finally, here it was. Depending on what we did with this information, this could be a means of weakening Moai. At the very least, we could drag Ten down, and perhaps if we were lucky, this might even extend into the upper ranks. In an era where personal information was such a large talking point, surely we could make an appeal to people's morals.

That said, I still wanted more concrete evidence. I had no proof that Ten was the only one I had given this burner out to, so that wouldn't be particularly damaging. Wasn't there something else I could find?

"Ideally, I'd like to actually find this registrar that Ten and his crew are probably giving out to companies, but I have no idea how we'd go about that."

"Mm, and I doubt he'd just give it to us."

"And I can't imagine Kawahara-san or Pon-chan having it either."

"Guess we'll just have to sneak into the higher-ups' houses, huh?"

Obviously, I laughed.

We pondered this for the rest of our lunch break but could not come up with anything, agreeing to consider the matter during the mock exams as we both headed back to work.

I waited in the classroom until the test takers finally arrived, taking their seats with aplomb. Naturally, I kept my cool as I handed out the test forms, but my mind was churning furiously.

Finally, I had a weapon.

What we did next would be vital. We now knew a crucial fact—we held a deadly weapon. Now, how could I best strike the enemy with it in order to cause maximum damage? There was no time to waste. Now that they had gone and slipped up, I had to drive my wedge into that chink and burst the dam.

I sat in the chair in the front of the room, my thoughts racing. However, the more frantic I got, the more my thoughts just kept circling back to the same place. In the end, I got nowhere. I forgot to even keep watch on the classroom—before I knew it, the fourth period was over.

Next period would be the last one. In this classroom, the air was permeated with the test takers' efforts, and their will to make their last stand. I would have to make my last stand as well and work my brain overtime. However, just being in the same room as these young people was not enough to give me the results I needed. Plus, my thoughts were clouded by my own jubilation. Perhaps finally, after so long, it had returned to me.

My joy was getting in the way of my own composure.

As I circled around and around the same points, my centrifugal force almost reaching its limits, for a moment it felt as though something sparked, and I was drawn back down to the purest form of a plan again. Would any Moai members give me the registry? Would one of the *companies* give me the registry? But then I realized again how absurd that was.

"What's most important is that everyone is happy. It's the simplest things that are always the most important and impactful."

Just as I was about to circle back to square one again, I heard *her* voice. It had been years since I last heard it, but there it was, as clear as day. A voice that could not in fact make everyone happy and did not exist in Moai now.

I stopped in place. I just had to get the register. I thought back to the day of the meet-up, when I had waited outside, and well before that, on the day of my final interview, what I had witnessed in the elevator lobby.

Then, I thought, *are professionals really all that impressive?*

There was little difference in age between us and someone who had been working for only a few years. Just as there was no immense gap between myself and the students who were taking their mock exams right now, I could not imagine any working professional being much more experienced and talented than we were. I mean, such people probably *did* exist, but most people had only scammed their way into a job by creating a false self, just like I had.

By that token, were there not professionals who made missteps as well? Just like Ten, who had let us on to a very important clue. Just as I currently held contempt for those in the corporate world, there was a strong possibility that there were those among their number who held contempt for the students who were coming up along the same path that they were.

A singular idea came to mind.

It was the sort of sham of an idea that I was ashamed to even call an idea, but I didn't think I was going to be able to come up with anything else. If Tousuke could not come up with anything better, I thought, this would do well enough.

Before I realized it, the time had flown by—the fifth period ended more swiftly than all those preceding. After giving the students a heads up on the exams they would be sitting for tomorrow, I released them. After that, I finished up my work, met up with the others again in the same room as that morning, confirmed the plans for tomorrow, and then we were dismissed for the day ourselves.

I immediately invited Tousuke to a nearby café. I picked as secluded a seat as possible, ordered an iced coffee, and launched into the conversation.

"You come up with anything, Tousuke?"

Tousuke grimaced and said, "Well, I tried," shaking his head. "Was pretty tough. How about you?"

"Well, I came up with one idea."

Just as I was about to start outlining my thoughts, our drinks arrived, and I shut my mouth. I put my lips right on the glass of iced coffee that was set before me, eschewing a straw.

"I mean, it's pretty stupid though."

"C'mon, let's hear it."

"Let's ask one of the companies that sent out the spam."

What I liked the most about Tousuke was how easy he was to read, but here what I saw was a very easily readable look of criticism, which was accompanied by a, "Come again? Sorry, I don't catch your drift."

"I mean, I told you it was stupid. I've thought about it though." I punctuated my next words carefully in order to make them as easy as possible to understand. "I thought, there must be some idiot professionals, right? Like, if we gave Hiro's name or Ten's name, and gave our contact info, and told them, oh, we've taken over the register now, then someone might actually be stupid enough to give us the register instead."

"You really think there's anyone that stupid?"

"No idea. However..." I took out my phone and showed him the inbox on my burner account. "This is our only lead." There, on the screen, was a whole list of e-mails that very kindly provided me with their company names and the names of their HR people, and their contact information. "Of course, maybe they're all more capable than I take them for, and maybe they all have strong crisis management skills, and no one will actually take us up on that."

"Only if we're being optimistic."

Exactly, I thought.

"But anyway, I think this is a pretty realistic approach. I'm gonna make some more burner accounts and give it a shot, but... you in? If I write up all the contents of the e-mails and everything, will you come with me to a net café or something and just help me send them out?" I looked Tousuke in the eye as I made this impassioned plea. He averted his eyes a moment, and then looked back at me.

"...All right. You *are* the commander, after all."

I was relieved to have my friend's assent, as well as some direction for the time being. It was fine if we didn't have a real path, as long as we had a destination.

"Oh, and as a token of my appreciation, I won't tell Pon-chan that you're into her."

"Uh, yeah, just...please don't."

How curious it was just then that it seemed like Tousuke had something caught in his throat.

Regarding what happened next, I think it will speed things along if I just start from the end. In summary: there was an idiot present.

Shockingly, even to me, one of the HR people I had sent messages to politely responded to me the very next day.

My e-mail to them had informed them that I had been newly appointed as the directory manager and was checking in on the present state of things, asking them to provide their current version of the register so that I could confirm everything. This HR person replied that they were using the latest version of the register as posted to a file-sharing service. They were even so kind as to include the URL.

The moment I got the mail, I called Tousuke. Tomorrow, we would meet at his place and formulate the next step of our plan.

"Sure, anytime tomorrow is fine. Trash pickup is tomorrow, so I'll be up early."

"I'll pop by at some point then."

"Sure thing!"

It was around noon when I rang a rather nonchalant-seeming Tousuke. I ate some convenience store noodles with *shirasu* as I chatted on the phone with him. My heart was smoldering with intensity. I had not yet accessed the URL that I had been provided, not wanting to be traced.

When I went to work that afternoon, I found that Kawahara-san and I were sharing a shift again. It seemed she had continued attending Moai meetings frequently since that fateful evening, and I could not help but smile as I greeted her, the corners of her own mouth far more upturned than before when she saw me.

"Something good happen to you, Tabata-san?"

"Huh? Oh, I found a silver angel in my Chocoball."

"Whoa, seriously?"

Little else transpired during our shift beyond that conversational misdirection. As always, Kawahara-san was waiting outside in the parking lot to greet me; we said our farewells, and I headed home. I munched a convenience store bento as I sat down at my computer, checking through my various burner e-mails, when I found yet another sincere reply from an HR rep. *Idiot,* I muttered towards my LCD screen, but of course, the screen gave no response.

For some reason, that night, I had a dream about Pon-chan and Kawahara-san. The fact that I'd had such an odd dream meant that I was not sleeping well; I always felt a bit off on such mornings. There was not much that I could do about something that I had only dreamt, so I pushed through the off feeling to change my clothes and eat a pastry and lazily check my social media, finally leaving the house around ten.

The sun was harsher today than I expected, so I abandoned the idea of riding my bike, instead detouring to the subway station. I appreciated being able to bypass several kilometers of travel just by riding in an air-conditioned box for a few minutes, avoiding ending up drenched in sweat. I climbed the stairs back to the outside to find that the sun was still just as it had been several stations ago, bitter about the distance that still remained between here and Tousuke's building. But obviously I lacked the financial means to demand that roofs be installed over every sidewalk in the area, so I would just have to bear with it. I resigned myself to walking in the blazing sun.

I had not walked along this road since the night I walked Kawahara-san home.

That evening, when I returned to collect my things, Pon-chan was still there. I wondered what the two of them had talked about while I was not around. When I showed up, they were just worried about Kawahara-san.

After a brief walk, I came upon the same FamilyMart that I had previously used as a save point. I stopped in again, picking up a bottle of tea to prevent myself from getting heatstroke, along with two canned coffees and two bags of snacks. I put in my chip card to pay, took my items, and stepped back outside. Just as I started heading towards Tousuke's place, still cursing the sun, I halted.

On the opposite side of the roadway, Pon-chan was walking along the sidewalk, from the opposite direction from the station. She was looking at her phone and did not notice me.

What was she doing in a place like this? I thought she lived near a station that would require her to make a transfer to even end up around here. As I wondered whether I ought to call out to her, Pon-chan continued toward the station. Perhaps because she was sweating, somehow her makeup did not look as put-together as usual. Of course, there was no need for me to share that impression with her, so I quit watching her retreating form and returned to heading towards Tousuke's place.

By the time I arrived at Tousuke's apartment, which was rather upscale for a student, sweat was dripping down my back. Even just stepping into the shade of the entrance was enough to cool me down immensely.

I climbed a number of stairs up to Tousuke's abode, which I had not visited in several days. I rang the intercom, hearing a noise from inside, followed by several seconds of apparently frantic activity. The door lock clacked open, and Tousuke appeared, wearing only his underpants and a towel around his neck.

"You're early."

"You in the middle of something?"

"Nah, I'm good."

I followed him into the apartment. I removed my shoes and trailed after his naked back into the living room. I had been in this room many times before, but somehow it felt different.

There was a faint, sweet fragrance of something that was not soap or food.

"Ah."

It occurred to me that several pieces of information I had acquired today were all fitting together, and a sound slipped from my mouth. I don't know how it sounded to Tousuke, but he looked at my face.

"Kaede, I—"

"It's cool," I interrupted. "These sorts of things happen sometimes."

Tousuke winced and said, "Well, guess so. Something like that..."

I borrowed the restroom to wash my hands, finding an empty contact case in the corner—something that Tousuke, with his perfect vision, had no need for.

I really should have teased him, but there was no time for that today.

I returned to the room and informed him of the snacks and coffee I had bought. Tousuke, now in shorts and a T-shirt, brought me some chilled juice instead. It felt like we were two friends settling in to play video games on our summer vacation, but in fact this was where our real battle began.

"I want to look at that URL on a computer. Can I borrow yours?"

"Still haven't pulled it up?"

"I figured we'd look at it together."

Tousuke booted his computer that was sitting on the desk, while I cracked open a canned coffee. After a few moments of waiting in silence, we heard the familiar Windows boot sound.

"All yours," he said.

As directed, I sat down in a chair that had probably come from Nitori and loaded up one of my fresh new burner accounts. This account, incidentally, I had crafted under the guise of a brainy third-year university girl.

"I still can't believe this actually worked," Tousuke said, peeking over my shoulder.

"Me neither. I feel bad for anyone who *joins* these companies."

I hovered the cursor over the URL I had received from the idiot HR rep. Then, I clicked, my mind prickling with the sudden fear that this might somehow be a trap.

Naturally, it was not a trap, but what I found was still a bit different from what I had imagined.

"Aw man, *seriously*?" I griped.

"What's up?"

"Needs a password. We can't view the register without it."

Of course, stupid as that HR person was, at least they were not stupid enough to hand over the key to the final lock, I thought calmly, though I was panicking slightly at this unexpected complication. I had imagined this would simply be a matter of opening up the webpage, downloading the register, and then discussing with Tousuke how to disseminate it.

"Guess we'll have to crack it."

"Code breaking, huh? We're like spies," he laughed, but this was no laughing matter. If we took too long, one of those HR people would probably contact someone from Moai to confirm things, and they would change the storage location. We had to figure this out before that happened.

Passwords...passwords...

"What sort of theme do you think it'd have?"

"Well, when we had these sorts of things in seminars, it'd be phrases that were popular at the time."

"I'd have no idea about that then."

I tried entering their head honcho's nickname, *hero*, but I hesitated to click, wondering if there was a limit to the number of log-in attempts.

"Tousuke, did you use this site in your seminars?"

"Yeah. I don't know a whole lot about it, though."

"Is there a limit to the log-in attempts?"

"Don't think so. One time I forgot my password and had to try reentering it a bunch of times."

This was good news. Turns out Tousuke's information mismanagement had come in handy. Relieved, I hit the Enter key, but sadly, no dice. Next I tried entering the name of our university, at which point I learned that there was an 8-character limit.

That also was not it.

"I think we've got a long road ahead of us here."

"...Well, let's take our time, the register isn't going anywhere."

It actually might, I wanted to say, but there was no real reason to make him understand that, so I kept my mouth shut. Instead, I asked a more vital question.

"If it's not some well-known phrase, what do you think they'd use as a password?"

"Hmm, maybe it's not something related to Moai."

"I mean, if not, then the possibilities are endless."

"Maybe some kind of catchphrase?"

Though I was sure it wouldn't be correct, I tried entering *risou*—ideals. Of course, it was wrong. From there, I tried entering every Moai related term I could think of, but I made exactly zero headway on breaching the register's authentication wall.

Maybe it was impossible to do this just by brute force. We would probably have to wait until someone showed up who was stupid enough to give us the password. But did we have that kind of time?

"What to do..."

I knew there was no point in getting worked up now. I stood up from the chair for a moment, cracking open the other canned coffee I had purchased. It was already pretty lukewarm, but I could feel the sweetness stoking my brain.

While I took my break, Tousuke took a turn entering any passwords he could think of, but of course the gates were not going to open for us that easily. I sat down on the floor, thinking. A password for Moai—I realized it was important to consider who would have come up with it. If it was Ten, then we were more or less done for. I had no way of understanding the principles of a guy like that. If it was someone else though, someone much higher up...

Still sitting, Tousuke gave a big stretch.

"Hmm, I wonder whether it *is* something related to Moai. If it is, I feel like you're the only one of us who can solve it."

"...Do you think they would use a date as the password?"

"Oh, you got somethin'?"

"June 21st."

I worried that I might be letting too much hope creep into my voice. Before asking me what those numbers meant, Tousuke entered them. I watched his finger as he pressed the Enter key. The tiny clicking sound sounded disproportionately loud.

"Mm, doesn't look like it."

I was rattled with disappointment as the "Incorrect Password" error message appeared on the screen for the umpteenth time, letting us know that yet again we had failed.

"So, what's with the numbers?"

"The anniversary of Moai's founding."

"Well, you've got a good memory. Oh, then, how about this?" he asked, once more entering English characters into the field.

moai0621

Again, he struck the Enter key.

"Oh!" he gasped, surprised. Behind him, I nearly jumped out of my skin.

I gasped in air, swallowing spit along with it. The login screen we saw on the monitor was now different from all the times before. There was a list of file names with one among them reading "Corporate Shared Register." Without saying anything, Tousuke hovered over the file and clicked. What popped up was an Excel spreadsheet *full* of student contact information.

"Kaede...! Kaede, you're amazing!" he said to me, turning around. I had no words to offer him in reply, partly as I was not accustomed to being praised and partly because I did not think it was all that amazing to remember the founding date of the organization I helped found.

However, that was beside the point. I was overcome by a different feeling.

"I mean, I didn't actually expect that to work."

It was something like joy...but only something *like* it. In other words, it was not *actually* joy. I don't know that Japanese even possesses a word I could use to describe that feeling, but it was perhaps one that I had felt before, albeit on a smaller scale. When *would* I have felt something like this, somewhere between the joy that some inkling of our will was still intact and the bewilderment of confirmation that Moai as an organization would be cooperating in these illicit corporate acts?

When?

Was it when Akiyoshi had run after me after class that day? No, I doubt it. What I felt then was only shock and confusion. So then, when did I feel this feeling?

"Oh, there's you, Kaede."

This was not the time to be sorting out my feelings. I peeked at the screen, and sure enough, there was a row of the spreadsheet with my name, department, and contact information. "Save this," I directed Tousuke, and a file labeled "Corporate Shared Register (For the Resistance)" appeared on his desktop. The evidence was now secure.

"So, what do we do with this?" asked Tousuke, dying to take action. I looked at him and told him what I had been thinking.

"We post this up online, along with the e-mail from that HR rep. I think if we get this up on some message boards and Twitter, the school will probably start getting some angry calls, which should deal a blow to Moai."

"Right, I see," he said curtly, the tone of his voice dropping, though he had been the one to ask the question. I wondered what was up, if perhaps he might have been stricken by the fact that our final battle was on the horizon. I tried not to search for too deep of a meaning in it.

Still, Tousuke breathed in deep, and then sighed. He clearly had something on his mind.

"Hey, Kaede."

"What?"

"Um, maybe it's a bit late for me to be saying this, but I've been thinking. Mind if I...?" he started, not looking at me. I couldn't imagine what he would have to say at a time like this.

"Sure, what is it?"

Tousuke looked back at me with a smile that said so many things he could no longer hold back.

"I..."

For an instant, the prickling silence seemed to halt even time itself in its tracks.

"Don't you think...it's about time to stop?"

"Wha...?"

The sweet scent in the room had long since vanished.

—✶—

Near the end of our freshman year, when I went to the cafeteria, I would sometimes catch Akiyoshi and Wakisaka eating together. I'd try my best not to be spotted, but occasionally one or the other would see me. I would wave if it was Akiyoshi or bow if it was Wakisaka, then sit down in some spot away from them and eat alone.

Looking back, I had achieved my initial goal from the time I first enrolled at the university—setting out for a quiet university life.

Moai had continued to grow in size and was now a full-fledged organization. Though it wasn't holding the sort of meet-ups they had now, we were borrowing large lecture halls for gatherings, and thanks to the alumni connections, we were able to invite professional guests to give special lectures. I only participated in our weekly meetings, which I had only done because Akiyoshi asked me to.

Akiyoshi was busy—with Moai, and her studies, and love. I, on the other hand, was just taking my classes, and working part-time, and meeting Tousuke, who I did not yet know would become a friend, all in a perfectly average fashion. There was no reason that the circles we both moved in would overlap; it had already been weeks since the two of us had spent time with only one another. Even during the latter part of the class where I had first seen Akiyoshi, we now had other acquaintances sitting around us. By that point, we no longer sat next to one another.

As her friend, it made me a bit sad, but I was living my university life my way, so it would have been downright boorish for me to criticize the way she was living hers.

"You should tell people what you're thinking," people other than Akiyoshi had many times told me, including teachers who were helping out with Moai, and unrelated alumni. None of them knew the philosophies by which I lived my life. However, arguing with them that they had no idea what they were talking about would be in direct violation of one of those philosophies—never rebutting the opinions of others—and so I would just give a weak smile and let it go.

Wakisaka hardly ever spoke to me. He just passively observed the Moai that we had grown into its current form, the human embodiment of resignation. Sometimes we shared small talk, but unlike Akiyoshi, Wakisaka never got particularly close with boring old me.

The days passed by without any major changes. Back then, I'm sure that Akiyoshi could never have imagined such a boring, unchanging university life. I could tell even from the outside that her life was hectic and full of excitement. I never thought of this as good or bad.

But eventually, those changes in her life had an effect on her as well.

That day, as usual, I had attended our once-a-week meeting. I had no particular opinions to share, only attending so that I could listen to the lively discussions about upcoming activities, so I always chose a seat as far back in the corner as possible. That day, I was sitting in the second seat from the back, by the window, just as I had been the day when I had first met Akiyoshi.

I have no idea why Akiyoshi thought that my presence was necessary at these meetings, but I had never asked her either. I cared just as much about the discussion that was going on. However, there was one phrase from within the chatter that I did hear clearly, that I can still hear even now.

I believe that at some point during the talking, someone

had made a comment to Akiyoshi, something along the lines of, "Oh, this is what I want to do, this is the course I'd like to take." Akiyoshi had then made a "Hmm" sound, as though she was thinking, looked over this someone's resume, and said to them, admonishing:

"I understand, but I don't think that's *realistic*."

I was sure my ears were playing tricks on me. Whatever the intention behind those words, I could not believe that they were coming out of Akiyoshi's mouth.

Realistic.

Realistic.

Realistic.

I turned the words over in my head, but no meaning came tumbling out. Here, at Moai, a group we had formed in order to seize our ideals, someone had presented their ideals and how to pursue them, and Akiyoshi had dragged out *realistic* as the hammer with which to smack it down.

I couldn't believe it. I didn't want to believe it.

Hadn't we come this far together, believing in nothing more than our ideals?

I kept watching her, hoping she might make some amendment to her statement. However, for the rest of the meeting she did not look my way.

That was the last time I attended our weekly meetings.

—*—

I was sure my ears were still playing tricks on me at Tousuke's proposal.

"About time?"

"Yeah. I mean, I think it's time to quit."

"Why?"

He grumbled a "Hmm," and spun his chair around to face me. "I've been thinking about this for a bit now, Kaede, but...are you sure it's really the best idea to destroy Moai?"

"We've been working on that very goal for months, so, *yes*, I do" I immediately replied. Tousuke made a troubled face, the sort of face that indicated he was only humoring me.

"That may be true, and I know I've gone along with this, but... hmm."

"Spit it out."

"No, I mean! I really do understand how you feel, Kaede." Normally very even-tempered, Tousuke was really making a spectacle of himself here. "Someone's altered something that you made, and I get that you're angry about that, but like, when you think about what those guys are doing right now, it makes you wonder if it's really something that needs crushing. I'm just wondering whether you might come to regret it."

"...I would not."

And first off, just what about it would he understand? What part of my feelings could he possibly understand? I would never have come this far if this was something I would regret. I never thought that he would say something like this to me now, after everything, nor that he would possibly try to look out for those Moai guys. I tried to imagine why.

"Let me guess, did Ten put you up to this?"

"Obviously not. Or well, maybe, in some way, I guess. We still hang out sometimes, but seriously, he *really* is a great guy! Though I mean, this register thing is seriously pretty bad."

"Right? So obviously, we have to destroy them. *We* never did this."

The two of us, full of our ideals, had never done anything this bad. Even if I were in the position Ten was in right now, I would have never allowed this to happen.

"So, what, you joining up with them?"

"No, it's just, when I saw that careless e-mail we got from that HR guy, I started thinking."

"Thinking what?"

"Even I might do something like this, like Ten or that guy. Maybe they just got carried away, or didn't realize they were doing something wrong, or something like that. There must be some other way to make them understand this. Even if we don't get rid of the current Moai, there must be people who have made that place their home, like you once did. That's what I thought after I went to that meet-up and saw the way Kawahara-san was at our takoyaki party."

I was dumbfounded.

"Like hell they didn't know what they're doing! Look at this spreadsheet. They're giving out people's personal information!

For money, or to solidify the ties between Moai and these companies, or something. In other words, they're using *us* as a bargaining chip to further their own goals. There's no other way to spin this."

That was right. And even if it wasn't, what did people like Ten—people who had no respect for people's boundaries and would tromp all over them—think about people like us?

"I'm sure you noticed it, at the barbecue."

I recalled the movements of their lips, how little they cared about belittling others.

"They're making fun of us."

"But they aren't."

I was taken aback at the speed of his reply. Tousuke stared back at me.

"We're making fun of them too."

"..."

"It finally occurred to me, recently. We've been making fun of them, putting all these labels on them, saying that they're shallow and annoying. And it's true, there's a lot of things that I hate about people like that. But that's not fair. We aren't all *that* different from them ourselves," he ranted, trying to appeal to me. Perhaps because I fell silent for some moments, he averted his eyes, startled. "Sorry. I'm not trying to lecture you, Kaede."

"Has that shallowness of theirs rubbed off on you? Is that why you put your hands on your kouhai?"

He did not appear to catch my meaning at first. After he mulled it over for a bit, his brows furrowed, and he let out a quiet sigh.

"That's not it."

"Didn't you tell me that you *weren't* going after her?"

"Well, yeah, that wasn't a lie."

"But the fact of the matter is that you went after Pon-chan when she was already in a moment of weakness because things weren't going so well with her long-distance boyfriend."

Tousuke put his hands on his face, head hung, saying nothing. Perhaps there was nothing that he *could* say in reply to this. Tousuke was my friend, but when something was wrong, I had to speak up about it. After a while of no reply, whether as a means of raising the white flag or simply because he could no longer bear the tension, Tousuke suddenly smiled, still looking down at the floor.

"Well, yeah, you're right." He covered his face with his hands, as if to hide his embarrassment. "But, well, didn't you say it yourself just earlier, Kaede? That sometimes these things happen?"

His joking words put me at ease.

"I did say that, but it was wrong."

Tousuke laughed again; I laughed as well. What the hell was this exchange we were having? We had shared trivial debates countless times in the years we had known each other. Every time, at some point, one or the other of us would erupt with laughter, and wonder what we were being so serious for, able to preserve our relationship with a smile. I was relieved to know that this was just one more of those exchanges.

What I needed was for him to understand more clearly what I felt about Moai without misleading, but I was sure that Tousuke would come to comprehend this in time. As I thought about it, Tousuke turned back to the PC and plugged a USB stick that had been sitting on the desk into the machine. Before I could figure out what he was doing, he pulled the stick out and curiously turned back to me.

"I'm sorry, Kaede."

"Huh?"

"I'm out."

There was still a faint smile on his face.

"Sorry that I said I could help. Over these last few months though, I've come to realize that maybe Moai isn't so bad. So, for now, this is where I get off." He looked down, not rising from his chair. "I'm sorry for egging you on."

The USB stick he held out to me, and the whorl of Tousuke's hair. I timidly accepted the USB stick from him, feeling that they were a set pair, and that if one or the other was not lost, they both would remain there forever.

"Still, I don't blame you for being upset," he said.

"So then…?"

"The way you're going about this just bothers me. I'm sorry."

His smile was stiff. I put the memory stick into my pocket and took a step back. My philosophy was never to get close to others, to avoid defying their opinions as best I could.

"Oh, right. Could you please try to keep getting along with Pon? I know she's a pretty different person from you, but she's a good kid. Though she is a bit sneaky, and a little too good at pretending to be asleep."

Seems she knows more than we thought, Tousuke's laughter implied. I took another step backwards.

"Why don't you try talking a bit more with Ten too? I'm sure that in terms of Moai, you consider him your enemy, but it might be a little different if you think of him as your schoolmate, Amano."

I took yet another step back, putting more distance between us.

"And then, maybe even their leader, Hiro. What was her real name again? I'm pretty sure I heard it at that meet-up..."

Already seeming resolved to our parting, Tousuke, cool as ever, looked up to the ceiling, as though he was merely having trouble swallowing something bitter.

"Oh, right, Akiyoshi."

Tousuke looked me in the eye.

It had been a long time since I had heard anyone speak that name.

"I'm sure if you just sit down and talk to Akiyoshi, you'll find out she's a good person too."

I turned my back on him, wobbled to the front door, and put my shoes on. As I opened the door and stepped outside, I heard only one short phrase from Tousuke, but I had nothing to say in reply and simply closed the door behind me.

"Come back anytime."

Just like the scent that Pon-chan left behind, I knew that before long, even those words would fade into nothing.

—*—

It was the third member of Moai, Tazunoki, who had given Akiyoshi, the one and only leader of Moai, the nickname Hiro. The three of us had been talking when we got on the subject of an RPG that had been popular at the time.

"I wouldn't say you're a brave warrior, Hisano, so much as a 'hero.'"

Normally, when Tazunoki said something like that, we understood that she was talking about what role we'd play in a video game, and we'd be embarrassed, humbled, or would just laugh it off. Akiyoshi, however, gave no such banal reply.

"I'm no hero."

It was then that Tazunoki, who seemed to be very fond of such grand statements as believing in the future, in hope, began to somewhat teasingly refer to Akiyoshi as "Hero."

What happened from there was rather idiotic. As the group's membership increased, one of the new members overheard this and, not realizing it was a joke, came to believe that Akiyoshi's name was actually *Hiro*. This little episode unfortunately stuck, and by and by everyone came to recognize Akiyoshi as Hiro, which she did not seem altogether displeased by, perhaps given its origin. Though I myself never referred to her in that way.

By now, Tazunoki, who inflicted this strange mark upon Akiyoshi, was a fourth year as well. Her own path had diverged from Moai, and she was relishing her university life. I believe she was presently in the US on a research exchange, or at least she should have been, according to the plans she had told me about when we happened to cross paths at one point in the middle of our third year. Now that I think about it, she had asked me to deliver a message to Akiyoshi, though I never did. I think it was, "Tell her I hope she's doing well."

I wonder if, deep down, she knew that message would never be conveyed. I think she had that way about her.

There was no way I would convey that message. The last time I had spoken to Akiyoshi had been the start of our sophomore year. It was the day I had made up my mind and said farewell to the new Moai, and the new Akiyoshi.

I had laid a whole plan for how I had intended to inform them of my decision, but it had never come to fruition. The timing was accidental; it was one of the rare times that we had actually bumped into one another on campus. I had been en route from the bike racks to my lecture hall, and the sky was disgustingly clear.

After a brief, perplexed, "Oh," Akiyoshi forced a smile that felt so natural it was almost *un*natural and walked up to me with a, "Hey there."

"...Hey."

"Long time no see, huh? What've you been up to?"

"I mean, I've been coming to school."

I have no idea how the tone of my voice sounded to Akiyoshi, but she stopped a half-step away from me. Still, she seemed to have no intention of dropping her crafted smile.

"You have class after this, Kaede?"

"Yep."

"Where?"

"Building B."

"Oh, me too."

She turned and started walking ahead. I followed beside her, maintaining the same distance. I wonder how we would've looked to others. Even if someone mistook us for close friends, it would be clear we were not lovers. There was an excess of emotion between us.

It was Akiyoshi who spoke up first.

"So, Kaede."

"Yeah?"

"You haven't been coming to Moai lately."

That much was true, so I merely replied, "Uh-huh."

"If you don't like the way things are going right now, we could change it a bit more."

Whatever I told her, it would not have mattered, so I merely replied, "It's whatever."

"I see..."

She fell silent. Unlike me, Akiyoshi was someone who hated silence. So, the words that she said next were probably meaningless, just a means to mend the situation.

"It's more fun with everyone around."

I believe that was the final straw for me.

"...Hey, so..." I looked at Akiyoshi, who was peering at the ground beside me, and spoke my intentions clearly. "I'm quitting Moai."

She looked at me, for the first time in some minutes. I remember her face in that moment. It was a mix of shock, and sadness, and perhaps even a hint of anger.

"Why…?"

Both that expression and that voice were all Akiyoshi, but I knew that the girl standing before me was no longer the Akiyoshi I had first met. She was just a plain, boring university student who had abandoned all her ideals. I'm sure that some people would think it's terrible of me to say this, but what had happened to Moai after that proved me right. That group continued to engorge itself, reaching its arms across the university as though it owned the place. All that Akiyoshi had once strived for had vanished.

Moai, the secret society, was gone.

With more whimper than bang, those fragile ideals had shattered.

I was disappointed in Moai and no longer turned my gaze to them. Deep down, however, I think I still believed that one day, Akiyoshi would take back her old ideals and her old self, go back to that time where it mattered not how others judged or criticized her, and return Moai to what it once was. But now, three years later, it still had not happened.

I had to do my part and carry on the will of the real Moai, the one that still cared about ideals. For the sake of all that this twisted Moai had destroyed, for the sake of my and Akiyoshi's old selves, the current Moai could not be permitted to continue to exist. I could not leave this twisted Akiyoshi as she was.

This could not be.

Of this I was certain.

—*—

I had believed Tousuke to be my friend, but the weight of his sudden betrayal had hung heavily on my shoulders ever since I left his apartment.

He had been the one to propose all this. *He* had talked about how much he hated Moai.

I returned home alone and practically threw myself into my empty desk chair, not even bothering to wash my hands. I immediately turned on my computer and plugged in the USB stick. On the drive I found, other than "Corporate Shared Register (For the Resistance)," several files that Tousuke had forgotten to delete. I opened them to find a resume that he had probably prepared for some class presentation, along with some other things I could not make heads or tails of, lacking the requisite specialized knowledge. They were irrelevant to me, so I deleted everything I did not need. Given that he had abandoned these files, I assumed he no longer needed them.

When I opened the register again, I was shocked at the sheer number of people who were included in it. Had these all been collected through events like that barbecue? I felt like it would be a lot more efficient to just go through everyone who attended their meet-ups.

It was a shared file, so the password for viewing had been the date of Moai's founding—which meant that it had been Akiyoshi who had set it. It was not *just* the date when Moai was first recognized by the university. It was the day when the two of us, just Akiyoshi and I, had come up with the name "Moai." Which meant that, naturally, Akiyoshi was aware of this list as well.

The question was, to what extent was Akiyoshi controlling this? If, and when, this turned into a public matter, and if the group's leader was proven to be calling the shots, it would become all the more perilous for Moai.

The head of a job-hunting group at a respected university was gathering and distributing people's personal information to corporations without permission. That was sure to get the young people and those with a distaste for academia fired up.

Come to think of it, whoever it was that was spearheading this effort, what exactly was Moai getting in exchange for giving this out to corporations? Operating funds? I was sure they had official sponsors, though. It had to be for strengthening ties to those companies, then. Or at least to give their members preferential treatment at interviews?

Whatever, I could just leave a question mark on that one, and others would come flooding in with malice to fill in the rest. That was how internet rumors and virtual lynch mobs were formed.

Now that I was on my own, there was nothing that I would accomplish by just sitting around thinking. I immediately converted both the register and the e-mail from that HR rep into image files, editing them into an easy to post format. It was not a difficult task. These were skills I had picked up in my university classes, so it was easily done.

With this, the bomb was now complete. Now I had to just plant it online and pray that it exploded.

I took a breath and thought about what Tousuke had said.

Speaking honestly, I could not say that I felt *no* guilt over this. However, my guilt was only in regard to those who were caught up in Moai who were not calling the shots in the way that Akiyoshi and Ten and the others were. What the present Moai was doing was wrong. However, like Tousuke said, there must have been people who had chosen Moai as a place of salvation, of acceptance, such as Kawahara-san. For the sake of people like her, it was not enough to simply hope for the destruction or atrophy of Moai. There was more than that. It needed to go beyond, to a future that denounced the Moai of the present and returned to its origins—a place seeking only ideals.

If I could make a place like that, I was sure there would be a place for Kawahara-san there. And there might even be a place for me.

There was no need for the present Moai there.

I loaded the edited images onto Tousuke's USB stick, ejected it from the computer, and placed it in my pocket. For the sake of caution, I had to deploy the bomb from somewhere else.

What Akiyoshi had once made into a lie, I would return to the truth.

Not only had the flames inside me not burned out, but now that I was on my own, they burned stronger still. Like pushing the first tile in a row of crooked dominos, I opened the door and stepped outside.

When I opened the back door of the drugstore building and stepped inside, giving an, "Evening," in what could only barely be qualified as a greeting, I found Kawahara-san huddled on a stool, her knees to her cheeks, staring at her phone screen. Her eyes were open wide, brows furrowed in such a way that I could almost hear them creaking. I had never seen a look like that on her face before, but I knew what it meant.

She was livid.

I crept along as closely as I could to the edges of the locker room, careful to avoid the sphere of her anger, returning a resigned, "Yo," to the "Howdy," I finally heard. There was a clear rage in the eyes that glanced my way.

It would be far too idiotic to ask, *Did something happen?* and so I refrained. You'd have to live under a rock or be a total eccentric to now know about what had happened at our own school that had gotten Kawahara-san so angry. I was neither, so I chose words appropriate to neither.

"It's pretty bad, huh."

"Yea—uh, I, serio... Ugh, I can't..."

Unsure of how to put her own thoughts into words, she just clicked her tongue loudly. It had been awhile since I'd seen the Miss Yankee side of her slip out, I thought as she slid her phone into her pocket and bowed her head at me.

"Apologies."

"I mean, I don't really know a lot about what's going on, but uh, it does seem like a pretty big deal."

"Big deal? Honestly it *really* pisses me off."

I'm sure that, given the time, Kawahara-san would have ranted to me about all the absurdities of the world then and there, but unfortunately it was time for our shift to start. Time flew by. After a while of working, I, as usual, found myself with too much time on my hands. As I constructed a crude sign while minding the register, Kawahara-san came by with the mop.

"Mind if I gripe for a bit?"

Straight to the point as ever.

"Wh-what's up?"

She huffed through her nose, as if releasing the air from her own anger-swollen head.

"Why are there so many *garbage* people in this world who laugh at the misfortune of strangers?"

"Uh-umm...I have no idea."

"Neither do I."

And with that, the conversation was over. Even with such a brief exchange, though, I knew *precisely* what she was talking about, and how it was that she had come to be angry at such people in particular. However, I had too deftly fashioned myself as an outsider. It was fine for her not to see me like that. If you don't make a habit of that sort of thing, you'll fall apart when things come down to the wire.

Normally, the only conversation we would need to share would be a few parting words on the way home. However, there was something I wished to ask her. When our shift was over, just before we left, I, as always, exited the locker room slightly after Kawahara-san, catching up with her as she climbed atop her scooter.

"Hey, Kawahara-san," I started, before she could say her

farewells. Perhaps because I had never done this before, she closed her half-open mouth and looked at me in surprise. I was clumsy at launching right into any topic, so I dithered a bit to cushion the blow. "Please don't worry too much over this. It's gotta be bad for your health."

As if proof that I had made the right choice in expressing concern for her, her mouth softened, and she bowed her head with a "Thanks," and then, "I'm okay now."

"I know it's not my place to ask as an outsider, but what do you think will happen to Moai?"

"Are you *actually* worried about that? Thought you weren't interested in them."

"Well, I mean it's just...I was the one who told you about Moai."

I had already prepared that response, along with the joking tone I delivered it with. Kawahara-san laughed.

"Mm, honestly I wonder. Right now, the head guys are all runnin' around apologizing and making all the necessary excuses to people. They haven't been upfront about who's to blame for this and stuff like that, but the senpai are saying that they probably have some plan for dealing with this."

"So, you're kind of just waiting to see how things will go?"

"The leader's got some upcoming debrief she's giving the members, but there's so many of us that it's gonna be hard finding a place to hold it."

"It'd have to be one of the halls if it's on campus."

"Pretty much."

It would probably seem suspicious of me to press any further, so I just said sincerely, "I hope this goes in some way that will let you rest easy."

"Thanks. Well, I guess whatever happens...happens."

"Sorry for keeping you."

"Nah, it's honestly just a relief to have someone who's not total trash care about me. G'night then."

With that, she dashed off, a smile on her face. *Good night*, she had said this time, instead of *See you*. This little change aside, I was grateful to Kawahara-san for being such an unwittingly good spy. With her help I was able to keep abreast of the upcoming activities and current vibe within Moai, all from the outside.

So far, it did not seem that they had come to any conclusions that could be conveyed to the full Moai membership, but I did know that at least there was going to be a debriefing for the members. It was a good sign that Moai's upper management seemed like it was trying to stand up and take responsibility for the incident, rather than brushing it aside in silence. Kawahara-san might have been livid now, but one day she would see that this was a turn for the better. It was in service of that that this was a good sign.

By "the incident," I was, of course, referring to the scandal—Moai's distributing students' contact information to outside businesses without their consent. Presently, I could certainly feel that there was *some* backlash happening, but at the same time, it was already at a point where things were out of my hands, and I was beginning to fill with a sense of dread.

It had been three weeks. The bomb that I had planted had already gone off more quickly, and with more terrifying force than I had imagined, drawing the attention of many and causing indiscriminate damage.

I had posted those images to a number of social networks and online message boards.

At first, I worried they might simply vanish into the sea of online postings without anyone taking much notice, but that worry swiftly vanished itself.

It was the social networks where it blew up in the earliest, most obvious way. Someone who saw the posting told someone else who was unaware of it about it, then that someone told someone else, and then it reached some radical account with tons of followers, from where it exploded all at once—an inciting incident which then set the message boards alight. I started seeing articles from web news outlets aggregating the various threads as well. The images were proliferated endlessly, and whether or not they were real accounts, more and more people who claimed to have been burned by Moai in the past began to appear, fueling the notion that this was not just an isolated incident and that Moai had been this sort of organization from the start.

As a matter of course, eventually people began asking Moai, the university, and even the company that had e-mailed me to comment directly on the matter. Some of them actually *called* or sent e-mails, asking whether this was true or not. However, it did not seem that any of them received any meaningful reply, and at that point, even Kawahara-san was only aware that there was "something going on."

Just when it seemed things were dying down, however, there was a secondary explosion. A weekly publication that was probably in need of a story sniffed out the commotion online and wrote an article, albeit a small one, about Moai. Reading the article, they appeared more concerned about the fact that they so shamelessly accepted this information from students, more than the fact that it was Moai that had done it. I have no idea where they sourced their information, but they had recorded proof in the form of comments from related parties that Moai members were receiving preferential treatment at interviews. I believe that the reason that people who only learned of this scandal through the article began to argue online that both Moai and the corporations were evil was probably because they believed it was the latter who were originally to blame. Humans truly are strange creatures, unable to abide the idea that someone else might be benefitting more than they are. Moai truly was becoming fodder for the people who, as Kawahara-san complained, enjoyed laughing at other people's misfortune.

Once again, this had far surpassed anything I had imagined.

I had never imagined that actual news outlets would report on this. The fact that real adults would be baited in this easily was proof that there was little difference in interest and motivation between us and those not far removed from us in age.

After Kawahara-san left, I quietly rode my bike home in solitude. I had not seen Tousuke since that day—nor Pon-chan, obviously. I wanted so badly to ask the two of them how they felt about all this, but I doubted I would get the chance to. There was nothing that I could do about it at this point.

I picked up some half-price bento from the supermarket without much incident, washed my hands and gargled, then immediately turned on my computer. The bento would have gotten soggy if I heated it up, so I ate it cold.

I opened my social media, and through my original, still clean account, did a search on Moai. More and more Moai haters were appearing by the day. Online, there was vitriol and derision—just looking at it was enough to put me in a hypnotic state. My mind swam, my heart rate rose, and I began to feel nauseated.

There were some defenders too, as well as the general consensus that all universities and corporations these days were doing things like this, but even that was drowned out again by the haters within a single scroll.

Moai had gone from being just another obscure organization to a source of entertainment.

I, too, was participating in this circus of questioning society. Just this morning, I had released another bit of bait out into the world. The effects could be felt everywhere.

This was my way of keeping the game close at hand as I was reluctant to let things grow so big that they might expand to a place beyond my reach. That said, I did not do anything especially new and fresh. I screenshotted an e-mail from a different company than the one I had originally edited into the image set and posted it from an internet café.

This posting had only one image and was a bit bland, so I appended a bit of text to the image as well.

"What are Ideals? A Question of Righteousness."

At first, I considered just leaving it there, but in a fit of emotion my fingers moved a little longer.

"What are the values of those who so brashly approach others, selfishly affirming or denying them?"

That was the end of the post. There was a bit of irony in there as well, directed toward Tousuke and Pon-chan. Once more, the self-styled heroes of the internet ran wild with this new image.

I assumed that this image would reach Akiyoshi at some point. I hoped it might help her have a change of heart. I hoped it would cause her some regret. I began peeking through a number of her socials, to see if there weren't any signs yet of said reflection or regret. However, she had not posted anything in some days. All that I came across were boring updates on recent meet-ups and other trivial nonsense.

Maybe it would take a little more time, a little more of an explosion. As I pondered this, continuing to enter "Moai" into search bars and scrolling, I saw it.

I thought I was just seeing things when I first scrolled past it. However, when I moved the scroll bar back up, I realized frivolously that my kinetic vision was less useless than I imagined it to be.

I stared, amazed.

Beyond my reach, there in the cyber sea, was an image.

There was no mistaking it.

It was a picture of Akiyoshi and Ten.

It had probably been taken in the middle of some wrap party. Both were smiling broadly, raising their glasses towards the camera. They appeared to be quite friendly with one another.

I assumed this was some recent event. Akiyoshi's hair was a fair bit shorter than in the old photo I had, and she seemed to be wearing makeup and some casual dress more akin to how I had seen her on the day of the mixer. At first, I assumed this had been posted up by some hapless Moai member who was unaware of what was going on, but that was not the case. The account seemed to be a burner, having posted up only two other pieces of information besides the photo.

Those two pieces of information were both phone numbers. One of the two seemed familiar to me. I frantically checked my phone contacts.

As I expected, one of them was Akiyoshi's phone number, unused in ages but still recorded in my phone—which meant I could assume that the other one was Ten's.

I had assumed that Akiyoshi would have changed her number by now. While I was taken aback by the fact that this meant I could still have a conversation with her anytime I wanted, it also meant that things seemed like they were starting to progress in a direction I had never intended.

I never thought that anyone would be *this* unscrupulous.

Momentarily it occurred to me that perhaps I ought to take a step back from fanning the flames of this scandal until I saw that the image had already been shared around, which meant that it was beyond my power to stop it.

Once more, I looked at the photo of the two of them.

Those smiles were built on fraudulent actions, hurting others, and abandoning their values.

I don't know if I did it of my own free will, or if I was merely swept up in the will of the masses, but I decided to lend a hand in spreading that image and information.

It was not my fault that things had come this far.

Moai was wicked enough to warrant this criticism.

The moment I realized this, my clicking finger moved with the lightest of motions.

It was the following week that the university officially announced they would be taking action against Moai. Before I realized it, summer break was upon us. From the university's perspective, this might be their sole salvation in protecting themselves from mayhem as much as possible.

I had already stopped attending my classes, commuting only between my home and work.

That day, as usual, when I arrived to my evening shift, I saw Kawahara-san arrive in the parking area at around the same time. She smiled at me.

"Evenin'. Uh...I'm okay now."

"Huh? Okay?"

"I'm not pissed off anymore."

Apparently, she had gotten the impression that I was frightened that she would show up angry every time we were on shift together. Still, what was with that smile?

"Well, I'm glad to hear that either way," I said as we headed into the locker room together, at which Kawahara-san sighed.

"I mean, now that a punishment has been settled on, I have to get prepared to accept it."

"Accept it?"

"I mean, I'm in Moai too. What's bad is bad, and I'm not wholly without blame."

"No, I'm pretty sure you're blameless," I said, completely earnestly, but she shook her head.

"It's not totally zero. I may not have been directly involved, but to say that I was not involved at all would be betraying myself."

"Ah."

This response did not mean that I accepted her opinion. It was an *Ah, I see.*

Kawahara-san was becoming yet another person who was completely drunk on her own self. Though I felt a sort of sadness, I offered her a smile and said, "That's an impressive way to think about it."

"It's not that impressive. I mean...I dunno, there seem to be a lot of people even within Moai who are upset about this. The debrief is gonna be this Saturday finally, and depending on what's said there, I might just end up pissed off again."

"Oh, finally, huh. Well, it'll be nice for things to calm down."

"Oh, if I do get pissed off though, I'm gonna need you to take me out for a drink or something."

I don't know how she took my momentary pause as I wondered how I ought to respond to this invitation, but she quickly added, "Oh, I mean, if you want to," with an odd little bow, before vanishing into the storefront.

Kawahara-san was beginning to seem like yet another vexing person. Trying to keep at least some consideration for my junior in mind, I considered the fact that I had now obtained the date for the member debriefing from the Moai upper management. I wondered if there was some way that I could listen to that debrief. This would be my chance to hear Akiyoshi's own feelings on the scandal and the actual facts of the incident. It would be fine to hear it through someone else, but honestly, I wanted to confirm the results of this battle I had waged for these past months with my own two eyes.

Plus, there was something of a sense of villainy lurking somewhere deep down in my mind. I wanted to see Akiyoshi's face when she realized she'd lost. However, I only felt that in half-seriousness. What I actually wanted was just to see Akiyoshi return to her roots.

That password. It gave me hope that it might not take much to make her remember the things she used to believe in. And so, if I could, I wanted to be present at that meeting.

There had to be some way. As I thought about it, Kawahara-san returned, and it was time for our shift to start.

Just as the last few days had been for me, it all went by in a blur—work, and eating, and conversation.

Everything but Moai.

—*—

"Hey, Kaede, you free next Sunday?" It was back when Moai was just the two of us.

"No real plans. How come?" I asked Akiyoshi without looking at her, as we walked through the courtyard after some boring lecture.

Back then we were just two people, friends, no unnecessary fetters to tie us down.

"I heard that there was a grad student who runs a non-profit holding a symposium on bullying. I was thinking I'd go meet them. Wanna go if you're not busy? Or wait, didn't you start your part-time job already? Would you be okay missing work Sunday?"

I was a little uncertain, but there was no point in lying, so I replied honestly, "I already requested not to work Sundays since you invite me to a lot of things like these."

For a moment she seemed dumbfounded, but the corners of her mouth soon perked up.

"You've been thinking about Moai a lot, haven't you?"

To be fair, Moai activities were not the only reason I kept my Sundays free, but there was no reason to douse my friend's spirits, so I decided to leave it at that.

"But do you really want to spend a precious Sunday thinking about bullying?"

"Well, this person works on weekdays and had grad school, so there aren't a lot of chances to meet with them. Plus, it's better than thinking about it on a Monday, right?"

"That's true."

I honestly didn't want to think about an unpleasant topic on an already unpleasant day.

"Apparently, the topic is how to care for the bullies as well, so I'm thinking there will be a lot of educators there."

"We aren't educators, though."

"But when we see bullying happening, maybe we'll be able to do something about it."

As always, I was no match for those bright, clear eyes.

"I am free, so guess I'll go. I'd want to be able to help a little if you were ever being bullied, at least."

"Well, c'mon, not a *little*, I'd want you to actually help me out! Mm, actually..."

The nihilistic smile she had tried to make was so poorly done that I remember it clearly still.

"I'm counting on you."

She was terrible at making expressions she wasn't used to.

—*—

Sometimes, I have to wonder what the four years we spend at college are all about.

The time of your life when you possess neither the feeling nor the responsibilities of truly living, when you can be almost nauseatingly free, not giving up your boyish spirit or latent pessimism. If it was a university student's privilege to wear that freedom as a badge, strutting around like you own the place, then maybe I wasn't a university student at all.

I used that freedom to accomplish nothing. I attained nothing. I just surrendered myself to that environment, waiting for the time to pass. Even my job hunting had only successfully been completed by imitating what those around me did right.

Was there anything I did that was of any real meaning?

If there was anything at all, it was what I had done in these past few months. These months of putting one foot in front of the other and truly living, twisted though they might have been.

And so, I wanted to know for certain that those few months had not been for nothing.

The day of the debriefing from Moai's management arrived. In the end, I could not think of any way to sneak into the meeting, given that both Akiyoshi and Ten knew my face. I at least wanted to be able to hear their voices in that case, so I decided to aim for secretly eavesdropping. It wasn't as if I could just slip a mic to someone in the crowd. Incidentally, I had decided to set my alarm for four hours before the meeting, thinking I could show up early and lie in wait for them somewhere and catch a glimpse of Akiyoshi and the others.

It was being held in a certain hall—one that I had not approached since that day.

I woke up from a pleasant dream and ignored the oncoming nausea to immediately wolf down two onigiri I had purchased at the convenience store, which I washed down with a dangerous tasting beverage called a "Monster" in order to beat my brain and body into shape. The sugar and caffeine made my whole body feel like it was on fire, and I could feel my heartbeat, which had been on the rise since I woke up, all the more clearly. Some of the nausea still remained, but there was nothing I could do about that.

No disguises this time. I was sure it would only make me stand out too much. I would have to be stealthy moving through campus, but I would head to this final battlefield as myself. This was my message to the twisted Moai.

Loitering around the house waiting was not making me any less fidgety or anxious. I downed the final sip of the energy drink and decided it was finally time to head out.

I slipped on my sneakers and stepped outside. Though it was still morning, the sun was already steadily beginning to warm the asphalt and concrete. I locked the door, cutting off my own retreat.

No one else in this great wide world knew that, at this very moment, I was heading into battle. No one knew—not the people in my neighborhood, or even Tousuke, or Pon-chan, or Kawahara-san. But why would they? It was better this way. I had spent most of my four years alone. No one ever stood beside me. No one except for her, that was. But that was all in the past now.

Right now, I was well and truly alone.

Once alone, once I accepted and resigned myself to that solitude, my body felt all the lighter, as though it were wrapped in a thin shell that made me all the more resistant to the outside air. It made me realize some things as well. When I was a freshman, I never admitted the fact that I was alone. I was only affecting a quasi-lonesomeness.

Unlike me, however, I'm sure that at that time, she was *truly* alone.

Ever since the day I met her, *she* was capable of believing in herself. That was how she could always stay strong, no matter how things really were. She didn't need anyone to stand beside her. I had foolishly believed that somewhere deep down, she and I were the same. In reality, we were just as different as we appeared. She had forgotten all about me.

How had the past two and a half years been for her, years I hadn't seen? She had been lifted onto a pedestal and flattered into losing sight of all that really mattered, but surely that was not all. Still, given how fundamentally I had misunderstood her, I wondered what she had been thinking. I wanted to know, but I also didn't. I was getting tired of disappointment.

I passed by other residents of the apartment complex as I headed down the stairs. We greeted each other with nothing more than a simple bow. I'm sure that not one of us ever once thought very hard about the others' lives.

My head was filled with thoughts of her.

My friend, who was no longer herself. Neither the sharp lines on her face I saw the day of the meet-up, nor the boring social feeds she updated every day, nor the washed out smile she wore in that new photo belonged to the real Akiyoshi who I knew back then. It made me sad, and though somewhere deep down I knew it was unreasonable, I resented her for changing.

Truth be told, the thought had occurred to me that if luck were on my side and a bond still existed, perhaps I could have a conversation with her. I had even tried calling her. However, luck aside, it seemed that bond was long ago severed as the number I dialed was no longer in use.

What would I have said though, if the call had gone through? Could I have told her she was wrong? Could I have demanded she go back to her old self?

It was her after all, so if that call had gone through, she probably would have said something like, "What's up, Kaede?" as though nothing were wrong. I'm sure she would have no idea that her performance was anything but perfect.

But it was obvious. During our very last conversation, she had tried, ever so passively, to keep me from leaving, but in truth, she didn't have the time to care about someone who was not an active member of her group. The proof of this was the way she only grabbed my sleeve to show her regret, but then swiftly let me go.

That was all.

It would be a lie to say that I was not at all sad, but some part of me knew this was inevitable. She was a special person. I was someone who had only moved into her field of view. So it wasn't as though I hoped she would remember me.

I just wanted her back, that special person. I didn't want this boring college student who just ran around like crazy trying to make connections for the sake of getting a job. I knew that she was not that shallow of a person.

I walked to the station, pouring sweat, and bought some tea in front of the station to keep my own brain from boiling. Though it was early on a Saturday morning, there were plenty of adults in business attire on the platform. When the train arrived, they all boarded with identical movements like they were being shipped out from a factory.

I didn't think about how drab or boring they were. Other than the difference in age, they were hardly any different from us. Sooner or later, I would join that assembly line too. I would have plenty of time to think about it then—to think about what a drab adult I am, what a boring adult I am. I could set those feelings aside until later.

A mere ten minutes later, I disembarked the train at the station closest to the area of campus in question, one I rarely visited. The only people who were at school on a Saturday were club members or researchers, or eccentrics. Still there was no reason for even them to be here this early. I could hear my own footsteps as I walked down the nearly deserted platform.

Sure enough, it was hot on the ground level. I probably should have at least worn a hat or something. I headed to the school entrance closest to the station exit, hoping to get into the shade as quickly as possible. I had no required classes for my final term. I did not know how many more chances still remained for me to visit the safety zone that was my university—not that I had any particularly strong feelings about this.

There was hardly anyone on the campus, aside from a runner who was probably just some random person from the neighborhood mixed in with a few people who looked to be students.

I sat down in the shade of a tree on a bench en route to the hall. I looked at my phone and saw there was still around three hours until the start of the meeting. Even if they had preparations to make beforehand, the Moai leaders probably would not arrive until an hour before at best. I had done this out of an abundance of caution, but it now occurred to me that perhaps my wake-up time was a bit excessive.

I drank the tea I had purchased. The cicadas were shrill around me, which gave me a funny feeling like I was some old person who had just gone on a walk for my health.

What could I do with all this extra time? Maybe I could find a nice cool café to kill some time in for a while. I was good at killing time. I had taken great pains to kill as much time as possible during my college years.

My brain never really did get used to hour-and-a-half lessons, and it wasn't as if I had enough acquaintances to run into one just by wandering around campus. I had just killed time alone and, occasionally, with Tousuke—an excessive amount of time killed pointlessly. My life as a student was probably a waste, but then, did such a thing as college years that *weren't* a waste exist anywhere? Moreover, there were people in this world whose hands were stained with sin *because* of the things they had learned in college, and people who lost their lives because of college itself, and even those who lost whatever brilliance may have once been inside of them.

Compared to all of them, I had suffered no losses. I was doing exceptionally well.

Thinking about it, even what I had been trying to do recently was only for the sake of bringing back the time that had slipped away. I would have never had to do it if Moai hadn't changed. This was no different from killing time. Of course, it would be a lie to say that I never once held hope for the passage of time. I doubted that was any different from other university students either. When I started school, and I met her, I'm sure that I held some hope for the future. I probably even thought that the day might come when I might encounter my own ideal self.

I don't believe that that time was a waste. Back then, at least we were trying to do something, trying to *be* something... weren't we? We were trying to overturn something, weren't we? Even if our methods were self-centered and incomprehensible, at least there was a light within them.

This time, I was the only one trying to overturn a lie, still carrying my ideals on my back. Though I may have made some detours along the way, I was still able to pursue my ideals, as my own self.

For the first time, I felt I was able to truly affirm myself. I could affirm all that I had done in these past two years and change.

My own philosophies.

The message on that image.

I wondered what might happen if I was found out, but then I realized vaguely that if I was, it would be the first time I had achieved any real meaning.

Just a few years.

Just a few years meant nothing. Just as there was no difference between us and high school students. Just as there was no difference between us and working professionals.

So, I had to tear it all down to nothing.

I would bring it back.

We would go back to that time.

From there, we could just build it back up again.

I could feel the temperature rising along with the feverish feelings boiling up inside of me. I probably did need to move somewhere else. At this rate I was going to end up exhausted before anyone even arrived. There were still three hours until the meeting. I could afford an hour's break, I figured, standing up.

Then, as I took one itty bitty little step forward...

"Um."

I took one little step closer to the future, unimpeded.

In the second I looked back; a million thoughts ran through my head.

There was actually someone here at this hour? Someone who would bother talking to *me*?

The ideals of my freshman year. The disillusionment of my sophomore year. The resignation of my junior year. The battle that was my senior year.

I don't know if I really did recall all of that at once in that moment that came as quickly as it went, but it felt as though I did. I don't know what was true at all at this point.

Whether we like it or not, though, when we don't know what is true, we have to decide the truth for ourselves.

I had to accept what I saw before me as I turned around.

There was Akiyoshi Hisano.

No more need for reminiscing.

THERE SHE WAS before me, in the flesh.

Akiyoshi... Akiyoshi was there.

There, without a doubt, was Akiyoshi Hisano.

Though she was a bit bedraggled with dark circles under her eyes, her clothes were the ones I had seen her wearing on the day of the meet-up, her makeup the same as I had seen in that photo with Ten. However, here before me was not an Akiyoshi whose attention was elsewhere, nor a smiling Akiyoshi, but the *real* Akiyoshi, plain and simple, looking at me with lost eyes.

It had been two and a half years since we last stood face-to-face.

It would be far too silly of me to ask what *she* was doing here. I almost certainly knew exactly why *she* was here. As the person most responsible, she would have wanted to arrive at the hall well before anyone else. Even so, I did not think she would arrive *this* early. I figured she would be a bit more cautious than that.

From the way she was holding her hand out towards me, I could tell that she had been worrying over whether or not to say something to me and had panicked when she realized I was about to leave.

As I froze on the spot, Akiyoshi averted her gaze and then looked back at me.

"So, um..."

She obviously was choosing her words carefully.

"Long time no see, Tabata-kun."

Tabata...kun.

"...Mm," I mumbled to fill the silence, if only as an expression of how uncomfortable I felt.

Not Kaede, *Tabata-kun.*

Both of them were undoubtedly me.

"Um, sorry for startling you," she said.

"I'm fine," I replied.

I'm sure that the two of us looked like nothing more than friends who had not seen each other in some years, which was in fact true. As I stood there wondering what I ought to say, Akiyoshi answered a question that I had not yet asked.

"So, I just..."

"..."

"I wanted to talk to you about something, if it's all right," she said, looking at me and then at the bench I had been sitting on.

Something she wanted to talk about. I could think of far too many things.

"Oh, right, so I tried calling you the other day, but I guess you changed your number. Your e-mail address too."

"...Well, it has been two and a half years."

This probably sounded like a dig at the fact that she had ignored me for over two years and then suddenly decided to contact me again now, but she just gave me a puzzled smile and said, "That's true," still staring at the bench.

She was clearly bewildered.

I could think of a number of reasons why she would be so lost, like, should she even have said anything to me? How should she speak to me? What should she talk about? Well, no, she said that she had something to talk about, so it wasn't the third one. I suppose in that case it was perhaps more a question of whether this was the right place to be talking.

As I began to fill with both fear and anticipation of what she was about to say to me, Akiyoshi took a deep breath, small enough that I hopefully wouldn't notice, then looked me firmly in the eye.

"How...have you been?"

"...All right."

"I see... Right, so, there's something I wanted to talk to you about," she again declared. I was plenty prepared to have a conversation here and now, but I offered no response. If I said anything, it would create the assumption that I was prepared to accept whatever she had to say.

Seeing her eyes head-on, they lacked all of the clearness they had once had. The cynicism that had been imprinted on her over the past two and a half years had now sullied her entire world.

"Um, have you heard the news?" She had never been so roundabout in conversation, either. I simply tilted my head in reply.

"Uh, Moai is, um, in pretty bad shape right now. There's been an issue, so we're going to have a meeting to talk to everyone about it."

"...I know."

Her well-groomed eyebrows flexed.

"...Yeah, so. Moai's in pretty bad shape."

I nodded back, if only to acknowledge the facts as facts, but her already wide eyes opened even wider.

"Don't you...have any thoughts about that?"

I understood what emotions she was moving through right now. Knowing this, I offered a meaningless reply.

"...I mean, I don't really know."

"We're in a lot of trouble right now."

"That's none of my business."

"But it's...Moai. The group we founded together."

"It isn't anymore."

I regretted that I had phrased this in a way that sounded like a criticism, slightly irritated at the way she had phrased this. I really shouldn't have. I could hear her drawing in a large breath.

"Yes it is."

"...It's not the same."

The look in her eyes shifted.

"Yes, I suppose...the things we do...might be different now..."

"They *are* different," I declared, pressing.

"What's different about it then?" she asked, as if posing a question to the class.

"...Beats me."

I meant to imply that she should know better than I did, but Akiyoshi seemed to have taken this in a different way.

"Beats you?"

I felt both disappointment and anger from her.

"You say that you don't know."

"I'm telling you I really don't know."

"You say you *really* don't know, and yet..."

Her face twisted in despair as her already unnatural tone grew harsher. She bit her lip once, and her brows furrowed. I felt that I knew what it was she was so upset about. Even so, I was the one who should be hurt, I thought. Everything had changed beyond my recognition.

I could tell from her expression that she already knew everything, and I assumed that she was about to unleash some kind of emotional tirade. However, she merely sighed, fighting to hold back what was clear on her face, just as the head of a massive organization should.

"You know, I did want to talk to you."

"So you said."

"...Forget it, let's cut to the chase."

It would be a lie to say that I was not frightened by this preface. It was idiotic to be afraid of something that hadn't even happened yet, but looking back on life, there's about a fifty-fifty chance of unfortunate futures one predicts coming to pass. That's why people are constantly afraid.

This was yet another of those times.

"I'm guessing...it's no coincidence that you're here."

"..."

"It was you, wasn't it?"

Somewhere deep down in my heart I had been practicing tilting my head in ignorance.

"What was...?"

The picture in my head had been more accurate than I anticipated, down to both our expressions.

"Moai."

She did not appear lost anymore.

"You posted on the internet about us exchanging personal information with businesses."

"You think I did that?"

"I do."

I could see the conviction behind her nod. It was not doubt or assumption. She was absolutely certain. Naturally, she was, of course, correct. The question here was how she had come to that conclusion and how exactly she felt about it.

Still keeping up the same bewildered expression I had predicted, I had to ask, "I'm not sure what you're talking about, but why would I do something like that?"

"I don't know."

She shook her head slightly, as if she truly did not understand it. I could see her trying to drop her hubris.

"But I know it was you."

The sound of my heart pumping more and more blood through my veins resounded throughout my whole body.

"What do you mean?"

Perhaps it was simply because of the temperature, but I swore I felt my blood curdling.

"I saw that image."

"Image?"

"When I saw what was written on it, I remembered right away."

"...Remembered what?"

"Your philosophy," she said, her forehead dotted with sweat.

I was silent. I was afraid that if I opened my mouth, she would hear my heart racing from within me.

I tried to swallow, but it didn't work.

I had been found out.

She...had noticed me.

Apparently, she took my silence as an affirmative.

"Why would you do something like this?"

What I had not expected was the tone of her voice, which carried no hint of an interrogation.

"Tell me."

This was not an entreaty. It sounded like admonishment. It was the sort of voice you heard from a parent or teacher scolding an elementary schooler who had done something bad.

I did not care for that at all.

"All right then, supposing that it was me, what *then*?"

"What?" Her voice took a sharp turn from the haughty admonishing tone that implied she just might forgive me to something tinged with an obvious rage.

I knew it. I knew that cajoling tone of hers was the kind that you use when you don't think of the other person as your equal. The old Akiyoshi would have never spoken in a tone like that.

"I'm speaking to you because I wanted to have a *real* conversation about this."

"Conversations aside, you did something bad, didn't you? It's none of my business, but giving out personal information to corporations? *You're* the one at fault here if you were doing something like that at a time like this, when everyone knows why you shouldn't."

"That's entirely true," she admitted with surprising forthrightness. "That's why I'm going to acknowledge that and accept responsibility."

"...You say that like it's something to be proud of."

Now I was simply taking inventory of my own thoughts and releasing my feelings aloud.

"I didn't mean it like that."

She flinched visibly. I could tell that I had struck her heartstrings, so I decided to speak my mind before her irritation could grow any more.

"I don't get it, but..."

There was no point in delaying this any further.

"Shouldn't you consider the feelings of someone who would do something like that?"

That preface was probably as good as a full confession.

"Maybe there was once, somewhere, a secret society that pursued its ideals."

In truth, I should have never said something this risky in

front of her. However, the way that her gaze and her voice and the way she addressed me had all changed in those two and a half years was like nails raking down my back. I had thought for certain, should a time like this ever come, it would be in my chest that I felt that pain.

"No one ever thought much of it when it was just a group that clung to its ideals, not inconveniencing anyone. Then, that organization began to grow at a disgusting rate, spreading out all over the school, its members laughing down their noses at others and getting in everyone's way. I doubt that there was only one person who was less than happy about this. Plenty of people have been fed up with Moai. It's just that one of those people...happened to do something like this."

I could feel the wounds on my back growing deeper, but I could not stop myself. The look on her face made me *sick*. I couldn't stand the fact that there was no hurt or remorse in those eyes.

I kept on talking, hacking up everything I had felt until now.

"There are people whose whole worlds have changed because of Moai. Their lives at school, and maybe even outside of school, have changed in ways they *never* wanted. Even though we founded Moai with the mission of becoming your ideal self, you've upset the people around you. There have been *casualties*."

Despite my clear accusations, Akiyoshi did not interrupt. She merely pressed her lips, looking at me in the way that any normal person would when enduring something. She looked as though she had forgotten her own position in Moai.

For just a moment, there was a brand-new Akiyoshi.

"Moai has been, without a doubt, a perpetrator, but it was because it never atoned for its crimes that this reckoning came. It's only obvious that something like this would have happened."

Just then.

Just then, as I spoke, I caught a glimpse of possibility on Akiyoshi's face. Perhaps it was just wishful thinking on my part, but... No, it was there. I thought that perhaps she might be coming to realize that what she had done was wrong—the error of her ways. If that was truly the case, then perhaps it was not too late. After all, if I was being honest, all this time I had considered that Akiyoshi, now but a normal person, might be a victim of Moai too. Perhaps she was nothing more than a hero who had been brainwashed by the masses and lost all her strength, without her even realizing it.

Perhaps in hearing what I was saying, she was realizing that right now. Maybe she was thinking back on her own mistakes and trying to bear the shame. Maybe she was having a change of heart.

That was what I wanted to think.

"Moai...it's been twisted."

I tried to direct the conversation to a more hopeful conclusion. I thought that there might still be a future where Akiyoshi might change her mind.

"But maybe what's happening right now might be a good thing."

The chances were slim, but there was still a chance that Akiyoshi had begun to feel that the current Moai was twisted as well but had merely been unable to stop it. Perhaps she merely could not fix it herself, perhaps because she was their leader, because the tide was too strong.

If so, there was still time.

"Maybe...it could be remade."

She was still just standing there, enduring as she listened. There was a single gust of cool wind. The shadows wavered.

"You could start over again."

The wish I'd held onto for all these months had finally been spoken.

"As the *proper* Moai."

I was a little proud of myself for being able to say it. To make it easier to speak to her, I quit staring down my own nose and looked Akiyoshi directly in the eye. Perhaps when we saw each other clearly, eye to eye, we would realize that very little had actually changed between us, even though we had both been battered by the winds of a Moai that had changed so much.

"I can help you, if you need me..." I offered. She lowered her gaze, ever so slightly. I had no idea what she was thinking, or feeling, but I tried to imagine.

Hopefully, she was remembering something. However, I should have remembered that in reality, unlike unfortunate predictions, our expectations betray us about eighty percent of the time.

Akiyoshi's lips began to move, crushing everything I had hoped for.

"Are you *kidding* me?"

For a moment, I wasn't sure I caught her meaning, then she

once more looked me in the eye, her own eyes bleary and seeming to contain every single ounce of strength in her body. Bizarrely, I could only describe her gaze as one you would wear when staring down an ancient rival.

"Are you *fucking kidding me*?!"

This time, I was the one who flinched, as everything she had been holding back came roaring out.

"Akiyoshi..."

"The hell?! What the hell is this 'twisted' nonsense? This 'good chance'? This 'we can rebuild it'? And what, what was it? A 'proper' Moai?!"

Obviously, this was not a question.

"You don't know *anything* about what goes on in Moai! You don't know *anything* about the past two and a half years! You try to destroy Moai and blame it on other people, and then you're gonna just sit there and say *that*?! You have *got* to be *fucking* kidding me!"

Akiyoshi wheezed, her shoulders heaving, as though she had been forgetting to breathe. I turned over the words that had come out of her mouth in my mind. The more I thought about them, the more bizarre they were.

I had worked so hard to try and guide Moai in the right direction, and I had even reached out to her in reconciliation. And yet here I was being vilified, all my words denounced.

When I finally let that sink into my bones, I felt my blood rush to my head.

"What are *you* saying? You know it. You *feel* it. There is something *wrong* with Moai."

"You know what? You keep saying that. But just *what* is wrong? Quit dancing around it!"

The look she had had in her eyes, as though she was actually seeing *me*, was gone now.

"It's obviously twisted. You're hurting people and doing bad things. You yourself said it just now, didn't you? That you're doing different things from the Moai we created."

I could hear her breath, ragged, through her clenched teeth.

"This time, yes, we messed up. And *yes*, there are probably people we've caused trouble for. But what's so wrong about things just being different?"

"I—"

Akiyoshi wasted not another second, launching an attack before I could put my thoughts into words.

"There's *nothing* wrong. It's natural for things to change as time passes. It's not like things that stay the same are somehow more righteous than things that change," she sniped, but I turned her words around.

"You *never* used to lecture people like this, Akiyoshi. You have changed for the worse."

"And so have *you*!"

Her expression shifted. I could tell that deep down, her sorrow was beginning to overtake her anger, ever so slightly.

"How did you end up like this?"

"Same to you. How could you have abandoned all your ideals like *this*?"

"I *haven't*!" she shouted, more loudly than anything she had said before. "I would *never* abandon my ideals! I still believe in making as many people happy as possible, that people should be able to live a life they won't regret, that people who have found their own happiness should do good in the world, and also, if it was ever possible, that we should live in a world free of wars and poverty and discrimination!"

"Then why the hell are you masquerading as some job seeker's club?!"

"You can't get by on wishes!!!" she screamed again.

Her voice sounded so full of hope, but compared to what she was saying, on the other hand...

"It takes means and effort and planning to make the things you want to see come true. That's what I've come to realize. There's nothing twisted about that! I'm just trying to make things *happen*! You should understand at least that much!"

"...How can you call that an ideal if you no longer believe in the power of wishes?"

To hear her say such a thing disappointed me all the more.

"You..."

With a voice that was half a moan, Akiyoshi's heavy-looking business bag slipped out of her hands and onto the ground.

"Just what have you accomplished in four years through all those *cheap* methods?" I asked. "How have you changed the world by helping out random job hunters? What did you change for the better by bringing in a bunch of idiots and ruining Moai's reputation?"

In response to my question, Akiyoshi, who now seemed

nothing more than just a girl, appeared to be desperately fighting back tears. So, this was where we had come to.

"Tell me, Akiyoshi."

In part, it felt as though I was questioning the meaning of my own four years. I waited for her to reply. I prayed that she would say something of meaning.

Finally, she looked me in the eye, trembling.

"...I was wrong."

I had expected to hear the truth from her lips, but there was not even a conversation in those trembling words. Yet, hearing them, somewhere deep down I was relieved. Even if we could not see eye to eye, at least she had come to realize the error of her own ways. I was happy, even.

I thought that she was ready to repent. Still, I wanted to hear it clearly, straight from her mouth.

"You were wrong about *what*?"

Now, her lips moved with certainty.

"So many times in the past two and a half years, I thought how much better things would be if you were still part of Moai, but I was completely *wrong*!!!"

What she was now rambling was a confession, one that I had never expected. I was taken aback. A giant question mark floated in my head; I had no idea what she was saying. In my heart I felt both joy and sorrow, but there was no time to consider this.

"But *you* pushed me away," I replied, "along with the old Moai."

"Pushed *you* away? What are you talking about?!"

"Your values changed, and you pushed me out."

"You left all on your own!"

"But you didn't try to stop me, did you?!"

"We made a *deal* that if you ever stopped liking how things were going you could leave anytime! That's why I asked you so many times if things were okay with you. Every *single* time, you said absolutely nothing, but now you want your *revenge*?! I was completely wrong about you as a person."

I was dumbfounded at this sudden personal attack.

"I'm not going to sit here and have my last four years criticized by someone like you!" she shrieked, shaking her head wildly.

I hated her new haircut down to every single swaying strand, though there was no point in my saying so. There was no need for me to stoop down to the level of someone who would attack me this way by criticizing her appearance.

"Seriously, I *don't* understand! Why would you do something like that? If you didn't like what has happened, couldn't you have just talked to someone around about it? Or if the people around you were no good, then couldn't you have just talked to *me*? Seriously, *why*?! I don't get it!"

"If you don't get it then there's no way I can make you. The only reason you don't get it is because you've never tried thinking about *me*, someone different from you!"

"I did! I really did! That's why I really wanted to talk to you that time, two and a half years ago!"

"And yet you're blaming something that you couldn't do on *me*."

Her face twisted, teeth gritting almost audibly, as though I had hit the mark.

"Whenever I tried to talk to you back then, there was always someone else there. Tazunoki or Wakisaka...san or whatever. All your groupies. So there *wasn't* a time."

Thinking back to that time made what she had been saying all the more unbelievable.

"You thought things would be better if I was there? That has *got* to be a lie. Even without me there, you had an endless supply of people you could rely on. And that aside, you seemed like you were trying to focus all your time on Moai, but then you were completely off in your own world mooning over that boyfriend of yours," I said with a sneer, when...

"*...What?*"

Her single syllable reaction was completely different from any other she had shown me that day. She now gripped at her own hair with her freed-up hands, in a gesture clearly not of anger but utter bewilderment.

I also felt lost. I had no idea which part of my words had driven her to that point. Certainly, I was in such disbelief myself that I had in part hoped to rile her up, but I had assumed this would only enrage her. I wasn't actually trying to hurt her.

I had no idea what it was that had so flummoxed her as she stared at me through those big, round eyes. It troubled me that her reaction was so different from what I had imagined. What I had hoped was to prompt her back into continuing the conversation.

"Wait... Don't tell me..."

I could see a subtle twitching of her cheeks.

"Were you in *love* with me?"

I had no clue what she meant.

"*...What?!*"

The voice that came out of me was of the same ilk as Akiyoshi's, just prior. My head was filled to the brink with question marks now. What on Earth was she saying?

"Is that...why you did this? Because of... Because of some grudge?"

What the hell was she saying? In *love* with her?

"Huh...?"

Love.

Obviously, I trusted in her as a friend, back then. I respected her. Frankly put, perhaps I did love her. However, it was equally obvious that it was not a love that I felt for her with the sort of nuance she was implying. She was not asking if I had loved her as a friend. She...was asking if I had loved her in *that* way.

"Th...that's not..."

Akiyoshi looked into my eyes as I spoke. I had never seen her make a face like this before.

Another unfamiliar expression.

"...You disgusting *creep*."

For a brief moment, her silhouette seemed to be dyed in all black. But there she was, looking at me with scorn in her eyes. My head felt hollow, and I could hear her voice resounding through every corner of it. I tried desperately to focus my ears on that reverberating voice, but each time I caught the sound, it carried the same meaning as the moment I had first heard it.

Loved her? *Creep?* I didn't understand.

On what basis, on what grounds would she say such a thing? She didn't get to decide what it was that I felt for her.

Or was it simply that I had just never realized it? Somewhere deep down, *had* I been looking at her in that way? Was she right? Had I just been trying to destroy Moai and make her atone out of some kind of grudge?

That...couldn't be.

"I...I didn't... I never..."

My blood began to boil.

This was unlike anything I had felt before. It was an anger that shook me down to my very marrow. The abandonment, the fact that she had changed, the verbal abuse, the fact that I was nothing to her now—all of it made me shudder. I had been misread, and with a flagrantly incorrect interpretation.

Akiyoshi had misread me.

That was all it took. Others might think this an incomprehensible reason, but that was all it took to make a sack of dark, venomous poison erupt from within me. Before I even realized it, that poison began gushing from my open mouth.

"Don't be *ridiculous*!" I shouted, in a voice so loud it startled even me. Akiyoshi's shoulders quivered in shock as well, but she quickly fixed her posture, scowling back at me.

"That's what *I* should be saying. I can't believe that you would get in our way over something like that. Something as *stupid* as that!" she spat. There was no trace of the old Akiyoshi left in her face.

I knew it then. I finally realized it—Akiyoshi was one hundred percent correct.

Mistaken.

I was mistaken.

I was mistaken in trying to do something about the twisted, new Moai, much less trying to set Akiyoshi in the right direction. It was already far too late for that. Would I ever have made it in time? No, I never would have.

I was already too late the moment I met her.

"I was wrong."

"...Yes, you were."

"I should have never made room in my life for someone as irritating as you."

Had I not, my past four years would have never been so wretched.

Akiyoshi appeared utterly bewildered. What was she so surprised about?

"You're just a monster who craves the spotlight. You only chose me that day at random just because I happened to be sitting beside you, because you needed someone to help you tend to your wounds. It didn't matter *who* it was."

"That's n—" she started to say, but then, Akiyoshi swallowed her words. I could see her slowly paling. My poison was seeping into her. Loathing the fact that she would dare to make such a face, I began spouting poison again.

"What the hell was all that about *ideals*? What about the greater good? You got me all wrapped up in your little plots when you were only ever in it for *yourself*."

I knew then that I had always wanted to say this. It wasn't

just Akiyoshi; every single one of them talked about ideals. They spoke of kindness for the sake of others. But when you peel back their skin, all you find underneath that is pure selfishness.

Akiyoshi, Tousuke, Ten, Pon-chan, Kawahara-san—they were all the same. When it came down to it, they were all just in it for themselves, just using others to fulfill their need for attention, or money, or their sexual desires, no matter who or what it was.

Using Moai as merely a place for them to affirm their sense of righteousness.

Using a senpai in place of a lover out of mere loneliness.

Using a gathering of friends as a tool for job hunting.

Using a kouhai as an outlet to sate one's desires.

And perhaps even...

"I was just an easy excuse for you. It didn't have to be me. I was just a stand-in, someone who would pay attention to you."

No, but if it was Akiyoshi, then those feelings, even after all this time...

"...You're probably right."

She nodded with a pained look on her face, as though all of my poison now ran through her veins.

That face burned itself into the back of my skull.

I couldn't hear.

I knew that her lips were quivering, but that was all.

It felt as though my ears had been cut out entirely. Then my heart, then my stomach. The wind blew through that hollow, chilling me to the bone.

I was struck by a sense of danger. I felt an impending doom.

I had to get out of that place before my legs were cut off too. However, I felt that there was still one last thing I had to say.

"I would have been so much happier without you. And so would everyone else."

I could not even hear my own voice, but I'm certain that those were the words that came out of my still remaining mouth. As half of my head was already gone, I had no idea if what I wanted to say had gotten across. I looked at Akiyoshi though my remaining eye and turned my back on her.

I got the feeling that at some point in the distant past I had wanted to see her face, but I no longer cared.

That was the last time we ever saw one another.

The next day, my missing ears grew back, but a heavy wind was still blowing through the hole left behind from my heart and innards. In the over twenty-four hours since that meeting, I had not so much as had a drink of water, certain that anything I ingested would just slip right back out through that gaping hole.

I had no desire to even get up from the floor of my apartment, but I was not so anti-establishment as to skip out on a scheduled work shift. So, I dragged my underprepared body out to work.

Though I had not slept the whole night through, somewhere deep down, the day before felt like a bad dream. I only knew that it was not a dream because I hadn't slept at all.

As I had not managed to listen in on the debriefing the day before as I had intended, what I should be doing next was to go to work and ask Kawahara-san about it. However, I could not recall the last time when what I *should* be doing matched what I *wanted* to do. I had already lost all interest in the matter. All my anger and frustration had fled from out of that void within me sometime during the night, as if even they despised me.

When I embraced the void, it only opened even wider. All that I had done in my fight against Moai and the group itself, all the name-calling, and even the fact that I had defied my very own key principles, all rang hollow.

In the end, I really was nothing more than a convenient stand-in for Akiyoshi. It felt as though Moai and everything that went along with it had been nothing more than a lark. My feelings were never even necessary. With time and my own memories rendered utterly meaningless, even my own existence felt pointless. Actually, no—maybe I had always felt that way about myself. I had just been mistaken in ever considering myself to be anything of consequence.

I was back to normal now. It was just a temporary nuisance that I had ever had any illusions otherwise. I now understood clearly that this was fruitless.

And because it was fruitless, it no longer mattered.

I was not hurting for money, and I sought no recognition from my part-time work. There was no one who I was hoping to meet. This was just practice, so when the time came, I stepped outside and rode my bike to the drugstore.

The dregs of the midday sun warmed the air around me, but strangely I did not feel the heat at all. I arrived at the drugstore parking lot, not really certain how I had gotten there. I remember feeling my feet slipping from the pedals a number of times along the way, but I could not recall what sort of people I had passed by, nor even how many traffic lights I had stopped at.

I dismounted at the usual spot and entered through the back door into the locker room. As soon as I entered, my eyes met Kawahara-san's. Normally, I probably would have wondered about what sort of mood she was in following the Moai debriefing. However, that no longer concerned me. I simply looked her in the eye and greeted her.

"Heya."

"...Hey."

I was not even particularly concerned that there was a slight unnatural feeling to Kawahara-san's usual curtness. There were only a few months of this left anyway. When I left this job, she would just forget me. I, nothing more than a senpai she could chat with on her work shifts, would become but a phantom in her memory. I was certain that we shared about an equal level of non-awareness of other people's emotions.

All throughout my shift, my body felt unsteady. I was not sleepy so much as I was experiencing a constant sensation of falling. I soon grew accustomed to this feeling and was able to stay on my feet despite my ongoing descent. Work proceeded without a hitch, and as per usual I found myself with time to kill. I went about my stocking and sweeping all while feeling as though I were being sucked down into the floor, while at the same time all my innards continued to rise inside me.

It was strange to think that at this rate, things would wrap up uneventfully and I would just go back to that apartment. For an empty person to go back to an empty room felt like a joke.

"Um..."

As I crouched down, restocking the CalorieMates, I heard a voice from behind me. I picked up the CalorieMate bar that I had dropped in shock, returning it to its cardboard case. I turned around, trying to bring down the impossible speed my heart was racing at. I had assumed it was some customer wishing to know where a certain item was, but in fact there stood Kawahara-san.

I stood slowly up, taken by surprise. She stared at me fixedly as my own line of vision shifted from a point lower than her own to a point higher.

"...Something wrong? Shouldn't you be at the—"

"It's fine, there's no customers here right now."

So then, what was it?

Her brows furrowed slightly. I wondered if she was angry about something.

"Something happen then?"

"No, I was just wondering if you were all right."

"Me...?"

"You've been kind of...absentminded since you got here."

Oh, of course, she was worried about me. That's what that expression was. *Out of it, huh?* I guessed she did have an eye for people.

"I'm fine. I mean, I think I've pretty much been absent for my entire life." I phrased it like a joke, but it was true. Kawahara-san did not laugh.

"Absent, huh? That's actually a pretty similar word to 'empty.' So yep, that's just me, absent as ever."

It seemed equally possible that she would laugh at this, or perhaps be worried, or maybe even get mad and say that I shouldn't say such things. Any of them would have been fine by me, but that was not her reaction at all.

"...Sorry," she said. "I don't really know what to say to that." Apparently, all I had done was make her uncomfortable.

"Oh, no, sorry for saying something so weird."

"I've been thinking about it, since yesterday."

"...Since yesterday?"

She seemed a bit flustered at my question, putting her hand to her mouth.

"Sorry, it's got nothing to do with you, Tabata-san. I'm really sorry. No, it's just...I heard someone else say almost the exact same thing, that they were empty inside. I had no idea what to say to it then, either."

So, she gets tangled up with a lot of weirdos too, I vacantly realized.

"I don't think you need to say anything to it. I'm pretty sure I really am empty. Me, and that other person."

"I can't feel that way," she said, then quickly bowed her head and added, "Sorry," as though even she had not expected her sudden rebuttal. "But seriously..."

It was a bit late for it now, but those appended words made me think that she really, truly, was a good person—a properly good person, unlike me. She bitched and complained about others, but in the end, she really was a good person who sincerely cared about others. Though I couldn't agree with her words, I thought I ought to at least formally thank her.

Just then, someone entered the store. We both gave a proper, synchronized, "Welcome!" The kind of greeting that would please a manager, rather than a customer.

Kawahara-san needed to get back to the register. She wrapped up the conversation with a, "Well then," and a smile that reached only her lips, bowing her head and turning her back.

I had to finish restocking the CalorieMates as well, I thought, stooping back down, when I heard one more, "Um..." I looked back to see Kawahara-san approach and then whisper low enough that the customers would not hear, "This is probably unnecessary information, but..."

I waited to hear the rest.

"Actually, the other person who said they were empty was Hiro-senpai, from Moai."

Dropping only that bit of information, she turned back to the register, not a single hair shifting out of place.

I wondered why she would tell me that. It made little sense, and I almost wondered if she was insinuating something, even though there was no way she could know about the relationship between Akiyoshi and me. But that wouldn't make any sense either.

It was indeed unnecessary information, but the fact that she had imparted such information to me did not pass me by. It remained somewhere stuck around my throat which had not yet been cut out, hindering my breathing.

I was not crouching now because I needed to straighten the CalorieMates up into rows—I was overtaken by a feeling that the room itself was swaying and was unable to stand.

I dropped to a knee. It grew difficult to breathe. My hands began to shudder. I was unable to bear the chill that rattled around my scooped-out chest and gut.

"Were you...in love with me?"

For some reason, it only now occurred to me what this feeling was that had been cutting away at me and now gouged at my throat.

I was *hurting.*

At some point, the room stopped swaying, and instead, my vision grew blurry. I quickly hid it before anyone could notice.

"So, um, Kawahara-san."

For the first time ever, when we finished work that day, I called out to Kawahara-san as she started to leave the locker room ahead of me. Seeing her turn around with wide eyes, as though she had been attacked in a moment when her defenses were down, I had to properly explain the reason I had called to her.

"Sorry, could I ask you to wait up for me...?"

It was an odd request, if you thought about it. Kawahara-san always waited in the parking lot for me before heading home, after all. And yet, she gave me a sincere, "Yes, of cour... Yes," nodding profusely before heading out the back door with a, "I'll be outside."

I shed my apron and work shirt, heading out behind her in my T-shirt and black linen pants. This time, instead of starting up her engine, Kawahara-san was waiting for me.

"Hey, sorry to keep you. Or uh...sorry this is so sudden."

"No, I mean, it's fine or whatever."

"There's something I want to ask you."

How to approach this? It would be strange to ask this out of the blue, wouldn't it? As I dithered, thinking that it wasn't as if she knew all that much about me anyway, Kawahara-san said, rolling her helmet around in her hands, "Let me guess... Is this about Hiro-senpai?"

"Wha..."

"Well, I mean, I just wondered since our conversation earlier kinda left off at a weird place. Sorry if I'm misinterpreting."

She wasn't, so I nodded humbly and said, "No, you're right. What I was wondering though, was why you told me that the leader of Moai was the *other* person who said they were empty?"

I feared she might have realized that there was some connection between us.

"Hmm..."

Still turning her helmet over, Kawahara-san looked up at the night sky. I followed her gaze up, but the lights of the drugstore were so bright I could not see a single star.

"So, um, apologies if this starts soundin' kind of rude, but..."

"It's fine, go ahead."

I nodded, fully afraid that the parts of me that had been injured were about to experience some brand-new damage.

"So, uh..."

It was almost a relief to hear the words spoken from so close to me.

"The two of you, or well—you might not actually know Hiro-senpai, but you do know that she's the head of a large organization, so bear with me. The two of you are *completely* different types of people, right? I'm sure that the stuff you do and your daily lives are completely different too."

That was true.

"But you're both depressed over something, clearly tearing yourselves down and saying that you're empty and stuff, yeah? So I think you're sort of both the same. You both have too much confidence in yerselves."

"Confidence?" I parroted stupidly, reflecting on this unexpected word.

"Yeah, you're too concerned about your own proper image, I think."

"I don't...think we are? At least I'm not."

I had never once thought that I was some kind of amazing person. Kawahara-san had made a grave misjudgment.

"I mean, it's not that I think you think you're a great person or whatever, but I think you're probably always thinkin' about bein' the right way and doing the right thing. It's more like, as people you're trivial to yourselves."

Trivial... To be fair, I had acted, felt, and lived my life in a trivial, meaningless way.

"Both you and Hiro-senpai are in different positions, but I think you both think it's obvious that you could be living a better life. That's just what occurred to me earlier. I mentioned her name because I thought that was weird, but, well, what I'm tryin' to say is, what I should've said to Hiro-senpai yesterday was: Everyone's empty inside. I'm empty too. And according to you, Tabata-san, so are *you*."

"No, I...don't think that's...true."

Instantly, I rejected her opinion. I had been breaking my own principles left and right since yesterday. However, that was how I truly felt. At this point, I even felt terrible for thinking that Kawahara-san was the same type of person as me.

For some reason, though, she grinned at me.

"It's fine. When there's somethin' you're lacking, you just need someone else to cover for you."

"Is that...how it is, then?"

"Yeah, there's always gonna be a senpai who'll stick it out with you even after you get drunk and lose your cool and make a run for it."

I could not comprehend or accept this logic, but I knew that she was trying to cheer me up, so I just said, "Thank you for the encouraging words," forcing a smile.

"No, I'm just glad I have you to prop me up. Honestly, I was feelin' a little in the dumps too."

"Did something happen?"

There I went again shattering my own philosophies, stepping all over someone's boundaries with my words. *Crap,* I thought, but she just gave me a strange little smile and asked, "You wanna hear about it?"

I nodded. She casually turned the helmet over in her hands once more.

"Moai's gone."

The words passed right in through one of my ears and out the other, before looping back around.

"...What?"

"Well, more accurately, it's still around but seems like it's gonna be dissolved. 'Least that's what Hiro-senpai said at the meeting yesterday. Was kind of a shock really. I've had a lotta fun since joining."

"Was that the university's punishment?"

"Don't think so. Seems like the school just imposed some penalty. Disbanding was Hiro-senpai's decision."

"...Huh."

Was this her way of taking responsibility? For some reason, my throat began closing up again.

"Guess it got bad enough they had to tear it all down."

"Well, hm, so actually, like, it seemed like it was a pretty sudden announcement and some decision Hiro-senpai just made when she was up there on the mic. Ten-san and the professors all lost their minds over it. Seems like that wasn't what they discussed."

"Wow..." What could that mean?

"I mean, I imagine that she's got a lot of responsibilities as the head of the organization, a lot of weight on her shoulders that we can't even imagine. But at the debrief, Hiro-senpai just looked so frustrated that I finally realized how seriously hard this stuff must be on her. Even though it's a bit late for that."

"So, Moai is being dissolved because that's what the *leader* wants?"

Even knowing that, there was nothing I could do about it. Still, now that things had gotten this far, I couldn't help but let a bit of worry into my voice.

"At the very least it seems like Hiro-senpai doesn't want to be involved anymore. One of the juniors who was set to take over as representative starting next year was saying that if the group does disband, they might just start operating as a different organization, but apparently most folks still seem pretty uneasy about that idea."

"...You're basically just being abandoned," I muttered.

Kawahara-san looked up at the sky again, mumbled a, "Hmm," then said, "I suppose that's true, but I do wonder if we'll be okay without Hiro-senpai."

There was some clear unease in the edges of her wry smile.

"Moai is run with the backing of a lot of alumni, but it's usually Hiro-senpai who forges those relationships. So, on top of the management issues, I just don't know if there's anyone who could truly take her place," she said, as though speaking about someone very dear to her. "I mean, she remembers the names and faces of every single member. After the debrief, she stood at the exit speaking to every single one of us. There were some people who weren't into that, but like, she spoke to me directly, and even remembered one of my personal goals that I had brought up in conversation before and offered me encouragement. Even in a huge organization like that with so much hard work to do, I don't think she ever wrote off even a single member."

She looked up to the heavens again, as though honoring the dearly departed.

Seeing her like this, I was certain that said leader would be thrilled to be missed in this manner. That even if Moai were gone, in a way, things had still gone *exactly* as she had hoped. Now, she would be memorialized as the leader who had been beloved by everyone, even if she had to step down to take responsibility for a scandal. Whatever happened to her though, that was no longer any of my concern.

I no longer wished to have anything to do with such an empty person who caused me so much pain.

"So, that's the sort of person who ran Moai."

She never wrote off a single person, Kawahara-san said. Yet, long ago, had she not found she no longer had a use for the stand-in known as me? And in exchange for doing so, she had found far, far more stand-ins who affirmed her better than I ever had.

I suppose that was what it all came down to.

"Sorry, I'm just blabbing on about something you don't even care about."

"No, I'm sorry for asking something of you that was so hard to talk about."

Whenever people apologized to me, I always ended up apologizing myself. The atmosphere still strange between us, we went our separate ways from the drugstore parking lot, respectfully of one another, neither of us with a smile.

I tried again not to think about anything as I rode my bike home. Once I arrived, opened the front door, and stepped inside my little box, I was able to relax a bit. Perhaps that was because it was normal for me to be alone here. Here, no one would realize how empty I was.

Except for myself, that is.

I turned on the lights, set down my bag, gargled in the bathroom, and then sat down on my chair in front of my computer. I had no reason in mind for doing this. It was merely that I always did the same thing every day—not going along with that flow would in and of itself seem to have some kind of intention.

On the desk was an unopened can of coffee that I had taken out and forgotten to drink. I popped open the can and took a sip. The low amount of added sugar was obvious in its taste. It suddenly occurred to me that this was the first liquid I had imbibed in a while.

I managed to finish the coffee without any of the fluids leaking out through the hole in my chest, then stood from my chair and opened the refrigerator, downing an oolong tea that was inside.

I sat down again and powered up my computer. There was nothing I really needed to do, but again, this was nothing more than me going through the usual motions. I casually checked my e-mail. There was nothing new of note beyond some self-help message from a job-hunting website. I had not opened the burner e-mails that I had made for the sake of job hunting and eliminating Moai in some time, nor did I intend to open them again at any point before the heat death of the universe. They would just be one more bit of flotsam lost to the digital ocean of the internet.

That was where they would end their time.

Suddenly, I found myself envying the ease with which time can just come to a shuddering halt and slip away in places like that. If the story of my own life or whatever were to end then and there, the void within me and all my pain would mean little. Or maybe that pain and nothingness could be twisted into some sort of lesson. Perhaps it might even be glorified.

However, the fact was, my life continued. Incapable of anything as dramatic as suicide, my life would carry on, that pain and emptiness I carried continuing to haunt me. It would never be glorified—it would merely be empty, cold, and painful, and continue to wound me. How much easier things would be if I knew it would end. How much easier things would be if I could beautify these feelings. The same went for knowing others.

I should have ended Akiyoshi's time within my heart two and a half years ago. Would things have been easier if I had been able to glorify her existence, if I would have kept that time sealed away inside of me?

I would never have gotten this hurt.

Ever since I met her, I had *only* been hurt.

I was going to have a normal graduation and begin working, passing the years with this hurt. One day, I might even get married. Throughout all those points in time, I would be carrying a hurt that I never needed.

Meanwhile, Akiyoshi's time might just stretch on forever. She would get a job, become a real adult, and...perhaps even be happy. By then, she would surely forget about Moai, and about me. Every few years, I would think about that fact, and the wounds within me would only grow deeper.

How very long a life can be.

I clicked the mouse at regular intervals, sounding almost like the ticking of a metronome, countless windows appearing and then disappearing from my computer screen, then reappearing again. Among them were sites associated with some of my social networks.

I looked at one to see that I was still logged in to one of the accounts I had made for spying on and posting inflammatory remarks about Moai. It was time to close the book on that account as well. It would be too pitiful for the little thing to just leave it, I thought, and intended to immediately delete it. However, I hesitated to click the button.

Something popped up in front of me. Someone had sent me a message.

I opened it to find it was from a sender I did not recognize. The subject line was "Spread the Word," and there was some sort of URL attached. My sense of caution having grown dull, I thoughtlessly clicked on the link and was taken to a page containing a single audio file. With equal lack of caution, I clicked the "Play" button.

There was some manner of rustling noise, followed by several seconds of silence.

What kind of stupid prank is this? I wondered, about to delete the message—when I heard a voice.

"Hello, everyone, and welcome. I am the official representative of Moai, Akiyoshi Hisano."

I instinctively thrust my chair back, knocking noisily into the low table behind me.

"Thank you for—"

I frantically gripped the mouse and stopped the recording.

What was this?

What the *hell* was this?

It was Akiyoshi's voice—a voice I had thought that I would never hear again, and yet there it was again already.

She was greeting someone as the representative.

Spread the word?

Should I even continue? Could I keep listening to this? After some hesitation, I decided I should at least find out exactly what this recording was and once more clicked the button.

"—taking the time out of your busy schedules to be here. As I am sure you are all aware, there was a recent article reporting that Moai has been exchanging personal information of students with certain businesses. Today, I would like to clarify the facts of the situation and speak about the future of Moai."

It was a recording of Akiyoshi's address at the debriefing yesterday. That's what this was.

Immediately, I understood what was happening here. There was someone among the members who had attended yesterday's meeting who had a very negative view of the situation. They had taken this recording and were sending it out to accounts like mine who were anti-Moai, hoping to spark more criticism.

I had my doubts—speaking as someone who wanted to destroy Moai. Would exposing a simple fact confirmation and group roadmap really be a measurable threat to Moai at this point? Moreover, any information delivered by a representative would be selective. Would there really be anything more worthy of critique than what was already available online? Was that what they were criticizing? The selective nature of the information? As I pondered this, Akiyoshi's address continued.

"First off, I accept full responsibility for this situation and for having neglected the management of this group. I have caused a great deal of trouble for everyone, for which I sincerely apologize. I am truly, truly sorry."

What seemed to have been a prepared speech trailed off into her genuine feelings. It was language that was both incredibly straightforward and practically invited nitpicking. However, I quickly realized there was no need for such nitpicking, nor any point in my saying such a thing; Moai's dissolution had already been decided.

I continued to listen, but naturally, Akiyoshi had no information to give about the situation outside of the literal facts. All that she said had already been alluded to on the internet or published in that article, with no additional footnotes, along with her own apology and a report that there would be no direct punishment nor official actions taken by the university against the members of Moai.

It was at this point that it occurred to me that I typically used headphones when I was playing something off of my computer. I took out the earbuds that I always had in my pocket and plugged them in.

I instantly regretted it.

With the sound flowing directly into my ears, I now felt as though I was actually in the room for the debriefing. I felt that cold wind blow directly through my stomach. Still, I could not pull myself away.

"In light of the preceding event, we have decided to limit Moai's events for the time being. The period of time has not yet been decided given specific details pending further discussion with the university. This does not mean that members will not be prohibited from gathering independently, but Moai itself will have limited official activities. Regarding the alumni meetings for juniors, individual introductions will be made during your senior year. We appreciate your understanding."

It was impossible for me to guess what was going on in Akiyoshi's mind as she read out what was likely a prepared statement in a flat, hollow tone.

"Regarding the handover of leadership..."

She suddenly trailed off.

Through the microphone, I could hear her take a deep breath.

"I...I'm really sorry. I've been doing a lot of thinking about what to say to you all about this, how I ought to take responsibility...but, no matter what I say, I don't think it's going to undo all the disappointment everyone is feeling right now. I'm really, really sorry."

Both the tone of her voice and the shape of her words were different from what they had been up to this point. I could tell that something was stirring within her.

Unlike the previous unclear picture I had, the stark image of

Akiyoshi bowing her head now leapt into my mind, giving me the illusion that she was speaking directly to me.

No, this was no illusion. I might as well have been in that very hall right then.

I could not pull the earbuds from my ears.

"I've been thinking about...about what to do about Moai."

I could practically feel how quickly her heart was racing through the wavering of her breath.

"This group we know as Moai..."

Finally, this was where the announcement of the dissolution would come, I assumed, just as Kawahara-san had described. It felt as though I was reaching the conclusion of some long-lost memory. So many things had happened, and all of them felt as though they had been makeshift and meaningless from the very start.

Finally, this was all going to be over, I thought. All I could think was that I wished they'd be over sooner. And yet...

"In the beginning, Moai was just two people."

Akiyoshi did not finish her story. For the first time in a while, I could hear my once hollowed chest beginning to pump blood throughout my body.

"We were a team. It was just a verbal agreement, just an excuse to hang out with a dear friend."

My body reeled. There, right in front of me, was Akiyoshi holding the mic.

"Since back then, all the way up until now, I've always enjoyed, always loved, what we do at Moai, and even though many things

have gone awry, I've still been able to live through my university days with hope in my heart."

My own deep breath overlapped with Akiyoshi's.

"However, at the same time..."

There were several seconds of silence.

"I..."

When I finally heard her voice again, it sounded as though she was trying to keep herself from running from her own feelings.

"I now believe that I used many people's powers and abilities for my own means. I sacrificed those people, and in turn, betrayed them."

She ruminated on every single word.

"I did my best to show my gratitude to all the people who supported me when I was nothing more than an empty person, but even so, I'm sure that there are those who I neglected. There may...even be some people today who feel that way. Even... Even those who are not present here."

Me.

"There are...people who would have been...happier without me."

I suddenly forgot how to breathe.

"Of course, I do know that there are those for whom Moai was a place to call home, those who enjoyed the things we did together. I cannot thank you enough. It's just that, I'm really sorry, I just can't...ignore the people who I hurt."

......

"I just wanted everyone to be happy. I believed that if Moai succeeded, and everyone could become their ideal selves, then even those who had left us would accept us. I believed in my ideals. But I know

that there are people who served as sacrifices. I know that I was just using Moai."

I could hear her wavering voice whispering directly into my ear.

"I am truly, truly sorry. I'm sure that this will sound irresponsible, but I believe this is the only way that I can protect the Moai that I built on those ideals, and all the people involved with it, from any further harm. I'm sorry. Moai is going to be dissolved. I truly, deeply apologize. There's nothing more to say. I...I'm sorry..."

I heard murmuring and rising sounds of confusion from the venue.

For the first time in some time, I remembered how to breathe.

The moment I did, I was struck by the most intense nausea I'd ever felt in my life and fled to the hall, racing to the bathroom.

I gagged, but I did not vomit, only managing to hack up a bit of bile into the back of my throat.

I realized then that I was in my bathroom at home, the earbuds hanging from my ears, no longer connected to anything. I returned to reality and left the bathroom. I stepped into the living room and immediately flopped down onto the floor.

I noticed my body quivering. The chill of the wind that was blowing into my heart was nothing compared to what it was before. It was unbearably cold, but in contrast, my whole body was on fire, so hot that I thought I just might turn into ash.

I felt it now—the regret, and shame.

Sweat trailed down my back.

I clawed at my suddenly burning skull.

Why did it take me this long?

Why would I not realize something so very important until *just now*?

Now, I finally realized it.

I had never truly wanted to see Akiyoshi in pain.

What I wondered about the most was why it had taken me this long.

Though all of the rage and resentment I had felt until now was not a lie, it vanished as quickly into regret and shame as if it had been.

All I had been feeling was hurt.

Because I had been hurt, I could ignore things. Because I had been hurt, I could cause destruction. Because I had been hurt, I could lash out. I hadn't been thinking at all about what would happen when I *actually* hurt someone else. Or rather, I'm pretty sure that I thought since it was Akiyoshi, she would understand. She would agree with me and accept what I did, and we could laugh it all off as a hilarious misunderstanding.

Why the *hell* would I think that?

How could I have never imagined the fact that Akiyoshi could be hurt by my actions? If I had, I'm sure I would have hesitated.

I would have...wouldn't I?

Then again...if I was that good of a person, I would have never thought of harming anyone in the first place, would I?

I had thought and decided my course of action, without considering the sort of person that Akiyoshi was. I had, in short, failed to acknowledge her as a human being. I had thought of her as some sort of fixed point in my memory. There, she was *only* a memory, incapable of being harmed.

I'd been thinking it would be best to cut off ties with her entirely and simply beautify the memories I had of her, or something.

And I had been doing just that.

I had at some point ceased to see the real Akiyoshi, simply glorifying her memory.

My disappointment was all my own fault, under the front of assuming that we were supposed to be friends. I had tried, and succeeded, at harming someone who had never stopped thinking of me as a friend. I did not hesitate in wishing to make her feel the same hurt that I did.

How could I have ever felt that way?

It was because I was hurt.

Because I had *been* hurt.

Even though being hurt never justifies causing it. It only ever leaves you with shame—and regret.

Honestly though, why was I hurting in the first place? I had always suspected that I was only being used. I'd hoped that Akiyoshi would deny that, but when she confirmed it, I was hurt.

It was only then that I remembered—Akiyoshi had started to say, "That's not true," but had stopped herself. She realized that there was no person in this world who could accurately make such a denial, didn't she?

People only use other people as substitutes. Everyone uses others as stand-ins when they need something. Friends, lovers, family, kouhai, senpai, bosses, employees, they all use other humans as a means to an end.

It's the same thing when one lonely person makes friends with another lonely person. The same thing when someone who feels no one understands them seeks someone who does. Even when someone collapsed from illness seeks a shoulder to lean upon, it's no different.

Even I did this. Akiyoshi, Tousuke, Kawahara-san—I was just *using* them.

Being used and hurt by someone is not a good reason for doing the same to others. Especially when there probably wasn't anything I should have felt hurt over in the first place.

Hadn't I needed her too? I must have been happy to hear her call my name.

That momentary happiness was probably more than enough.

She was a stand-in, but that meant that I was able to fill the gaps in my heart.

I *needed* to fill those gaps.

She had been someone who could fill that void.

I might have been saved if I could have merely filled in that void that had opened up in my chest. I could have just done that, but instead I hurt a friend.

What the hell, me?

Now, instead of Akiyoshi's voice that had been echoing in my mind since yesterday, my own words that I had flung at her now played on repeat.

What. The hell. Had I *done*?

Not only had I denied her personality—I had denied her entire existence.

Now, for the first time, I understood the meaning of what I had been doing, what it meant to hurt someone.

I wished from the bottom of my heart that I could apologize, for the first time in my life.

But no matter how long I waited, Akiyoshi did not appear before me.

—*—

"What were you like in high school, Kaede?" Akiyoshi had asked me one day, a few months after we first met.

Without putting much thought into it, I answered, "Not much different from now, really."

It was not a lie. I felt that I had probably had a bit more faith in people then than I did currently, but honestly, all I wanted was to forget that blue, painful, fragile time of my life as quickly as possible.

"How about you? I'm guessing you've always been like that," I said. I'm sure it sounded a tad bit tasteless.

Akiyoshi's quirks—her basking in attention, her dogged belief in her ideals, the way she unilaterally declared that I was her friend—all seemed like congenital conditions that I doubted would ever be cured, and I had rather resigned myself to that. However, as we sat there in our usual spot in the cafeteria, she shook her head.

"I have no idea what your 'like that' is referring to, but I think I was pretty different in high school."

"What, was college a fresh start for you then?"

"It wasn't a 'fresh start,'" she chuckled. "When I was in high school, I never really got to say the things I wanted to say. I was weirdly afraid of criticism. On the other hand, I *did* also fight with my friends a lot."

"Seriously?"

"Seriously."

I was deeply surprised. I had been certain that she had been born without any concern for whether she stood out to others, and I was sure that as long as she remained that way, my own anxieties would start to fade away as well.

"So, when did those circuits get rewired?"

"Circuits...?"

"I mean, what made you decide that you no longer needed to be afraid of criticism?" I asked.

She lowered her eyebrows bashfully.

"I'm still afraid."

I was dumbfounded, but then she continued, "Oh, okay. I get what you're saying now. No, so I mean, it is scary. I'm always worried about whether someone is going to criticize me. It's just that, in high school, that's as far as I ever got. So, it's not that my circuits were rewired, so much as they developed?"

At the time, I couldn't really grasp what she meant by "developed."

"If you know that something's going to be scary, aren't you better off just not provoking that scary situation at all?" I said, speaking exactly what was on my mind. Back then, it was only in front of Akiyoshi that I could speak my own thoughts. She thought a bit and then shook her head again.

"I don't think that growing up means ignoring your own weaknesses. Your weak self is still going to be there, but humans can't change their own foundations that easily. It's about recognizing that part of you and growing past it. It's fine if some folks are satisfied enough just with recognizing that, but not for me. So, some things might be scary, but...what's important is to keep moving past that 'but,' even if it's only an inch at a time."

Nothing about Akiyoshi would ever indicate that she was "inching." As always, I was stunned to hear her say something so embarrassing with such deep confidence.

—*—

I hadn't understood anything—not anything at all.

Though I was practically doubled over from the pain in my gut from retching and the uncomfortable speed at which my blood was coursing through my veins, on impulse I decided to leave the apartment.

I scarcely noticed as I missed a step as I rushed down the stairs, twisting my ankle. The pain in my joints was outweighed by the pain throughout my whole body.

I reached the parking lot and clambered onto my bike but found myself unable to really pedal. I toppled over once, taking a number of other bikes down with me, but somehow or other,

I was able to depart. I pushed the pedals with my weak knees, straining to move as quickly as I could.

I was headed for the apartment building that Akiyoshi used to live in. I still remembered its precise location. I wanted to see her, to speak with her, straight away, right now. Focused on that, I pedaled with all my might.

I wanted to apologize, from the bottom of my heart.

For doing something so terrible. For hurting her.

The wind whipped by me, and I collided with a pedestrian's bag along the way. Their shout of anger was lost on me. Normally, I would of course have apologized, but right now, I didn't care about anything but Akiyoshi.

No, that wasn't true.

No, it wasn't true at all.

To be honest...to be honest it wasn't just right now. I had *never* cared about anything else except Akiyoshi. That was why I had done those things.

As this truth dawned upon me, once more my innards were racked with pain, and I wanted to hurl.

I pedaled frantically, until the student apartment building where I used to hang out all the time came into view. I passed the bus stop that Akiyoshi always used and practically tumbled off of my bicycle in front of the entrance, leaving the bike where it lay.

I hurriedly entered her apartment number into the buzzer and pressed the doorbell. I did not feel nervous, only guilty, and crushed by the weight of the friendship we once shared, a friendship where we were perhaps nothing more than convenient for one another.

I waited a short while after pushing the buzzer, but no reply came. I tried pushing it again, but the result was the same. Just in case, I ran around the back of the building, picking out the balcony to check. The lights were not on inside.

She wasn't home yet.

For a moment, I wondered if I should just wait there, but I didn't think my heart could take that. I headed right back to the entrance, picked up my discarded bike, and climbed atop it.

This time, I was headed for the school campus, our base of operations. I had left my phone and everything else back at home, so I could not contact anyone. I had no idea what time it even was. But there was no time for thinking, I simply had to move.

Once more I pedaled with everything I had.

I soon arrived at the university. It was dark, and there were hardly any lights to guide me beyond the light of the moon, but the campus gates were open. I rode right on through onto the main grounds.

Where was she? Where in the world could Akiyoshi be? I hoped to God that my uncanny timing would be enough to simply come across her or something.

As I rode, looking wildly around me, I heard a violent sound from the front wheel of the bike, and before I knew it, I was hurtling across the asphalt. I landed on my elbows and knees, smacking my head lightly on the sidewalk curb. I gingerly stood up, feeling all the pain you might imagine, and looked for my bike.

I found it nearby, the front of it horribly twisted as though I must have crashed into a guard rail.

The fact that it was broken did not bother me in and of itself, so much as the fact that I had lost my speedy means of transportation.

I wanted to see Akiyoshi that very moment.

Once more I felt that pressure in my innards, bile rising. I spit it out on the ground along with all the grit that had gotten into my mouth.

I tried to run, but the pain in my knees got in the way of that, but when I wasn't running, my innards hurt even more. It was though a hot iron bar was being shoved into me.

The research lab—or was there a Moai club room now or something? Or was it already gone from the university? Through my bleary mind, I realized that there was only one place for me to go.

To the research lab.

I headed for the research building as swiftly as my legs would carry me. Faster—faster now. I had to get there quickly, before Akiyoshi went somewhere else. Quickly, before it was too late.

Quickly...

I suddenly stopped in place—but not for any particular reason. No one had passed by me, nor had any strong wind blown me back. It wasn't even that the pain had grown too unbearable for me to walk. But perhaps it was something like that. It was as though I had suddenly woken from a dream.

Why was I doing this?

Sweat was dripping into my right eye—I couldn't see clearly, but the scenery I could see through my unimpeded left eye was so much clearer than before, the air so much cooler. Perhaps it was that my injury had knocked some sense back into me, or perhaps this would have happened right about now regardless. I was released from my reverie.

I had been freed from the illusion that Akiyoshi would still accept me after all this time. Even my own desperation of just moments prior seemed bizarre.

What was I going to do once I saw her? What did I think I could possibly do?

I wanted to apologize for hurting her and tell her I was sorry from the bottom of my heart.

And *then* what?

Even apologizing would solely be for my sake. I wanted to be forgiven, to be friends again, for her not to think poorly of me. There was nothing that *she* would get out of it. And why would I even think in the first place that she would forgive me? After what I had done, after the mess I had made?

Would I *ever* be able to take everything back?

Both my breathing and my heartbeat sounded different than they normally would—almost painfully present in my ears. My knees and elbows throbbed with pain.

I should go home, I thought.

Yet again, I was failing to consider Akiyoshi's feelings.

There was no way she would ever want to see me again.

Regardless of the fact that I had once been her friend, I had spat those rancid, poisonous words at her and ruined all that she had worked so hard to build in her four years. Who would find someone like that anything but *despicable*? Why would she ever want to see me? There was no good reason for having to meet with someone you hated.

That would only give you a good reason to hate them further.

But could there be a situation like that? What...if there was?

I stood there thinking, through the clanging in my skull. Then, a single thought occurred to me, one which I wondered if I ought to carry to fruition. I fretted over this, but even as I fretted with every fiber of my being, I started moving towards the research building again. I stared straight ahead, moving my feet forward step by steady step to close the distance.

My arms hurt, and my legs hurt. My innards and every part of me hurt, yet...they also didn't.

Taking far longer than it ever should have, I finally reached the building in question.

Unlike the rest of the building, where classes had finished and it was fully darkened, there were a number of lights on in the research lab. It was like a beehive—that was the only place where the larvae could be found.

The lights in the room I was headed for appeared to be on. I had no idea if she would be there. Even if she was, I had no idea what I could even say to her. Still, I had to see her.

I pushed the door open and headed into the building. It was cooler inside than out, and it suddenly felt as though my own skin was thinning.

Thankfully, the elevator was working. I rode up to the fourth floor and walked down the dark hallway. More thankfully still, there was only one room in the hall from which lights flooded out from the high windows.

I proceeded with certainty.

I stood before the door and knocked without hesitation, receiving a reply.

"Come in!"

The one I wanted to see was beyond this door.

I grabbed the knob and pushed the door open.

"Good evening."

"Wah!" The one who raised her voice was a woman right beside me, who was not the person I expected to see. "H-hold up!" she shouted, looking at me. "You're really banged up! Wh-what?"

Before I could reply, eyes still adjusting to the first bright lights I had seen in a while, someone else, a man sitting in a folding chair with his arms crossed, cut in, "You have some business with me?"

"...Yes, I do."

"Doesn't that all hurt?"

"It does."

More importantly though, I started to say, when the woman, probably a member of the research team, stepped away with a, "I'll go get some things!" running out of the room and leaving the door open behind her.

"Sorry about that busybody," he said, as I stood there speechless.

"It's fine," I replied, shaking my head again, bowing to this utterly resigned individual. "Been a while, Wakisaka-san."

"Since we talked, I guess. Saw you not that long ago. So, what's up? Why're you all bloody?"

Bloody? When he said this, I looked at my arms, finding I was far more injured than I realized. I quit looking before my brain could register how painful it should be.

"There's something I wanted to ask you," I explained.

"My, never thought I'd see the day. The great Tabata-kun wants to ask *me* something! Sure, honestly speaking, I'm shocked you'd even come to see me."

Not even appearing surprised by my injuries, he picked up a cup that was on the table and put it to his lips, then said casually, "I thought you hated me, after all."

I had no idea how I ought to reply to something so straightforward, but once I got over my hesitation, I bowed my head.

"My apologies."

What I was apologizing for was not for hating him but for barging in here to see him despite that fact. I could have bent the truth, but if I did that now, so much more of what I was about to say would probably start twisting into a lie as well, so I just bowed my head again.

"Whatever, I already knew it. Pick your head up," he said lackadaisically, despite me having confirmed my dislike for him. I did as I was told and straightened back up, finding him looking back at me with his usual world-weariness. "I've always appreciated that honesty of yours, Tabata-san. It's normal for people to have things that they like and that they hate. I am a little curious as to why, though."

"Why…?"

Why was it? I thought for a moment. What were the right words to express what was in my heart? I thought long and hard, before I realized there was no reason to be driving myself crazy over this. I'd already decided this from the very start. After being so stricken with shame and regret after listening to Akiyoshi's speech, I should have known. I should have been perfectly aware of it.

Now though, when I tried to say it, the words caught in my throat. I was dripping sweat from every pore. My insides ached once more.

Wakisaka was waiting. I took in too deep of a breath, ignoring how shrill my own voice was, and told him, "I think…"

And told him.

"…I think that I thought that Akiyoshi would never look my way again."

My feelings were like mud I was dredging up from the bottom of my heart.

There was the truth of how I felt, with no attempts to hide it. I had only just realized what had been there all along.

It was still difficult to agree with Akiyoshi's assumption that I had feelings for her in a romantic way. Still, it wounded me that my precious companion, the only one dear to me, would ever turn her attention to anyone but me.

And the things I had done had hurt her more deeply than anything else ever could.

I had to face those facts. I had come here so that I could.

As I spoke, I felt the air around me grow thinner. It grew harder to breathe, my heart rate rising to its limits.

It hurt so much to accept my own feelings.

The corners of Wakisaka's mouth quirked up.

"I see. I'm sure it's trite of me to say, but there's no person in the world who focuses all their attention on only one other person and nothing else. Plus, she was *definitely* looking your way."

"...I know."

I did know. If I had just thought about it, I would have realized that.

"Anyway, I'm guessing what you wanted to ask about was Akiyoshi-san?"

"Yeah, um...you are aware that Moai is over now, yes?"

"Obviously."

"That was my fault."

Despite my stating this clearly, there was still some part of me that was afraid to admit my own wrongdoings, and I could feel my stomach constricting.

I wondered what he thought about this. I did not expect doubt or anger. In fact, just as I predicted, he merely said, "I see," a response that hurt far more than either one. "So, how'd that come to be?"

This was a perfectly natural question, though I wondered if I should answer it, the weaker parts of me urging me to convey the story while omitting the parts that were less convenient for me. However, I told him everything—by which I mean, the whole story of how I had tried to destroy Moai, and how I had hurt Akiyoshi.

I still lacked the strength to suppress the weaker parts of myself. It was just that it would have been so much more frightening to wallow in the misery of that weakness.

As soon as I finished speaking, without the slightest hesitation, Wakisaka opened his mouth and said, "You really *suck*."

There was no hint of reservation in his voice.

"I do."

"Akiyoshi-san used to talk about you all the time, at least until you quit Moai," he said, staring right at me. "She might've badmouthed you a bit, but I'm sure that's just a reflection of her faith in you and your deep friendship. She was obviously in the wrong in some ways in this situation, but you really betrayed her trust."

"...You aren't wrong about that."

Other than Akiyoshi, he was the first person to actively criticize me about this matter. Coming from such a clear-cut angle, it struck me straight on.

"So then, that all said, what *was* it you wanted to ask me?"

Whether it was out of kindness or indifference, I was thankful that Wakisaka could be so objective about this. He had given me the opportunity to speak about the reason I had come here.

"I was wondering..."

Though I very clearly disliked Wakisaka, it took an extra second of breathing to prepare myself for being disliked by him.

"...if there was anything I could do for Moai."

I knew this was a selfish thing for me to ask, and it took even more courage to say it than it had to admit that I disliked Wakisaka. After I had been the one to tear things down, after I had hurt Akiyoshi. But I had to say it, even knowing that I would be despised, vilified, scorned.

Though I had fully expected it, I heard Wakisaka let out a deep sigh that cut directly through all my confidence.

"What is it you think that you *can* do?" *At this point*, he did not include, but I could hear it in his tone.

I steeled my wavering body, holding back my legs from running.

"...I'm s-orry, I have no idea. I really don't know. But I was just thinking that, maybe there might be *something*."

"Why're you asking me?"

"...Because we're outsiders."

Wakisaka looked neither pleased nor displeased at what could have been taken as a rude remark.

"As far as Moai is concerned, I am now an outsider. So, as someone who was helping Moai out *despite* being an outsider himself at one point, I wanted to ask your opinion." For some reason I could not get out the words, "And that's why I came here."

Wakisaka folded his arms and stared at the wall of the lab. I followed his gaze to see a wall with a narrow opening in it. "Now, this is just a simple question, but..." he started. "What exactly was Moai to you? What would have been the point of destroying it, just to build it back again?"

"Ah..."

I was about to say that it was for Akiyoshi, but I stopped myself short. That wasn't true; it simply wasn't. If I said it was for the sake of someone else, that was just me shifting the blame again.

I thought hard about what he meant by that question. I was not considering what sort of answer Wakisaka would want to hear, so much as genuinely posing the same question to myself. I searched for the plainest words possible.

Then, I found them.

It wasn't that I had remembered it. It had always been there, just on the tip of my tongue.

"I..."

I had been pretending that I hadn't seen it. I had been hiding it from everyone.

However, it was the truth and nothing less.

"I always...I always wanted to be there."

It was true. That was all. That was all there ever was.

Nothing more.

That was the one thing I could not say to Akiyoshi.

If only I had been able to, perhaps...perhaps there still would have been time.

If only it had been at any other time.

If it had been two years ago, a year ago, a month ago.

It wouldn't have been too late.

If only I could have just worked up the courage to pick up the phone and call her, arrange a meeting, and tell her that I still wanted to be a part of Moai. And yet, I hadn't. At every turn I stood in my own way of doing something so very simple.

It wouldn't even have been pathetic, or embarrassing, and even if it had been, the fact that I had lacked the courage to step outside of my own feelings made me all the more pitiful.

I had no idea.

I had no idea what it had meant to bottle up my own weakness.

But now…I understood.

It was already too late. I could not turn back time. That place, that time…it was already beyond my reach.

"I wanted to be in that place forever. That's…all I…that's all I really wanted."

My breathing grew unsteady. It was hard to speak.

The throbbing pain in my heart persisted.

Through the pain, I thought Akiyoshi must be hurting even more with a pain I could not even comprehend.

Hearing my words, Wakisaka nodded with a blank stare and a solemn, "Gotcha."

"Even if there was something you could do, though," he continued, "there's no guarantee you'd be able to reclaim that spot you want so badly."

I knew that.

"Are you all right with that?"

I inhaled and exhaled deeply several times, gulping.

"I think that would make me sad."

There was no use in hiding it anymore. No use in hiding it and causing any more hurt.

"But I know that there are people for whom Moai is an important place, just like it was for me in the beginning."

"I see." He nodded, more deeply than he had up until now. "In other words, you basically want to help out your own former self."

I let the meaning of those words sink deeply in and nodded.

"...Yes, I think that's it."

He was right. There was no more florid way to put it.

For several seconds after I replied, Wakisaka looked at me, his head tilted as if in thought. Then, the corners of his mouth quirked up. That was the first time I had seen him smile that evening.

"By the way, would you mind letting that nice, young lady standing there behind you in?"

I turned around to see the woman who had rushed out earlier standing awkwardly in the doorway with a first aid kit in hand. As I bowed and cleared the path, she marched right in, pointed to a folding chair, and said, "Sit down!" I dutifully obeyed.

Wakisaka let out a chuckle at this.

"Sorry, she's a bit of a busybody," Wakisaka said, standing up and picking up his bag before starting out of the room. I started to stand in turn, ignoring the woman who was currently applying disinfectant to my arm, but he turned and faced me before I could call after him.

"I'll be in touch later," he said.

He left the room just as the woman pushed me back down into the chair. Unable to refuse this act of kindness, I sat there, obediently receiving my treatment. As she worked, the woman smiled gently, as if remembering something.

"He's a busybody too," she said.

I stared fixedly at the small slit in the wall.

I wish that spring would linger a little longer, I thought, threading my arms through a long-sleeved shirt. I sipped some coffee and ate a slice of toast with some salad I had bought from the convenience store, opening up a message on my phone that pressed, "Hurry up and get out here!"

"I can't wait to see you."

The message had started with that polite greeting and ended with those words. It had occurred to me the last time she had contacted me, but being cute while still being polite must have been some special technique she had picked up.

Once I was finished with my coffee, I rinsed out the cup and set it in the sink. I put on my jacket, clumsily picked up my business bag, and with that, my everyday look was complete. Normally, once I entered this mode my body started feeling rather heavy, but the fact that I was heading somewhere different from usual put me a little bit at ease.

I checked the clock, seeing that there was still twenty minutes until the train I intended to catch. It was fifteen minutes from my home to the station. As a now serious professional who had only been late a few times since I started working, I always left the house with plenty of time to spare. I shared a simple greeting with my neighbor, who must have just gotten back from a run around then. I was thankful for this apartment and its thick walls, which prevented this lady from hearing the fights I had with my girlfriend.

It was a fifteen-minute walk exactly to the station. Though it was still spring, the sun was harsh, and my forehead beaded with sweat.

I passed through the turnstile and waited; the train arrived shortly. One of the reasons I liked my new place was that the nearest station was the first stop on the line, so I could always find a seat. It would be about an hour's ride until I arrived at my destination. I ended up nodding off while I thought about the things I was going to say, frantically gathering myself up and rushing off when we reached my transfer point.

After fifteen minutes of rocking along on the subway, I arrived at the station nearest to the university I had once commuted to every day. It was a Saturday, so there were few people there, so I purchased a canned coffee from one of the vending machines on the platform and took my time enjoying it.

After watching one more train come and go, I finally headed for the university. I took the escalator up, in accordance with my physical strength, which was declining slowly by the year. I passed through the main gates and headed for my final destination, one for which I needed no maps: the largest cafeteria on campus. I was a little disappointed to think that there would be no food service running today, considering how much I used to enjoy the fried fish there.

The closer I got to my destination, the more students appeared. When I rounded the last corner to the cafeteria entrance, a cheerful girl greeted me. A bit regretfully, I ended up returning the greeting with a bow and a bit of a reserved business smile.

There was a table set in the front of the cafeteria with three students sitting at it. I spoke with the first girl I locked eyes with, knowing that she was just as nervous as I was.

"Hello. I'm Tabata Kaede."

I pulled out my business card holder from my inside pocket and handed her a card. She politely accepted it, confirming my business and company name, and checked it off with a marker.

"Thank you for joining us here today," she said. "Just inside you'll find some materials and refreshments. Please help yourself."

"I will. Thank you very much."

This time I intentionally gave as natural seeming a smile as I could and stepped inside the cafeteria. The mild air-conditioning was pleasant feeling. Just as the girl had said, there I could get some tea and pamphlets to collect as I moved within, finding that the tables I recalled the cafeteria having had all been neatly removed and replaced with a large circle of chairs. I looked towards the projector that had been set up on the end, wondering if the host of the event would be standing there, when suddenly a woman leapt out from the crowd.

"Good morning! Thanks for making the time to come here."

"It's been a while."

The relief on my face at seeing someone who I recognized was probably the most natural expression I had worn all day.

"Yeah, you've been avoidin' me for a whole year, Tabata-san."

"Have not. Our schedules just haven't lined up. Oh, right. Tousuke told me to tell you he was sorry he couldn't make it."

"Some *girl* again?" she asked, wrinkling her nose. None of the piercings she once wore in her ears remained. She was now a pinstripe-suit-wearing adult.

"Seriously though, thanks for coming on such short notice.

Honestly, I figured you didn't wanna talk to me anymore, so I never bothered you while I was a student. I was surprised you agreed to this."

"Yeah, I think that came across in that 'Seriously?!' you texted me. But anyway, if I turned you down, I'm pretty sure you'd just kick me again."

"Listen, that was *years* ago! And we were *drunk*! You really do like to hold your grudges..."

"Rich coming from a tough girl like you."

As we tittered at each other, the "*Test, test,*" of a mic check echoed throughout the cafeteria. I looked up to see a tall, nervous looking boy setting up the microphone stand.

"Ladies and gentlemen, thank you so much for your attendance today."

The boy started off with a polite introduction, followed by a number of instructions for us. Kawahara-san and I moved to our designated positions and sat down in the tidy rows of chairs, reading over the materials. I had to applaud them on the production value of these pamphlets.

"Pretty professional, huh?" Kawahara-san said from beside me. "Obviously, I invited you here because I wanted to get you involved with the students, but honestly, it was mostly because I wanted you to see what we've built up over the past five years."

I looked at the bashful look on her face. Sure enough, either this was a trick, or she was a genius.

Finally, the appointed start time arrived, and though it seemed that some of the participants were still not present, we went ahead and began forming groups with the students. For the first groups, the professionals were sorted out based on the students' prospective industries, so Kawahara-san and I were separated. Just before we parted, she threatened me with a, "If you bully any of my kouhai, I'll kick you again."

I was urged to sit in a chair placed in the middle of a circle with a number of students seated around me. They all gave me a loud, hearty greeting of, "Thank you for coming!" which I replied to with another awkward smile.

"First period will now begin. If you have any questions, please ask one of the circulating members. Have fun, everyone."

Regardless of how nervous the glimmering gazes pointed my way made me, we were given the signal to begin. The students once again greeted me in unison. I felt like I had suddenly been appointed teacher or something.

"Good morning. I'm Tabata Kaede. Pleased to meet you all." I decided to start off with some small talk. "This is my first time participating in this conference, so I'm actually pretty nervous. I hope I can ask you all to please be gentle with me. Um, well...I was invited here today by Kawahara Risa, who was the group representative as a senior two years ago."

Unable to say anything particularly interesting in front of this attentive group of students, I decided to just launch into an explanation of the work I did. I explained about our company, our duties, our primary clients, and the benefits—the sort of things that one would speak about at a job fair.

My clumsiness was somewhat inevitable; I had never listened

that closely during my time as a student. I should have pinched more techniques from those speakers back then. Of course, if you told my student self that one day *I* would be the professional, standing up there talking to students, he would have never believed you.

The students gave me their undivided attention, faces serious. Once I was finished talking about my work, it was time for some Q&A. As I fielded questions about the job-hunting process and making connections, wondering what I would do if I was faced with an actually difficult question, one of the students, who happened to be wearing a name tag, raised their hand. I remembered reading about this in the pamphlets—the ones wearing name tags were members of the group.

"If you don't mind my asking, what were some good experiences you had during your time as a student, things that you learned a lot from, if any?"

That was their question. It was probably a question from the manual.

The word "growth" was proudly emblazoned as one of the key principles by which this group operated, so that was surely what they were interested in hearing about. Good experiences, things I had learned a lot from—one thing immediately came to mind. But having no idea how much use it would be for them to hear about it, I immediately dismissed the thought.

But then...I reconsidered it.

Maybe it was fine if it was no use to these kids. It was fine to learn about things that you had no actual use for. Then, you could make choices that would *actually* benefit you.

I looked one time across the whole group and then began to speak.

"Well, I wouldn't call it good, but there was one experience that I learned quite a bit from."

I took a slightly deeper breath than usual.

"I hurt someone important to me and came to regret it." I could feel the air within the circle growing heavier. The weight of the air seemed to match the tone of my voice.

"When I was a student, I hurt a very dear friend, and I completely destroyed something that she had valued."

One baby-faced girl, probably a freshman student, stiffened.

"By the time I came to regret it, it was too late, and there was no way to undo the damage." I carefully chose the words that would best get my message across. "And it wasn't as though I hated this person. On the contrary, I held her in such high esteem that when I saw her going down what I thought to be the wrong path, I decided it was my job to correct her behavior. What happened was the result of my own selfish actions. There might even be some of you here who have gone through a similar experience yourself."

One boy nodded weakly.

"Even now, I still regret it. This might sound arrogant of me, but I'm glad that I was able to acknowledge that regret. The regret of causing that hurt is still rooted within me and makes me strive to be as honest with other people as I can. It makes me think about sincerity."

Even though I had no idea if that was yet something that I had achieved.

"Realizing that I hoped to never again do something like that, to never again harm the people that I hold dear, was the experience from my time as a student that has had the greatest influence on me, both in terms of my professional and my everyday life. I still strive, a little more each day, to be a safe haven for others. To be someone who would never harm those special people—which might sound a little awkward to hear, but that's the truth."

Somehow, I had managed to tie things back to my opening words.

Now that I was speaking about it, for the first time something occurred to me. Perhaps giving this talk was the reason I had come here. The reason for all the time that had passed since then.

I gauged the students' reactions, wondering if I should prompt them for the next question, when I looked up.

Then, our eyes met.

My eyes met *hers*.

The whole time I had assumed it was one of the group members who had been circling the room, but when I saw her out of the corner of my eye, standing there behind the students, watching, there was no doubt.

Our eyes met, and I stopped breathing.

She nodded once, hesitantly. Her eyes still on mine, her lips parted once and then closed. Kawahara-san had told me that she hadn't planned on attending. Standing there in her suit, she just stared at me.

"Tabata-san, are you all right?" the group member who was sitting in the circle asked me, and time began to move again.

I quickly apologized with a, "Sorry," then concluded, "I hope that answer was sufficient?"

By the time I looked up, *she* was already gone. I thought she might have just been an illusion, some convenient illusion born from my own scars.

Finally, the first period came to an end, and I gave the suitable farewells as I stood. I had to look for her, just in case. There was nothing I had in mind that I would do if she was there, but still…I had to try.

I searched desperately through the announcement of a break period. Surprisingly, I found her quite easily. I spotted her from behind, heading alone for the cafeteria exit. Before I realized it, I was already stepping towards her.

It was fine if she was an illusion. There was nothing that I hoped to do, nothing that I *could* do. And yet, my legs moved.

I only started considering what to do after I started after her. Finally, I found myself outside, looking all around. She was walking down the boulevard. I saw her shoes crunch down on the fallen leaves on the ground.

She was no illusion.

There were no obstacles between me and her slender back. If I hurried, I would be close enough to tap her on the shoulder.

We had only known each other for a few short months, but the one I knew I was supposed to be standing beside was right there.

I thought about calling out to her, but I was halted by an overwhelming fear.

Every action you take has a chance of making someone else unhappy.

I didn't want to be hurt. I was afraid.

...And yet.

I want to see you again. I want nothing more than to see you again.

Maybe now, you would accept me, with all my mistakes and all my weaknesses. Me, someone so different from you. It's because of you that I became the person I am today. You made the lies that I told a reality.

My pace quickened, and I caught up, just behind her. Obviously, I was afraid. I was still *me*, after all.

She might just ignore me. She might even reject me.

But that was fine.

She could ignore me. She could reject me.

If that happens, I just need to get hurt again.